"*Recruits* is a truly awesome work that holds the potential for appeal across genres and age groups. Enormously engaging and thought provoking. The concept itself is remarkable, and the writing is absolutely beautiful."

—**Kim Neimi**, former executive vice president, NBC Universal

"*Recruits* is mind-bending storytelling, part *The Matrix* and part *I Am Number Four*. The story holds to a remarkable combination of the immediate and the beyond. This forms an adventurer's feast of the most addictive sort."

—**Tosca Lee**, *New York Times* bestselling coauthor of *Forbidden*

"Wow! *Recruits* is a remarkable feat, combining adroit storytelling with a delicious mixture of the now and the fantastic. Locke's writing shows a wonderfully fluid grace. The story brings to mind the poignant beauty of Arthur C. Clarke's best novels, as well as such modern works as *Avatar*."

—**Phyllis Tickle**, former senior editor, *Publishers Weekly*

RECRUITS

Books by Thomas Locke

LEGENDS OF THE REALM

Emissary
Merchant of Alyss

FAULT LINES

Double Edge (ebook)
Trial Run
Flash Point

RECRUITS

Recruits

RECRUITS

THOMAS LOCKE

Revell

a division of Baker Publishing Group
Grand Rapids, Michigan

© 2017 by T. Davis Bunn

Published by Revell
a division of Baker Publishing Group
P.O. Box 6287, Grand Rapids, MI 49516-6287
www.revellbooks.com

Printed in the United States of America

Library of Congress Cataloging-in-Publication Data is on file at the Library of Congress, Washington, DC.

ISBN 978-0-8007-2789-5

This book is a work of fiction. Names, characters, places, and incidents are the products of the author's imagination or are used fictitiously. Any resemblance to actual events, locales, or persons, living or dead, is coincidental.

17   18   19   20   21   22   23   7   6   5   4   3   2   1

This Book Is Dedicated To:

Jennifer Leep,
Dave Lewis,
Jessica English,
and the incredible team at
Revell

What a joy
To work with trusted and gifted friends

I

Ten years ago this month, they started drawing the train station, one positioned on another world.

They had the same image burning in their brains, in their *hearts*. The station was a tube pinched at both ends, like a twisted candy wrapper. They argued over how big it was. A couple of miles long at least. And the trains, they were all glass. Not like trains with windows. Glass trains. And the tubes they traveled in, glass as well. But that wasn't the best part.

The trains came and went all over the tube. Top, sides, bottom. Gravity modulation, that was definitely Dillon's term. Sean assumed his brother got the concept from some sci-fi novel, but Dillon insisted it came to him in a dream. Whatever. They drew the station on sheets from sketch pads and pasted them all over their two rooms. Walls and ceilings. Forget posters of rock groups and models. Even as they entered their teens, there was nothing they wanted more than to build on the dream. Leave the same-old behind. And fly to a world they were somehow sure was more than just a figment of two imaginations. So they kept drawing, adding cities of lyrical majesty that rose beyond the station. They were connected to this place like the ticket was in the mail. Ten years had changed nothing.

The idea came to them when they were seven. Nowadays Dillon claimed it was his concept. But Sean knew his twin was just blowing smoke. Dillon had a highly convenient memory. He remembered things the way he wished they were. Sean decided it wasn't worth arguing over. Dillon tended to go ballistic whenever his remake of history was challenged. But Sean knew the idea was his. Totally.

Still, he let Dillon claim he was the one who came up with the concept. The one that powered them through the worst times. Kept them moving forward. That was the most important thing. They had it in their bones.

Only that spring, the concept and all the bitter yearnings attached to it actually did change into something more.

···

They were coming from the school bus, walking the line of cookie-cutter homes in suburban Raleigh. They lived in a development called Plantation Heights, six miles northeast of the old town, the cool town. All the good stuff was farther west. The Research Triangle Park. Duke University. UNC Chapel Hill. NC State. Five different party centrals. That particular Friday afternoon was great, weather-wise. Not too hot, nice breeze, Carolina blue sky. Two weekends before the end of the school year was also good for a high, even if they were both still looking for a job. Just two more of the local horde, searching for grunt work that paid minimum wage at best. But their eighteenth birthdays were only four months and six days off. That summer they would take their SATs and begin the process of trying to find a university that would accept them both. Because they definitely wanted to stay together. No matter how weird the world might find it, the topic had been cemented in a conversation that lasted, like, eleven seconds.

The biggest focus for their summer was to find something that paid enough to buy a car. Their rarely used drivers' licenses burned holes in their back pockets. Their desire to acquire wheels and escape beautiful suburbia fueled an almost daily hunt through the want ads.

Dillon looked up from his phone and announced, "Dodge is coming out with a new Charger SRX. Five hundred and seventy-one ponies."

Sean tossed his brother his backpack. "I'm not hauling your weight for you to go trolling for redneck clunkers."

Dillon stowed his phone and slung his pack. "You and your foreign junk."

"Seven-series BMW, V12, blow your Charger into last week."

"For the cost of a seven-series we could get two Chargers and take our ladies to New York for a month."

"The kind of ladies who would set foot in a Charger would rather go to Arkansas, buy some new teeth."

They turned the corner and saw a U-Haul partly blocking their drive. Two hefty guys were shifting furniture from the truck into the house next door. Moving trucks were a fairly common sight in Plantation Heights. The development held over three hundred houses. Or rather, one home cloned three hundred times. Which was how Sean came up with his name for the residences and the people who lived here. Clomes.

They stopped, mildly curious over who was moving in next door.

Dillon said, "For a moment there I thought maybe Big Phil had decided to relocate us."

"Fat chance."

"We're going to walk in and he'll tell us we're turning urban. We'll move into a downtown loft. Burn the polyester and go Armani."

Sean had a quip ready. He always did. Two o'clock in the morning, he'd be woken up by some comment his brother had dreamed up, literally. The response was always there, just waiting. Only this time his retort died unspoken, because their new neighbor came out his front door.

Adult clomes basically came in two shapes. The fitness freaks had skinny moms and overpumped dads. They talked about their bikes or their yoga or their weekend trips to hike around Maui in an hour. The other clomes wore their sofas like lounge suits. The farthest they moved was to the fridge or the backyard grill. They talked about . . . Actually, Sean didn't really care what they talked about.

Their new neighbor definitely did not fit in Clome Heights.

For one thing, he only had one hand.

The left sleeve of his shirt was clipped up, hiding the stump that ended just below his elbow. He limped as he walked. He was lean and dark complexioned, like he'd been blasted by some foreign sun for so long his skin was permanently stained. This man could have taken the biggest guy in Plantation Heights and turned him into a clome sandwich. One-handed.

When the guy turned around, they probably saw the scar at the same moment, because Dillon dragged in the breath Sean had trouble finding. The scar emerged from the top of his shirt, ran around the left side of his neck, clipped off the bottom third of his ear, and vanished into his hairline. Military-style crew cut. Of course. The jagged wound was punctuated with scar tissue the size and shape of small flowers.

Their neighbor spoke to the two movers in a language that didn't actually sound like he was talking. More like he *sang* the words. And they responded the same way. How three big guys could sing and sound tough at the same time, Sean had no idea. But they did.

Then they saluted. Like Roman soldiers in the old movies. Fist to chest. Another little chant. Then the movers got in the U-Haul and drove away.

The guy then turned and stared at them. Which was when Sean realized there was something mildly weird about two teenage kids standing in the street, gawking at this guy like they were looking through a cage at the zoo. For once, Sean's nimble mind came up with nada. He just stood there. The intensity of that man's look froze Sean's brain.

Their neighbor said, "So. You must be the twins. Kirrel, correct?" He waved his good hand at the front door. "Want to come inside for a cup of tea?"

Dillon managed, "Uh, we've got homework."

The guy seemed to find that mildly humorous. "That is the best excuse you can manage?"

Sean probably would have stood there all night if his brother had not snagged his arm and pulled him away. "Have a nice day," he said.

Dillon waited until they were inside to say, "'Have a nice day'? Really?"

"Go start your homework, why don't you." Sean moved to the front window. But the guy was gone. The street was empty. Silent. Just another day in Clomeville. Except for the man who had just moved in next door.

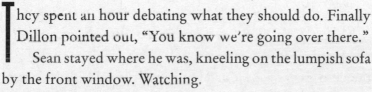

They spent an hour debating what they should do. Finally Dillon pointed out, "You know we're going over there."

Sean stayed where he was, kneeling on the lumpish sofa by the front window. Watching.

"It's just a matter of time. You know it, I know it. Today, tomorrow, two midnights from now after we haven't slept. We're going."

Sean's forehead streaked the glass as he nodded. "I'm just getting used to the idea."

"What's the worst that could happen?"

Sean's breath frosted the glass. "We discover the guy is a serial nutcase and we wind up buried in his cellar."

"Okay, sure. But considering the alternative of another summer unemployed and trapped in Clomeville, that's not so bad, right?"

Sean swiveled around. "You've got a point."

They were midway up the neighbor's front drive when

Sean said, "Text somebody. Tell them to call us in twenty minutes. If we don't answer, tell them to call 911 and say they've got to come to this house."

"Good thinking." Both of them got busy on their phones. When Dillon was done, he gave Sean a queasy look. "Maybe this isn't such a good idea."

"Too late." And it was.

The guy was already standing there by his open front door. Watching them with those bottomless eyes.

...

Sean was almost through the living room when he realized what he was seeing.

The house smelled of fresh paint and disinfectant. And disuse. It had stood vacant for a couple of months, long enough for the air to grow stale. He and Dillon had played with the idea of sneaking inside and building their teen version of a man cave. But realtors tended to be very careful about setting the alarms.

Sean had never been inside this particular place. The former residents had been old and quiet and private. The development had enough residents of this type to make them a third class of citizen, really. The only sign they even existed was the car that went up the drive—the garage door already sliding open, the car rolling forward, the door sliding down, show over. At night, lights streamed around curtains. Lawn care was handled like the garbage. Sean didn't know the neighbors had moved out until the For Sale sign appeared.

At least this guy didn't have curtains. Maybe a passing jogger would hear their screams, glance inside, and call for backup.

The floors were nice, real wood laid down with round pegs. The planks were polished and as bare as the walls. No photographs anywhere. A couple of boxes, not much. But that wasn't what halted Sean in mid-stride.

Dillon was already in the kitchen when he turned and said, "What is it?"

"Everything is new."

Dillon came back to stand beside him. "So?"

"No. I mean, *new*. All this stuff, it's still wearing the sale tags."

The guy stepped up beside them. He stood maybe an inch or so taller than Sean. Both of the twins had gone through a serious growth surge when they hit thirteen, racing each other toward the six-foot mark. Which would have been great if they liked basketball. Which they didn't. They both were into soccer, and the spurt just killed their game. The center of gravity they'd both relied on was completely thrown off. So they wound up not making the team when they shifted to high school. And the hole in their schedules and identities remained unfilled.

The guy said, "What's your name?"

Sean turned and realized the guy meant him. "Sean."

"Are you always the observant one?"

Dillon said, "Not always."

The guy smiled at him. At least, Sean thought it was a smile. A flicker of tight lips. A small dimple to each cheek, there and gone. "And your name?"

"Dillon."

"I'm Carver."

Dillon couldn't help it. "Carver, really?"

"Yes. Sean, you just won the right to go first." The guy turned and limped into the kitchen.

Dillon remained standing beside Sean. Talking in the low murmur they had used since childhood. "Carver. Great. All the furniture in his old home was probably too blood-spattered to ship."

Sean didn't respond, since he had been thinking the exact same thing.

Carver said from the kitchen, "Let's get started, gentlemen."

...

As spooked as he seemed, Dillon still managed a quip as he entered the kitchen. "What, no tea?"

"Later." Carver indicated the chairs around the kitchen table. Also new. "Be seated, gentlemen."

The kitchen was showroom bare. Not even a towel by the sink. The cabinets looked as though they had never been opened. The chairs scraped overloud as they sat down.

Carver inspected them both, then said, "I suppose you're wondering what this is about."

Sean licked his lips. Eyed the rear door. The empty back garden. Freedom. His brother didn't speak.

"I am here," Carver said, "because you contacted us."

Okay. That was new.

Sean asked, "Us?"

He waved his stump. "Set that aside for a moment. This will be hard enough for you to fathom without trying to explain who sent me."

Dillon opened his mouth but did not speak. Sean liked that—how this guy had managed to shut his brother up.

"Normally we do not connect with anyone as old as you two. Less than half your current age is the norm. At seven or eight years, as you count them, the individual is still open to possibilities. By your age, generally the perspective on life is firmly established. When adults tap into the force, they seek to manipulate it, fashion it into something they can apply to their concept of reality. But in your case there are two extenuating circumstances."

Carver dragged back a chair of his own. "First, you are twins. You share the same conceptual structure. To be contacted by *both* twins is extremely rare. The last time this occurred, we were gifted with two of our most potent adepts."

Dillon was watching his brother now. The stare open and unblinking. Sean totally agreed. He told Carver, "You said two things."

"I did, yes. The second is, this world has only once before produced a recruit. But that individual changed the course of history. So we have decided to give you this opportunity. See if you are still trainable."

Sean said slowly, "I'm hearing the words. I'm not understanding a thing."

"Anything further will just open up more questions. That is another reason why we identify all candidates when they are much younger. They do not need to have everything explained. They are too excited about simply being given the chance."

Dillon was still sitting there playing the mummy. So Sean asked, "Chance at what?"

"To grasp for what they have already sensed is possible. That you were made for something better. That you can rise *beyond*. That you can accomplish something greater than the life your current existence proposes. You have sensed it ever since you drew the first component of the station beyond your reach. You already know there are new realms to explore."

Sean felt himself blown back in his chair by hearing their dream spoken aloud by a guy he had never met.

Dillon asked, "You've been watching us?"

"Not long enough." Carver tapped his good hand on the wooden tabletop. "Before we begin, you must remove all electronic devices. Your watches, phones, everything. How long did you tell your friends before they will call the emergency services?"

Sean and Dillon said it together. "Spooky."

"How long?"

"Twenty minutes."

"Tell them everything is safe here, you are all right, and they should stand down."

Sean liked how he kept his gaze as steady as his voice. "Is it? Safe, I mean."

The dimples came and went a second time. The only sign of weakness this guy had shown. "Your safety is assured. As to whether everything is all right, well, that depends upon how you perform."

Sean rose to his feet. "Give us a second."

They retreated to the living room, where Dillon said, "What should we do?"

"I think . . . What do you think he means, 'perform'?"

Dillon shrugged. "Maybe how loud we scream?"

Sean decided. "Okay. Enough." He texted his friend. Waited while Dillon did the same. A shared breath. Then they returned to the kitchen and handed over their phones.

Somehow Carver made a solemn act of accepting the devices. "Gentlemen, you just passed the first test."

"Are there many?" Dillon asked. "Tests, I mean."

"Only if you keep passing."

"And if we don't?"

"All this never happened," Carver replied. "And I was never here."

Dillon dragged out the word, "Okay."

"Dillon, sit down. Sean, come here." He moved to the bare, whitewashed wall beside the rear door. "What you see here before you is not a wall. It is in fact a portal. I want you to walk through it."

Sean reached forward and touched. The paint still felt slightly tacky. "Seems real enough to me."

"To your physical senses, yes. This is what I meant by preferring to work with younger children. Their ability to sense beyond the physical is much keener. Can you perceive anything other than what you are viewing with your eyes?"

Sean found himself fighting the words around a racing heart. "Only that this is seriously weird."

Carver's frown was as quick as his smile. "Take a pace back. Now observe."

Their new neighbor then stepped forward. But he did not strike the wall. Instead, he simply vanished.

Dillon said, "Wha . . ."

Carver reappeared. "Now I want you to do this. Extend your senses beyond what your mind is telling you are the physical limitations. And follow your extended awareness."

"Through the wall," Sean said.

"No, no, no. The wall is not there. Not if you act properly and use what you already know exists within you." Carver looked from one twin to the other. "The image of the transport complex you both have spent years wishing you could visit, these dreams you both have shared for so long that define the hunger inside you—these are *real*. What is more, this signifies your higher potential. We meet together today in order to determine whether the seed planted in each human at birth has taken root. Despite everything about the physical universe that keeps you trapped. Despite all the reasons you have to lose hope and confine yourself to the mundane. We need to answer this ultimate question. Are you ready and able to move *beyond*?"

Sean was following him now. Even though his mind kept trying to shut down. Even so, he said, "What if I can't?"

Carver leaned in close enough for the bottomless gaze to almost swallow him. He growled, "You will not fail. You are going to walk through that portal and enter into a new and higher level of existence." He then nudged the small of Sean's back. Instantly Sean felt like a second belt had been fastened to his waist. "You are now linked. When you pass through, remain as you are. I will draw you back."

"*When* I pass through," Sean repeated.

"Correct. Now go."

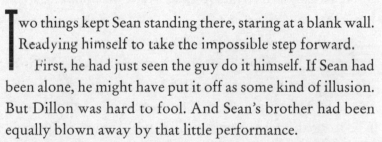

Two things kept Sean standing there, staring at a blank wall. Readying himself to take the impossible step forward.

First, he had just seen the guy do it himself. If Sean had been alone, he might have put it off as some kind of illusion. But Dillon was hard to fool. And Sean's brother had been equally blown away by that little performance.

Second, Sean felt in his gut that this was real. The whole deal. The guy in maimed condition, the impossible words, the incredible challenge.

Forget logic.

This was what he had spent his entire life waiting for.

A chance to break free.

Only he had never figured it would be like this. Being told to do the impossible.

Except that, if he could do this—actually follow the guy's lead and walk straight ahead, find that portal—it wasn't impossible. It was . . .

Sean stepped forward.

That single step changed everything. Because it wasn't just a movement of his feet. It was a change at every level of his life.

Sean felt something shift deep inside. Deeper than his bones. At a level he did not realize he possessed. At least, not consciously. But he knew, even as he moved, that this was where the idea and the image had both first taken form. At the place about four inches below his navel that was burning now with a fire that actually did not burn at all. It filled him with a sense of power.

He actually shaped the words as he stepped forward. *We're meant for something big.*

And the wall was not there to stop him.

Sean slipped through a greyish mist and felt a slight grip to his being, like he moved through a spiderweb. Then he was through. And gasping with the shock. And totally excited. And freaked. And wanting to shriek with the incredible thrill of having *done it.*

Because he had arrived.

Inside the train station they had fashioned over years. *He was standing inside his dream.*

The place was huge. Bigger than the state coliseum where they'd been for a couple of concerts. Five times that size. The ceiling was lined with the glass tubes he had been drawing for ten long years. So many tubes they looked like tiny, transparent ribs. Then he saw the trains, and they were glass as well, of course, and they were flying, fast as anything he'd ever seen. And then he saw the people. Tiny specks that dotted the . . . the *ceiling*. They were walking *upside down*. And there were more people around him. Walking right-side up. And more still were on the walls to either side, everybody moving calmly, like it was what they did every day, hurrying to where the tubes opened and the glass trains stopped and people got on and off and the trains started back up, whooshing away and disappearing into those translucent tubes. And people stepped onto moving walkways and they whooshed too, only they were to his left and right and above him and beside him, and they were so *calm*.

Then he saw the man.

He stood directly in front of Sean. Tall and black, not normal African American dark-skinned. This guy was as black and polished as a gemstone. And he was really, really angry. If glares could kill, Sean would have already been reduced to a molten puddle.

Then he felt the tug at his waist, and he was hauled back. He was sorry to leave this incredible place. But not at all sad about leaving that guy. It was probably a bad idea, but Sean didn't like this guy or his glare, not one tiny bit. So he planted his knuckles at the base of his chin and gave a little finger wave. *So long, suckah.*

Then he was back in the kitchen. "Oh, man."

"That was amazing," Dillon breathed. "You just went *gone*."

Sean tsk-tsked. "Grammar."

Carver said, "Tell me what you saw."

Sean said to his brother, "You have *got* to check that place out. It is exactly like we drew."

"You mean . . ."

Sean pointed at the freshly painted wall. "The station. It's *right there.*"

Carver smiled. "Good. Very good. Anything else?"

"Other than people crawling on the walls?"

"Modulated gravity."

"Told you," Dillon said.

"And the glass trains, they were sooo cool. Where was that place?"

"For later."

Dillon was already up and moving. "I want in."

"Wait," Sean said. "There's this guy. He doesn't want us there."

Carver nodded approval. "Excellent observation. You focused well for a first outing."

"Who is he anyway?"

"Again, for later. Dillon?"

"Get out of my way, bro."

This time Sean was able to watch as Carver manipulated the air behind Dillon's belt. "All right. Through the portal. Stay until I draw you back. Ready?"

"Man, I've been ready for years. Longer."

"Go."

Dillon took a breath and stepped forward.

And rammed straight into the wall.

"Ow." He stepped back. Another breath. And launched himself even harder. This time Sean actually winced at the collision.

"Ow again." Dillon looked angry now. He hated nothing

more than the thought of Sean leaving him behind. Everything was a contest for Dillon. A fight.

"Hang on a sec." Sean stepped up to his brother. Close in, like they were planning a strategy on a soccer pitch. He planted his fist at the point below Dillon's navel, right where he had felt that surge. And realized he still felt it now. "This is where you move from."

"Talk English."

"Just *listen*. This isn't about fighting. You can't batter your way in. So take a chill pill. Go on, do it." He waited until he saw the flames fade in his brother's gaze. "Good. Now focus here where my hand is."

Dillon was never good at exposing the real heart Sean knew beat as fiercely as a forest fire. But for a fleeting instant, he showed Sean what was beneath his rage. He whispered, "What if I can't?"

"You are *not* going to make me do this on my own. Got it?"

Dillon opened his mouth, but only to give a couple of tight breaths. Sean watched him stow the fear down where it belonged. Deep.

Sean said, "There's a power. Feel it? That is your ticket out. You reach with that power. Not at the wall. *Through* it. Okay, on my count. One, two, three, go."

Dillon stepped forward and disappeared.

Carver said, "That was excellent. You have the makings of an instructor. This is a rare gift."

"I know my brother."

"No, no, this is something more. You identify the force, you utilize it, and you explain it in a manner that another person can understand, even when his own mind is fighting him." Carver patted his shoulder. The first time they had ever touched. "Well done."

Sean was still glowing as Carver tugged on the invisible cord, and Dillon stepped backwards into view. Like the wall just melted around him. Like he was moving through a white-washed pool. And Dillon was grinning hugely and saying, "Time for one good scream, then let's do that again!"

But before Sean could add his own confirmation to that idea, another person stepped through the portal. And suddenly the kitchen felt overcrowded. And a much less friendly place to be.

The black man glowered at Sean. "This one disrespected me."

Sean knew an enemy when he saw one. "Back at you."

Carver said, "Steady."

The black man snarled. He said to Carver, "You are wasting everybody's time. They are unacceptable. I fail them as of now."

"I have been given a month," Carver replied. "They passed the first two tests. They trusted against all logic. And they transited. On their first attempt."

"It does not change anything. I am the Examiner assigned to this case."

"Your position does not grant you the powers to fail a student who has passed."

Sean could see the guy just hated that. Really twisted him up. The man replied, "They will fail. It is only a matter of when."

Carver's tone hardened. "I have a month."

"You know the pressure we face. This squanders valuable resources."

"May I remind you," Carver replied, "of the last time we identified candidates from this locale?"

"That was a fluke."

"We are still reaping the benefits of that so-called fluke."

The Examiner wheeled about. "I will take great pleasure in proving you wrong. And ensuring that your seniority is stripped away once your assessment is proven as flawed as I know it to be." He melted away.

Carver walked over and punched the wall. "Bureaucrats."

Sean liked the man more than he thought possible. "You have *got* to meet our dad."

Carver turned around. Forced his anger aside. "My apologies. This should be a time for celebration."

Dillon asked, "What's got that guy's panties in a twist?"

"As I said, it is very rare to find a successful candidate anywhere near your age. Plus there is the locale. Most successful candidates come from communities where these abilities are fostered and talented children are praised." Carver stared at the blank wall. "The Examiner refused me permission to come here. I went over his head. I argued that if twin recruits can emerge from a society that degrades hope, that scorns the promise of better things . . ." He sighed. "We will see who is right."

Sean felt the same visceral force reaching out, only this time it was connecting him to the maimed man. "Were you a soldier?"

"I was. Yes. I still am."

"What was your rank?"

He frowned in the effort to translate. "Beneath the top leader. General, you call them. One rank lower."

"Colonel. What happened to your arm?"

"Again, later. Where was I?"

They said it together. "Celebration."

"Exactly. I am recalling a word we heard often in our observations." Carver showed them genuine warmth. "That word was Charger."

4

I t was hard to say who was more excited after the taxi dropped them off at the Dodge dealership, Dillon or the salesman. Dillon spoke the words that were there shimmering in the salesman's features. "You mean it? I can take any car I want?"

"So long as we can drive it away today."

The salesman was named Chet, who weighed a touch under nine hundred pounds. He didn't swoon at Carver's words. He did, however, quiver.

Dillon wore an expression Sean had last seen in some black-and-white film, where the guy has just heard that the girl he's been yearning over for the past ninety minutes actually loves him too. "There's one right over there."

The car was silver, which was the only thing that kept it from being a total redneck mobile, as far as Sean was concerned. But give Dillon access to some paste-on flames, and Sean was certain his brother would correct that.

Carver said, "Tell me what I am seeing."

Which was when Sean realized Carver was trying hard not to laugh.

Right then and there, Sean started getting annoyed. The only person allowed to laugh at his brother was him. Especially now. When Dillon was about eighteen feet from his second-biggest dream come true.

Dillon, however, only had eyes for the monster on wheels. "That is a Dodge Charger SXT. Six-point-four-liter V8, power shifters, twenty-inch wheels . . ." He looked at the salesman. "What's the interior?"

"Red on black, sir. Special SXT stitching. Glove leather. And don't forget the ten-speaker Beats audio system—"

"With the five-hundred-watt puncher." Dillon sighed. "Perfect."

"Would you gentlemen care to take her for a drive?"

"After we complete the purchase," Carver replied, reaching into his pocket and handing over his plastic.

Carver and Dillon headed for the desk where Chet wedged himself into a chair and started writing. Sean walked over to the dealership's front window and stared sullenly at the sunset view. The flags flapped in the late May breeze. He checked his watch, then used his phone to call home. He told his mother that he and Dillon were on an errand, so they'd have dinner with a friend. He hung up and hoped the word actually fit. That Carver was a friend. But he had his doubts. Serious ones.

Carver walked up beside him. "I know this is not your preference."

Sean heard the quiet underlay of accent, like a spice too

subtle to actually be tasted as something separate. Which only made his suspicions grow.

"You would prefer the . . . how do you say it . . . Beemer?"

Knowing the man had monitored their most private conversations really rankled. "I don't want anything from you. Except what you won't give. Some honest answers."

"I have not lied to you and I never will."

Sean turned so he could look over to where Chet walked Dillon around the SXT, explaining the features. "What kind of guy buys a seventeen-year-old stranger a fifty-five-thousand-dollar car?"

"The car is mine."

"Oh. Right." Sean had enough heat to meet the fathomless gaze. "Do you even know how to drive?"

Carver showed no heat. "Theoretically."

Sean turned back to the sunset. "Great."

"Tell me what is troubling you."

"I just did." But the man stood there, waiting, so he said, "I want to know what you're expecting to get in return for this."

Carver nodded. "I understand." He pointed to the car. "You think I am doing this so you will be in my debt. That is incorrect. This is intended as a reward."

"Like walking through the wall wasn't enough?"

"Look at your brother. The young man who could not do what you did until you taught him how. He showed a fear you did not even feel."

"I was scared."

"No. You doubted. But you knew no fear." Carver gave him a chance to argue. Then he went on, "Your brother has a warrior's heart. He is simple in his actions and his aims. He responds well to instruction and reward. He needs to be focused in the correct direction. I am speaking to him as one soldier to another."

Sean liked being able to look at him directly. It felt like he had crossed over some threshold, meeting the man's gaze. "What are you enlisting him for?"

"An excellent question." Carver aimed his stump at the pair. "Let us complete this purchase, and then I will answer."

5

Thirty minutes later, they were seated in Dillon's favorite restaurant. Actually, Sean liked it well enough. When Carver asked where they wanted to have dinner, Dillon responded by turning the wheel and heading for the Hillsborough Street Grill. Every other birthday, Dillon got to choose. He had selected the Grill ever since his seventh year. How Dillon had first learned about the place, Sean had no idea. Osmosis, probably. A whiff of grilling sirloin burger on the breeze.

"Four thousand years ago by your counting, a planet discovered a set of hidden records which declared that theirs was not the only world where humans existed," Carver told them. "That actually there were many others where humans were the dominant race. At first they refused to believe it. But through this newly discovered record, they also learned how to harness the energy that propelled you through the portal. And they realized the records were true."

Sean asked, "How many others?"

"We are still determining this. For example, your own planet was not discovered until two hundred and seventeen years ago."

"So the records of other worlds isn't complete," Sean said.

"Exactly. Why, we have no idea. There is a great deal we do not know about the Ancients. We do not even know if they themselves were human. Or why they chose to plant humanoid colonies as they did. Or even *how*."

Sean's own response surprised him. Everything Carver was telling them promised to overturn both his perspective and his life's direction. A tiny part of him wanted to run screaming from the room. But mostly he felt . . . The only word that fit was *okay*. Because hovering there in the background was the image of *their station*. What Carver told him built a foundation for that new reality.

Sean asked, "How many worlds that you know about?"

"One hundred and nineteen. Of them, eighty-two are members of the Assembly."

"Are we the last to be discovered?"

"No. There have been seven more since. All as far-flung as your Earth. We call them outposts." He wet a finger in his glass of water and drew an oval on the tabletop. "You are here, in the galaxy's far edge. The main cluster of human-occupied planets is here, midway out the galaxy's opposite side."

"So, a long way."

Carver shrugged. "You have seen for yourself, physical distance means very little when you can open the portal."

The Grill was jammed, as always. It had been a destination of choice ever since some foodie magazine claimed it made the nation's best burgers. The restaurant was noisy enough for their conversation to stay private.

His brother's response disturbed Sean. Dillon stared moon-eyed at the beast parked out beyond the front window. As though a new car was more interesting than hearing their lifelong dream was not actually a dream at all.

Sean nudged his brother. "Anytime you feel like joining in here."

Dillon turned around. "Sorry."

"Sorry doesn't cut it tonight." He elbowed Dillon again. "Pay attention."

"Sure."

Sean didn't like this easy agreement. It promised trouble. Dillon normally responded to being nudged by slugging him.

He turned back to Carver and asked, "So they discovered some secret records, but they don't know where they came from or even how long they've been out there?"

"Correct. The records were hidden in a manner that you will only understand when you progress."

"*If* we progress," Sean said.

"When." Carver was firm on this.

"Your Examiner doesn't agree," Sean pointed out. "He thinks you're wasting your time."

"He is not my Examiner. He is yours. And Examiner Tirian likes everything neat and orderly. Tirian wants to identify the candidates early. As close to birth as possible. So they can be monitored and trained."

"Then we get discovered . . ."

"You are everything he detests. You come from a rogue

37

planet. You have no proper background or training. You are revealed by accident, a random scan of your planet that takes place every few years."

Sean liked this. How he could be comfortable enough with the stranger to come up with the next strand of thought. "And up we pop."

"Out of nowhere. Clearly connected to the concept of a higher force, a greater potentiality."

"And our Examiner, he doesn't like that."

Carver actually showed teeth. "He was livid. He wanted to pretend you did not exist. That you were an anomaly. The empire would best be served by ignoring your existence."

Dillon caught that word. "Empire."

Carver swiveled the gun-barreled gaze to Sean's brother. "Correct."

"But you said the planets are separate."

"One Race, Many Worlds, One Aim."

The way Carver said it, solemn and stern, left Sean in no doubt he had just heard a motto. Or pledge. Or something. "And that aim is . . ."

Carver sat. Waiting.

Dillon offered, "Peace?"

"Good. Very good. Sean asked what you were being enlisted into. There are two threats to peace. The first is internal. All worlds within the Human Assembly pledge to protect the rights of their citizens. There are regular reviews by specialists known as Counselors. If a government fails a review, there is a warning. If the situation is not corrected, the planetary Ambassador and the Counselor are assigned power as temporary governors, or Monitors. In the worst case, the Praetorian Guard are called in."

Dillon scoffed, "You think our Earth gets a passing grade? For real?"

Sean could answer that one. "We're not signed into the empire."

Carver's gaze sparked approval. "Every few years, the Counselor assigned to your sector returns with a specialist team. All human planets are surveyed by a group known as Watchers, who are trained and very sensitive to potential recruits."

"You mean, like, telepathy?"

"Thought transference is not possible, though some technologies come close. No, the Watchers scan at the level of energy, hunting for traces of the same force you harnessed in order to transit. All potential recruits emanate this force. Some Watchers describe it as a flavor, others as a sound. Three months ago they performed the first scan of this planet in almost a decade. And discovered you."

"Better late than never, right?" Dillon grinned. "Except for Tirian."

Sean asked, "So how does a planet get to join your Assembly?"

"There are guidelines set in place. The Counselor assigned to your Earth covers what is known as an outpost sector, in this case containing eleven planets. Every so often, the Counselor will seek to identify a likely leader. They approach, explain who they are and what they represent. So far, not one of Earth's leaders has accepted the empire's challenge. Until that happens, the Counselor is forbidden to do anything except observe. Once a leader has accepted the challenge, the Counselor offers support, advice, resources."

Dillon said, "Counselor sounds kind of, I don't know, wimpish."

"In most cases, Counselors serve as advisors. They and Ambassadors and planetary Justices are also responsible for overseeing a world's level of adherence to the planetary code. In a sense, they represent the empire's might. They are selected through a very grueling process. Your Examiner wishes to become a Counselor, and eventually an Ambassador or a planetary Justice."

Dillon asked the question for both of them. "So what are you?"

"Right now, I serve as your instructor."

"No, I mean—"

"I know what you mean." Carver set his stump on the table beside his empty plate. "I am an officer in the Praetorian Guard."

Sean felt the burn rise in his gut. "And the second threat?"

Carver waited for them to answer that one.

For the first time that evening, Dillon became totally involved. "Aliens? Really?"

Carver did not share their thrill. "The first assault came so soon after the records were discovered, some think the records were revealed because of their coming invasion. As though we had to be under serious threat to realize what had been hidden away. Understand, we have no idea how long our heritage had remained concealed. But very soon after these records popped up, one of the neighboring worlds was overrun."

"By what?"

"This answer must wait. Fear can form a barrier to your progress."

"Sooo . . ." Dillon hesitated, then had to ask. Which was good, because it saved Sean from needing to do it himself. "These aliens, they're seriously scary?"

Carver shook his head, denying them an answer. "Listen very carefully. You met the Examiner. We have one month. There will be tests, not every day, but often. Fail one, and I am required to wipe your memories. You will forget everything."

Sean recalled what Carver had said in the kitchen. "You were not here. We did not meet."

"Correct." He reached into his pocket and passed over two slender hard-shell packs. "Inside are headsets. Place the large element over the center of your forehead. Wear them at night."

Sean did not touch the box. "This is the mind-wipe thingie?"

"No, you will not see that, you will not recall it, and if you proceed as you have started, it will not happen." He nudged the boxes. "These are instructional. You will be taught as you sleep. If you are indeed open to instruction. Tonight will determine this."

The two brothers made the boxes disappear. Then Dillon asked, "But if we pass, we get to fight aliens? For real?"

Carver's gaze remained locked on Sean. As though he needed to get a message across. What exactly, Sean had no idea. "The key to success is a combination of discipline, determination, and confidence. Repeat those words back to me."

The guy was stern enough, strong enough, serious enough, for them to actually do what he ordered.

"Focus on this. Not what comes later. Direct your attention and your energy toward meeting the next goal." Carver slipped from the booth. "That mindset offers the best chance of success."

Sean and Dillon had separate bedrooms connected by a bathroom. It was a silly arrangement as far as Sean was concerned. How much could it have cost to put in a second bath and give the kids some privacy? As it was, two of the bathroom's walls were basically nothing except doors. There were a lot of things Sean didn't like about the place they called home. Their bedrooms had biggish walk-in closets, but the bedrooms themselves were narrow and hardly larger than the closets, like they'd been designed for princesses-in-training. Sean had always known it wasn't the closets or the narrow bedrooms or the silly plastic cross-hatchings they stuck on the windows or the blinds that constantly broke down. Or the one bathroom where there should have been two. Sean had always been restless. He had always felt like the home trapped him and Dillon more than it nurtured.

The bathroom doors were open so he and Dillon could talk. They used to do that all the time. Now, not so much.

Dillon murmured, "So . . . this whole deal. You think maybe it's real?"

Sean decided not to mention the silver beast parked in the drive next door. The same machine, minus the red paint and the side flames, that Dillon had as his computer's background. "We're wearing crowns to bed and you're asking me this?"

The things did actually look like the tiaras they'd seen in movies, when the young princelings were trotted out to greet the world. The circlets had snapped into place as soon as the boxes were opened, silver wire that could be flexed and folded with ease. A flat plate about the size of Sean's thumbnail fitted snug over his forehead. Another two were set on his temples.

Dillon said, "Not to mention how we were handed these things by a military officer from the other side of the galaxy, right?"

"Right."

"He could still bring out the knives and surprise us tomorrow."

"Doubtful."

"Yeah. I mean, he knew about the Charger."

"And the Beemer."

"Really?"

"He told me while Chet was walking you around the car."

"Old Chet. We sure made his day."

"The guy is still quivering."

Dillon went quiet. Then, "I don't know how I feel about them listening in on us."

44

Sean didn't respond. He knew how he felt. It made him burn.

"But I guess it's okay, since we spent the day traveling to our train station."

"With the modulated gravity."

"Right. Just like we imagined."

"We didn't, though. Imagine it."

"Sure." Another pause, then, "I wonder what that means. Modulated."

"Means you can walk on the ceiling, I guess."

"So we study all this stuff," Dillon said. "We pass the tests. And we go fight aliens. Sounds like a good life to me."

Sean nodded. He had been thinking the same thing.

"I don't like the idea of getting mind-wiped if we fail."

"We won't," Sean said. He hated a lot of things about this deal. Most of all, he hated the fear he felt over this prospect. Now that he had done it. Now that he had accepted the reality of something more. "We can't let that happen."

7

The dream was waiting for Sean. That was how it felt. One minute he was thinking on what Carver might have in store the next day. The next he was seated in class. Geography. Sean recognized the chip in the edge of his desktop. It was one of his favorite classes, that and French. Both held the promise of distant lands and endless adventure.

Except Carver was standing at the front of the class. "Ready to begin?"

Sean looked around. "Where's Dillon?"

"He was invited. He did not come."

Invited. For some reason, the word caused Sean to feel a rush of very real fear. The vision wavered, and Carver almost vanished. He heard the man say, "Hold fast."

He did, but only to say, "I won't go without him."

Carver frowned, but he did not say what momentarily stained his features. Instead, he said, "This is an optional course."

"Dillon won't fail for not showing up?"

"Correct. There will be opportunities offered you both as you proceed. Chances to grow in optional directions."

Sean stretched out legs he knew actually weren't there. But it didn't matter, as logic had no place in a dream where he was talking to a man who held the mythical future in the palm of a hand he no longer had. "So let's get started."

Carver pointed at the blank blackboard. "Pay careful attention."

And then the instructor vanished. Not even a poof. Like he had never been there. Which was good for a laugh, since Sean wasn't actually there either.

As soon as it started, Sean was locked in. The blackboard melted like a movie screen coming to life. The background was blue like the sky at dawn. The letters were gold. They swam into view, and as they appeared a woman chanted in a language that was not spoken but rather sung. Her voice sounded almost regal, a remarkable mix of age and timeless wisdom and music. Sean could not see her, and did not care.

Eventually she asked him, "Would you like to speak with me?"

"Sing," Sean corrected. "Sing with you. And the answer is most definitely yes."

He spoke the words in the language he had heard the movers use. A language that carried a promise to go farther and faster than he had ever thought possible. And he was not just speaking the words as they appeared on the blackboard that was no longer there. He was joining. As he spoke, he realized here was the secret of this race, a unique component of their culture. Speaker and listener not only communicated words but also shared a hint of the underlying emotions. Sean and his instructor sang back and forth, and in doing so, shared the moment.

It wasn't possible to weep in his sleep. Even so, Sean knew that was what he wanted. The experience of learning this language called Serenese was that intensely beautiful.

Saturday mornings were usually good for a lazy snooze until whenever. Dinner that evening was the one meal the family tried to have together. But the past couple of years, nobody had tried very hard. Sean knew something was wrong between his parents, and it was getting worse. He was pretty sure Dillon knew the same thing. But they never spoke about it. Living it was already tough enough.

Only that Saturday, Dillon's alarm went off at five thirty. They were due next door at six.

As Sean described the dream, Dillon buried his face in his cereal bowl and refused to meet Sean's eyes. When he was done, Dillon spooned up the last bits, then asked, "Do you remember any of the language?"

"I think so."

"Tell me some."

The words swam up unbidden, easy as his own English. Sean told his brother, "You need to come with me next time."

Dillon stared. "What did you say?"

When Sean explained, Dillon got a sad look and did not speak again until they had crossed the two yards and entered the open front door. When Carver entered from the kitchen, Dillon asked, "I'm not in trouble for not showing up?"

"There are no down-checks. Either you pass or you fail," Carver assured him.

Sean didn't like the misery he had caused in his brother. They fought constantly. There was growing friction in many areas of their lives. But they faced the outside world together, and he hated how Dillon started the day feeling like he might be left behind. So he repeated the words he had said the night before. "I'm not going without Dillon."

Carver's frown did not return. Instead, he merely said, "Noted."

...

They spent three and a half hours learning how to tie an invisible knot. It was partly a harnessing of that same gut-level force and partly a manipulation of their hands, and because they had two hands and Carver only one, they could not get how the two were supposed to work together.

So Carver grew a second hand.

At least, that was how it seemed, as they watched the fore-arm and hand slowly emerge from the closed sleeve, remaining long enough to show them how to fashion the knot using the same energy they had used to travel, the force Carver had formed into a new hand. And then disappearing again. Leaving the stump and the empty sleeve.

Dillon asked, "How come you don't keep the hand around all the time?"

"Both of you go to the transit station and have the other draw you back, and I will tell you."

"I'll go first," Dillon announced. And without hesitation, he went.

"Leave him for a moment," Carver said, speaking for the first time that day in the musical tongue of Serenese. "Can you understand what I am saying?"

"Yes. Is this your home language?"

"No. It is the universal tongue of all Counselors and senior officers. Serenese is spoken by the world where the records were discovered. We think it may hold a link to the power itself."

"By joining with others," Sean guessed.

"Correct. The earlier you learn it, the faster you learn other lessons."

"Can Dillon come to class tonight?"

"We'll see." Carver must have understood the distress, for he added, "It is very rare for a recruit to accept dream-time tutelage at this stage."

"Is this what we are now, recruits?"

"So long as you continue passing your tests. Bring your brother back."

Sean pulled on the line that he had been holding, the one that should not have existed. His conscious mind kept trying to draw the physical reality back into the kitchen where they stood. But all Sean needed to do was remind himself of the life that waited across the hedge, in the home next door. He had no problem drawing on the line and pulling his brother back. None at all.

When they had each done it three times, Carver announced himself satisfied and said, "After our next exercise is completed, I want you to practice this another ten times each."

Dillon asked, "Do we have to stop after ten?"

"You will experience disorientation after a while," Carver replied. "When that happens, stop and eat something. Wait until it disappears. When you become very weary, stop for the day."

"So do we stay here in the kitchen, or can we go do this somewhere else?"

Carver cocked his head, like he needed a different angle to observe Sean's brother. "That is an excellent question."

Dillon positively glowed.

"The answer is, you must become comfortable with your destination and be able to call it up. Once you have arrived at this point, I will teach you how to form a portal. Then you can travel from anywhere. But only so long as you follow very strict guidelines. You must never, ever attempt to travel to an unknown destination. These rules are in place to protect you and others. All public destinations are known as transit stations. They too follow very rigid guidelines. You must never veer from these rules. This forms a component of your tests."

"Identify the goal, form the doorway, then take the step forward," Dillon said. "And never travel outside carefully established boundaries."

"Correct. This will form the first half of your next test.

Traveling to the destination without my assistance in forming the portal."

Dillon reminded him, "You were going to tell us about the hand."

"The primary form of trade between planets is technology. I have an implant that permits me to re-form what I lost. Unless I am with recruits, I never show my wounds. I reveal this because you need to understand the risks."

Sean had not spoken once that entire morning except when Dillon had moved through the wall. It was his way of letting Dillon not feel like he was being left behind. Dillon had responded as Sean hoped he would, forging ahead with the fierce determination that was just one step off the fighting rage Sean knew he felt. That was Dillon's way of handling anything he didn't like. By combat. Sean could not have been more different. He wasn't afraid of fighting. He just didn't see the point.

They lunched on sandwiches Sean and Dillon made, heavy on the mayo and horseradish. The fridge was crammed with unpacked sacks ordered from a local deli mart that delivered. Dillon piled on rare roast beef while Sean sliced a tomato and washed lettuce. Carver ate the same way he had the previous evening, observing them for an instant, tasting cautiously, then eating everything without comment. Sean found Carver's habits as interesting as his almost-hidden accent. And the sleeve that wasn't always empty. Shadows of a life that lay just beyond the unseen portal.

When they were done, Carver opened the kitchen door. "We move outside."

An awning had been erected, tall enough for Sean to be able to lift his hands over his head and not touch the striped cloth. It covered almost half of the fenced-in yard. Dillon looked at the unkempt shrubs, the patchy grass, and declared, "You need a dog."

"I won't be here that long." Carver motioned them to the center of the awning. "Today we begin your first lesson on combat."

Dillon showed the day's first smile. "Now you're talking."

There were two components to this. First they had to shield themselves. Connecting to the force was coming more easily now, especially after the morning's repetitive exercise. Going to the transit station was hardly boring. But after the morning's exercises, it felt almost normal.

Which of course meant they were moving on to a totally new definition of normality.

Shielding required drawing the force completely around them, forming a sort of lumpish globe. Sean wasn't really sure he was successful until Carver tossed a handful of dirt at Dillon and then at him. In both cases, the grit formed a slowly swirling veil before sliding off and falling to earth. Which Dillon declared was, "Another item on the list of coolest things ever."

Defense and attack. Carver repeated the words until Sean felt like they were tattooed on his skull. First ensure safety, then apply force suitable to the threat.

The attack sequence was basically forming a fist from the power and punching forward. Carver brought out a weighted bag that he hung from a metal stand in the middle of the shaded space. Their job was to make the bag swing. For once, Dillon was way ahead of the game. His first punch toppled the bag. Carver's praise brought out the day's second grin.

Once Sean got the hang of it, he was ready to move on to the next thing. Unlike his brother. Dillon was in heaven. He punched and punched and loved it when Carver added to the challenge by flinging grit at them, ensuring they kept the shield in place as they punched. Carver made them accelerate the punches, then moved them farther from the bag.

When he was satisfied both brothers were handling the challenge, he turned toward the back door, saying, "One hour of practice, then you return to transits."

Sean went through the motions mostly because his brother was having such a great time. But he was already bored. Another hour of this held about as much excitement as math.

Which was when Dillon hit him with a rock.

"You're not paying attention."

The rock struck him on the side of his head and *hurt*. Sean didn't think. He just whipped around and slammed the invisible fist right into Dillon.

His brother might as well have been shot from a circus cannon.

Dillon soared through the air and struck the wooden-slat wall dividing Carver's backyard from the neighbor opposite Sean's own home. The barrier was mostly decorative and was definitely not meant to take the kind of blow that came from an invisible fist striking a guy wrapped in an invisible shield.

The wooden wall went down like a disappointed lip. Dillon spilled into the neighbor's rosebushes.

He wasn't hurt—his shield held—but he came up steaming just the same.

"I didn't mean—" Then Sean realized that Dillon wasn't all that interested in having a conversation.

Sean had just enough time to wrap himself in a shield before he went spinning like a top. Dillon had struck him on the side rather than straight on. Sean whirled about so fast he could actually hear the grass squeak beneath his shield. Which would have been kind of cool, except for how he took out Carver's brand-new outdoor grill and then slammed into one of three decorative fruit trees. Almost dislodging the roots.

"Stay down," Dillon growled.

Sean started to offer a couple of comments, questioning his brother's right to give orders. But he decided the words would be wasted. So he stayed down, but only because he figured he didn't need to stand up to strike.

This time Dillon's fall took out the corner posts supporting the canvas awning. The structure flopped down, enveloping him.

Clawing his way out from beneath the striped tent only made Dillon madder still. Now the fist came at Sean straight from above.

The hammer blow punched Sean's shield into the ground like a human-sized nail. From his position thigh-deep in the earth, Sean sent punch after punch at his brother.

Dillon's head stayed down and his feet clawed the earth. He kept raining down his own strikes on Sean. *Bam-bam-ditty-bam.* The blows pounded Sean ever deeper into the hole. Sean could hear the earth grinding around him. He was almost chest deep now, and too mad to care. Dillon had his back against the house's foundation, with a pair of major cracks opening behind him. He didn't seem too worried about that either.

Nobody could get Sean anywhere near as mad as Dillon. He was trying to work up a wedge that he could use like a launcher, send Dillon flying into next week, when the rear door opened up and Carver weaved his good hand. Instantly the air emptied of force. The earth spilled in around Sean's legs, and Dillon fell with a *whoof* to the ground.

Sean was terrified. Completely and utterly scared, so deep in the fear funk he could not even shape the panic into words.

Dillon looked up, his face compacted with grit, and showed his brother the exact same thought. That they were going down.

But Carver did not seem the least bit put out. Instead, he surveyed the collapsed awning, the cracks to his home's foundation and rear wall, and the chest-deep hole Sean was struggling to climb from. Then he reached out and rebuilt the side fence.

When he spoke, Sean realized Carver was working hard to hide his laughter. "That's enough combat practice for one day."

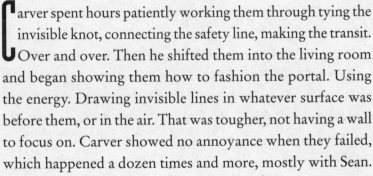

arver spent hours patiently working them through tying the invisible knot, connecting the safety line, making the transit. Over and over. Then he shifted them into the living room and began showing them how to fashion the portal. Using the energy. Drawing invisible lines in whatever surface was before them, or in the air. That was tougher, not having a wall to focus on. Carver showed no annoyance when they failed, which happened a dozen times and more, mostly with Sean.

Sean felt unbalanced by having released his rage against Dillon, as though he had exposed a dark edge that tainted him. This troubled state impacted his ability to transit. But Carver remained patient, bland, watchful. What was more interesting was Dillon's response. Sean's brother looked increasingly troubled every time Sean failed. As though the whole thing was his fault.

When they had both successfully transited five times, Carver called a break. Sean moved to the bathroom and was inspecting the place where Dillon's rock had struck him when his brother appeared in the doorway. He carried a plastic briefcase that he set on the sink. "You're still bleeding."

"I know that."

Dillon opened the case to reveal a miniature pharmacy. "Whoa. The dude has got himself a portable operating room."

Sean stared at the case and its contents. The rage turned to something sick. There on display was every risk they might be facing with future tests.

Dillon found a bottle of hydrogen peroxide, wet a towel, and said, "Turn around."

Sean did as he was told. His brother probed. "Ow."

"The blood's stuck to your hair."

"Leave a little skin, why don't you."

"I'm trying to be gentle. Hold still."

"Ow again."

"Almost done." Dillon dropped the pink-stained towel in the sink and opened a tube of antibiotic ointment. Dabbed a bit, capped the tube, shut the case. Said to the sink, "I shouldn't have thrown the rock."

Sean had a hundred different responses, but they remained unspoken. He could not remember the last time Dillon had apologized for anything. "It's okay."

His brother's relief was evident. "We're good?"

"Until I leave you stranded on some ceiling."

Dillon grinned. "Dude, you did some serious damage to the colonel's house. Your strikes made a crack in the foundation big enough to let the night in."

"I don't think it matters."

"What do you mean?"

"Take a look around. The soap is still in the wrapper. The towel you just used still has its sticker."

"I don't . . ." Understanding dawned on his face. "Carver doesn't sleep here. He doesn't stay here."

"If you could transit whenever you wanted, would you stick around Plantation Heights? I mean, think about it."

But Dillon's mind was tracking in a different direction. "This house, the furniture . . . Carver is here for us."

"We already know that."

"Yeah, but this is, I don't know . . ."

Sean nodded. He understood. "Totally different."

"The dude comes in, does his instruction, then picks up his lunch bucket and transits off to . . ."

"Argonistan. Back to the house and the kids and the two-headed dog."

Dillon's grin was infectious. "I want me some of that."

Sean started to ask, *Even if it costs you an arm?* But he decided there was no need to point out the risk. Because he already knew the answer to that one. For both of them.

...

They were both exhausted by the time they completed ten transits each. Which was a little strange, since nothing about the transit was the least bit physically demanding. But by the time they halted, Sean's entire world felt slightly out of focus. His muscles ached. Correct that—his *bones* were sore. Dillon sat across from him at the kitchen table, his shoulders slumped, his eyes vacant.

Carver told them to quit for the day, led them back to the front door, and saw them off with, "It will come more easily tomorrow."

For once the silence at their dinner table was welcome. Sean had no idea what was on the television droning from the next room. Dillon did not speak once the entire meal.

Their father, Big Phil, was an accountant with the state's Department of Agriculture. When they were young, Dillon thought his father said he worked for the Department of Oatmeal. The name stuck. The Department of Oatmeal pretty much said everything people needed to know about Big Phil and his wife, Gladys. Sometimes at night Sean and Dillon tried to remember the last time their parents had hugged. Forget kissing. Or had a conversation that wasn't punctuated mostly by silences and unfinished sentences. They never fought. They never yelled at the twins. That would have required too much effort. The most excitement the twins ever saw Big Phil show was at the neighborhood cookout, when their dad got together with other dads and compared how long they had until retirement. Big whoop. Their mother managed the local CVS. She left in the morning tired and came back exactly the same.

When dinner was over and they had helped clean up, Sean dragged himself upstairs and collapsed with his clothes on.

Dillon appeared in the doorway. "How do I make the link at dreamtime?"

Sean wanted to tell him to go away. But his brother's quiet desperation managed to filter through his fatigue. "Carver said it was an invitation. Try accepting the idea before you sleep."

"Okay, thanks."

"De nada." Sean dozed off in mid-word. A couple of hours later he got up, drank three glasses of water, undressed, brushed his teeth, and went back to bed. Dillon snored softly throughout.

He was back in bed before he remembered the circlet. He wanted to say, *Not now, not tonight.* But he got up anyway and fitted the dingus into place. The language-dream started up as soon as his head hit the pillow, or so it felt. And truth be told, the lessons were fun.

Sean woke the next morning to the sound of Dillon's alarm clock. He had forgotten to set his own. He lay in bed, wishing he could get his mind to focus, when his brother called, "Breakfast in ten."

Only Dillon did not speak the words. He sang them.

10

That Monday, school was a serious trial. Of course, it was never much better, especially since they had been dropped from the soccer team. But today was particularly rough. The lingering effects of the weekend's exercises fitted around Sean's brain like a blanket. Everything came through slightly muffled. Whenever he managed to fully focus, all he could think about were the wasted hours he was forced to endure in class.

In elementary school the powers that be had decided it would be best to separate him and Dillon. The idea was, the twins could then develop their own identities free from each other. That lasted, like, three days. Until the teachers got together and compared notes and realized that the twins were bouncing back and forth between classes, working the system. No reason, except they liked playing with everybody's heads. So they were dumped in the same class. Permanently.

Today Dillon was one seat removed, and the desk between them was empty. First class was geography, the teacher was one of Sean's favorites, but still he felt like the lesson was just another dentist's drill working on his poor head.

Dillon positioned his notebook so Sean could see and wrote, *Arghhhh.*

Sean shifted his pad slightly and replied, *Another nine days of this until summer recess.*

Just shoot me.

That was pretty cool, waking me up yesterday with a little tune from the Serenese hit parade.

Dillon smirked at his page. *I have to tell you, bro, I wish I was there right now. The lady singer is hot.*

You saw her?

No need. I know a hottie when I hear one. By the way, she's only got eyes for me.

Not what she told me last night.

We spending this afternoon walking through walls?

We'll find out in—Sean checked the wall clock—*five hours and eleven minutes.*

Dillon groaned. *I'm dying here.*

Two different ice ages came and went between first period and the lunch bell. Sean drifted off twice, something he normally never did. He was rewarded in math by the teacher slamming the ruler onto Sean's desk. When Sean jerked back to full alert, he smacked his head-wound on the side wall. At least Dillon showed the courtesy to wince.

At lunchtime they walked the hall together. Completely disconnected from the scene. Actually, the noise hurt Sean's ears, like he was hungover for no reason. Up ahead the din rising from the cafeteria was a drill waiting to take aim at his skull. Dillon must have felt the same, because he was moving slower than Sean. They let the tide sweep around them until the hall was empty.

Dillon muttered, "I don't know how much of this I can take."

"Right there with you."

Dillon leaned on a locker and swiped at his face. "Is it always going to make us feel like we've got the flu?"

"I don't—" Sean stopped in mid-complaint when he heard a girl whimper.

Together he and Dillon hurried on down the empty hallway.

The cafeteria jutted from the rear of the school to their left. Straight ahead were the playing fields. The gym was off to their right. Sean rounded the corner and heard the girl say, "Get *away* from me."

Sean instantly recognized the guy's voice. "All I want to do is talk."

He and Dillon stepped into view as the girl snapped, "I am so totally through talking to you."

The hall leading to the gym held glass-fronted display cases containing trophies for academic and sports achievements. All the stuff nobody ever looked at. There were semi-hidden alcoves where the cabinets ended and doorways opened, janitorial and coach offices and stuff. Eric was standing with his back to the hall, holding Carey Havilland in one of those niches as he said, "We dated for, like, five months. That doesn't mean enough for you to listen?"

"You're not talking. You're threatening." Carey struggled against his grip. "Now let me *go*."

Carey Havilland possessed a beauty that Sean thought of as lyrical. As though she had been born for a different age, one where sonnets were written in her honor. But life had not been overly kind to her. The first week of school the previous year, she had lost her mother in a traffic accident. Carey disappeared for a while, and when she came back, the teachers all treated her like she was made of crystal.

Carey was not fragile in form, yet there was a tender quality to her gaze and her smile that had Sean and Dillon both wishing they could make everything better for this amazingly sweet and beautiful girl.

She was defined by things that set her apart from the cliques of other lovely girls. She wore no makeup. She chose clothes that looked utterly out of fashion. Not punk, not grunge, not chic. Carey was basically friends with everyone, and yet she never dated. Until Eric entered the picture.

Eric was the star of both the football and the basketball team, the guy most likely to go where he wanted and be whatever. One day Eric became the guy driving her home. For a while, Carey and Eric had been the school's hot item. Then abruptly the whole deal was off. Sean and Dillon rarely talked about Carey, because they both wished they could be the guy at her side.

Now Sean watched as Dillon started toward them. Like his brother was connected to alarm bells at some level below thought. The cry went out, and super-Dillon sprang into action, while anybody else would still be figuring out what they had just heard. Which was, "You're *hurting* me."

"You heard Carey," Dillon said. "Step back and let her go."

Eric's problem was, he thought he deserved the world on a string. The guy everybody else sort of envied and hated and wished they could be. Eric was graduating in nine days and already had a scholarship to play ball at UF. He was blond and he was big and he always got what he wanted. And what he clearly wanted just then was for Dillon to, "Bug off."

"No problem," Dillon said. "Soon as the lady says everything's cool."

Eric switched stances to look behind him. He took a second to recognize Dillon. "You got a death wish, Kirrel?"

"This is your last chance."

"Guys, remove this garbage." Eric turned back to the squirming girl. "Carey and I have unfinished business."

Sean did not actually see who Eric was speaking to until the two guys appeared by the gym doors. He realized this was not just a confrontation. This was a setup. For the first time that endless day, Sean's vision clarified. The guys were the largest of Eric's crew, two hulking brutes Dillon called Frick and Frack. They liked to walk the halls between class, pretending not to notice as they bounced smaller beings off the walls. Tossing pretend apologies over their shoulders as they marched and chuckled. *Sorry. Yuk-yuk.* They wore their grins now, and Sean realized they had been stationed where they would guard the gym after Eric pulled Carey in there and used the empty sports center to teach her whatever lesson he had in mind. From the sheer terror on Carey's face, she had long since figured out this was her fate.

Which was when Sean stepped between the pair and Dillon. Frack said, "Two for the price of one."

Without turning around, Dillon asked, "You okay with the Frickettes?"

Sean decided now wasn't the time for a little chat, as the brutes were closing in. When the first one reached for his neck, Sean extended the force from his gut, forming the same invisible fist he had last used to crack the house's foundation with his brother playing hammer. Only this time the guys weren't surrounded by any shield.

The Frickettes went tumbling. They slammed through the gym's swinging doors. Both doors drummed the side wall and gave off a massive *boom* that echoed through the empty chamber. The pair tumbled across the court, coming to rest beneath the nearside basket.

Sean followed them inside and ordered, "Stay down."

The Frickettes were slow in rising, but rise they did. And growl. Sean assumed it was the sort of noise they used to terrify the opposing team's defensive line. Frack actually lowered himself into a three-point stand.

Sean said, "Really? You think that's going to work?"

Maybe it was the previous day's lingering effects, but he could not have been calmer if he'd been sprawled poolside reaching for the sunscreen. Sean didn't want them walking around describing how some force out of nowhere dismantled their worlds. So he waited until they were up close and personal. Then he reached out, like he was actually shoving them away. And slammed them against the far wall. Just one punch was enough to fell both Frickettes. This time they didn't get up.

Sean walked back into the hallway to discover Dillon had Eric up against the janitor's door. The star athlete's blond hair was all messed up. His team jacket was ripped at the sleeve. His eyes were slightly glazed. Which was hardly a surprise. Because Dillon was gripping him with one hand and slamming him against the steel door leading to the equipment room. Each of Dillon's invisible hammer blows dislodged the door's upper hinge a fraction more. The sound was very satisfying. A thud, a squeak from the metal door frame, a grunt from the school star. Another thud. Another squeak. Another grunt.

"Dillon."

"Yo."

"Eric has gotten the message."

"You think?" Another thud. Another grunt. "What do you say, Eric. You going to leave Carcy alone permanently?"

With every shove against the door, Dillon's force compressed Eric from hairline to sneakers. Like he was working up a bowl of mashed athlete.

Sean said, "Enough, Dillon."

"Yeah, maybe you're right." Dillon let the guy go.

Eric slumped down and sat sprawled against the seriously damaged door.

Dillon leaned in close and said very softly, "You touch her again, I'll know. And I'll hurt you."

Sean couldn't be certain, but he thought he saw a flicker of something pass through the guy's vacant gaze. Confusion, definitely. Maybe a little fear. Just then, though, the high school star was too busy trying to draw a decent breath to do more than cough.

Sean asked Carey, "You all right?"

"Yes." She leaned over and picked up her purse. But her hands were shaking so hard she upended the thing and all her stuff spilled out.

Dillon dropped to his knees and scooped up the scattered items. "Here you go."

"Thanks. You're Dillon, aren't you?"

"Yes." Dillon offered her a supporting hand and pretended not to see the tears. "We could go sit on the bleachers outside, give you a chance to catch your breath. Sean can go get you a Coke. Would you like a Coke?"

"I guess . . . A Coke would be good."

"Sean?"

"On it." But he stayed there, watching as his brother guided her out the rear doors.

Sean had never heard his brother talk like that before. Smooth and calm and caring. Like he was born to play the guy in the white hat, only neither of them had realized it until right then.

Which made it kind of amazing when Carey said, "My knight in shining armor."

Dillon's grin was the only goofy thing about him. "Come on, let's go pretend this never happened."

11

Dillon basically coasted through that afternoon, apparently carried by the bliss of helping a beautiful damsel in distress. One who claimed to be in his debt. Sean had actually heard Carey say the words. Between the next two classes Sean was tempted to remind Dillon of the chances he had, attaching his star to a girl that good-looking. But he let his brother float for a while longer. Besides, the disconnected feeling he'd had all day had begun to solidify into something else entirely. A deep sense of foreboding drifted in the school's air, coagulating just overhead, like his own personal cloud of doom.

Their last class was interrupted by Carey showing up. She nervously smiled their way as she handed a note to the English teacher, who announced, "Misters Kirrel, it appears you are summoned by higher authorities."

The teacher had that manner of speaking, like she was quoting poetry when she was correcting their punctuation. Sean liked her well enough, though the odes she loved to read out loud were good for a last-class snooze. But there was no chance of dozing off now, not with his heart going like the beast beneath the Charger's hood.

When they were in the empty hallway, Dillon revealed his own share of the tremors when he asked, "Is the thing with Eric coming back to bite us?"

"They don't tell me anything." Carey served as part-time office assistant. Sean had heard her describe the job as a totally new level of boring. Even so, her presence definitely perked up every male student's visit to the principal. She went on, "When I showed up for my three minimum-wage hours, Ms. Levitt handed me the pink slip and said go. I went."

Carey still carried herself with a mildly shattered air, as though her world had been reknit but with one part missing. She tried for bright and almost succeeded. Sean doubted anyone else would know just how close to the edge she was. He liked how Dillon touched her arm, a friend who wanted to offer strength in a hard time.

Dillon asked, "You doing okay?"

She did her best to make light of it. "I got the jitters in the middle of class. And I can't stop looking over my shoulder. Otherwise, I'm okay."

"I could hang around, play your personal security."

Carey smiled, like she had been waiting all day for Dillon to offer. "Maybe we should discuss this."

As they approached the admin offices, Sean's feeling of impending doom grew stronger still. "Are we up for the firing squad?"

"I haven't seen Eric or his crew or the coach." It was Carey's turn to pat Dillon's arm. "If they show up, so will I." She pointed them to the bench that students referred to as the hot seat and disappeared into the inner sanctum.

Dillon asked Sean, "You okay?"

"Worried. Tired. Semi-stressed."

"Carey's got our back."

"Looks like it's your back she's interested in."

Carey emerged and said, "She's got someone with her. You okay hanging here awhile?"

Sean was about to reply, "Like we have a choice." But Dillon was already up and swinging around the counter, back into her private space. Like he chatted with beautiful people every day of the week. And Carey welcomed him with a smile. A real one.

Sean didn't know whether he felt jealous or not. Just then, the sense of a storm beyond the horizon was all he had room for.

Dillon was still over there, talking softly and making Carey laugh, when her phone rang. She answered, hung up, and announced, "Okay, guys. You're up."

They walked into the office and found Carver seated across from the principal. Only it was a Carver transformed. Gone was the missing hand, the scar, the casual wear. In their place was a gentleman in a very fine suit, polished shoes, Rolex, even a gold class ring. A new alligator briefcase rested in his lap.

"Sean, Dillon, come in. I assume you know Colonel . . ."

"Carver."

"Colonel Carver says you have proven to be of remarkable help in researching a book project?" Clearly Ms. Levitt was having difficulty actually fitting the components of that sentence together. So she fashioned it into a question.

Sean for one found no need to respond. Beside him, Dillon remained mute as a post.

"And your book project . . ."

"Is on new directions in military response," Carver replied. "The required research is considerable. And I have a very tight deadline."

"Yes. You said. One month."

"Actually, we are down to just twenty-eight days."

"So you would like to have me excuse these students from their final two weeks of class."

Sean piped up, "Nine days."

"Indeed."

Carver said, "I have been granted a research stipend. Which I would use to pay for the time of these two students. And they would also be rewarded with quite a considerable amount of learning."

Ms. Levitt was not convinced. "Are either of you gentlemen interested in military matters?"

"Not until we started working on this," Sean replied.

"Now I'm fascinated," Dillon said.

"But it's pretty exhausting," Sean said. "We put in some long hours."

"Day and night," Dillon agreed.

Carver said, "But they can earn in one month what many of your students can't attain in an entire summer."

"And we haven't been able to find any other job at all," Sean said.

"I see." The principal was a tight woman. Tight features, tight hair, narrow glasses over a tight gaze. Thin lips. Narrow voice, like she was always slightly winded by the need to speak at all. "Well, I'm afraid I can't simply allow them to forgo their schoolwork."

Sean knew what was coming before Dillon took a breath. His brother was going to whine. As in, the last nine days of class were a total waste of good air. The teachers were counting down the clock as much as the students, who mentally were already poolside. Nothing got done. Which Sean knew was totally the wrong thing to say to a woman who was readying her narrow little arguments.

But Dillon was too far away to nudge. So Sean punched him with the force. One little blow. Quick and light as he could make it, straight to the ribs.

Dillon whoofed out all the unspoken protests.

"Are you all right, young man?"

Dillon shot his brother a sour look. "Something in my chest."

Carver glanced over at Sean. Cast him the quick dimples. The slight unfrosting of that hard gaze. There and gone. He turned back to the principal. "I understand your need to follow protocol. Which is why my superiors have set up a conference call with the school superintendent."

She faltered. "I beg your pardon?"

"That was why I came here today. I assumed it would require a higher-level entreaty. And we really do not have time to spare."

"Every hour counts," Sean agreed solemnly. Carver wasn't the only guy who knew how to swallow his laughter.

Ms. Levitt toyed with her pen. "I suppose we could permit these gentlemen to miss their final three days."

"And be released from school for the remaining days at lunchtime," Carver suggested.

Sean added, "Please."

She offered him a smile that remained about ten thousand miles from her narrow gaze. "I suppose that might be possible."

Carver was already moving. "I assure you, madam, these gentlemen will be well rewarded by your kindness."

...

Carver had somehow managed to drive the Charger to school, but he showed no interest in getting back behind the wheel now that Dillon was around. Which meant Dillon's day was about as complete as it could get. He was leaving school behind the wheel of a new SXT, after rescuing the girl he had no business even talking to, and hearing the principal say his school hours had just been cut by sixty percent. Sean crammed himself into the rear seat and wondered why he felt none of his brother's delight. But there was something to the day, a faint odor of caution and menace. Or perhaps he was just not used to things going their way.

When they pulled into the drive, the front door opened, and the Examiner scowled down at them.

Carver said, "He's early."

Dillon showed his second dose of fear that day. "We're going to be tested? Why didn't you say something?"

"There was nothing to be gained by alarming you in advance." Carver turned so he could address both of them. "You know the drill. Create the portal, pass through, return. Then in the second portion, raise the shield, defend, attack. You have already successfully accomplished both tasks. Remember your lessons. You will do fine."

Sean followed them up the steps and into the house. He pretty much managed to ignore the Examiner's irate presence. Something at gut level told him the Examiner was not the reason for how he felt. Which was not a good thing. If there was a threat out there worse than having his mind wiped, it had to be bad indeed.

Carver asked, "Which of you wants to go first?"

"I am the one to make that decision," the Examiner snapped.

Carver just sighed.

The Examiner pointed to Sean and said, "You. Out."

"Go wait in the kitchen, Sean."

Sean wanted to tell Carver how he was feeling, but their instructor remained in the living room. The door was shut and Sean could not hear anything beyond a faint murmur. Ten minutes later Dillon walked in, flushed but pleased enough to declare, "Piece of cake."

When Sean took his place in the living room, the Examiner's frown seemed somewhat displaced. As though things were so far removed from his expectations that he was being forced to rethink his assessment. Which should have been good for a grin. But the sense of unease remained, even as Sean successfully created the portal, passed through to the train station, and allowed Carver to draw him back.

Sean performed three more transits. Throughout the test, the Examiner did not actually look his way. Carver, however, appeared genuinely pleased.

When the Examiner remained silent after the fourth transit, Carver opened the kitchen door and said, "Outside, both of you."

Carver positioned them under the repaired awning, then said, "Raise your shields, then on the Examiner's word you attack."

The Examiner protested, "Once again, those are instructions I should give."

This time Carver did not back down. "Follow the protocol you practiced all weekend."

Tirian glowered at Carver and said, "Shields up." A moment's pause, then, "Attack."

Sean sent the blows at Dillon, he got the licks in return, they both plowed furrows in the bare earth, same as before. Again, Sean was fairly certain the guy did not bother watching. After a few minutes the Examiner said, "Enough."

Sean nodded in response to Dillon's wide grin. Inwardly he tried to identify what had him so knotted up. He wondered if maybe that was all it was, learning to accept that the bad old days were truly behind them.

The Examiner did not seem to be able to hold on to his customary heat as he said, "This changes nothing." He took a step, like he was walking off the rear porch, and vanished.

Carver sighed once more, then said, "Inside."

When they were seated around the kitchen table, Carver

said, "What the Examiner in his wisdom failed to inform you of is that you are ahead of schedule."

Dillon said, "That's good, right?"

Carver looked at Sean's brother, like he was trying to decide how much to say. "It is better than that. You appear to be accelerating. You have both managed to attend night class. Your skill with the Serenese language is improving. Your shields are well grounded, your attacks almost natural. Your training overall is moving at twice the standard rate."

Sean asked, "So we'll be done in two weeks?"

Carver's implacable gaze turned his way. "You are so eager to be rid of me?"

"No," Dillon said. "Definitely not."

Sean replied, "I just want to be done with the tests."

"The tests will continue for several years. Longer, if you specialize. But the risk of being mind-wiped ends with the conclusion of tier one. And yes, that could come more swiftly than expected." Carver glared at the empty space beyond the kitchen door. "No matter what the Examiner might think."

"Well, all right." Dillon grinned at his brother. When Sean did not respond, he asked, "What's eating you?"

"Ever since midday I've had this feeling that something's seriously wrong."

Carver waved that aside. "Such unsettled moments are part of learning to transit. Your entire definition of reality is being redrawn. Be patient. Rest when you feel the need." He pulled out a drawer in the table and withdrew a manila envelope. "I have something for you."

The "something" turned out to be two sets of keys to the Charger.

And two packets of cash. Fifties and twenties.

"I prefer to pay you in advance," Carver said. "Now go out and celebrate. That's an order."

12

They went back to the Grill. Of course. Sean did not even bother pointing out that Raleigh was home to hundreds of other restaurants. As far as Sean was concerned, it really didn't matter where they ate. He still carried his burden of worry. Even Dillon noticed it, despite the fact that the guy was living inside a buffet line of dreams come true.

Toward the end of their meal Dillon finally groused, "Think you could check your cloak of doom with the lady at the door?"

"Sorry. Maybe you should just drop me off at the house."

"No way. Like you said, we're in this together." He pointed at the half-finished burger on Sean's plate. "You want that?"

"You can *not* still be hungry."

"No, man, but this is too good to leave."

"Go for it." Sean glanced out the window at the westering sun. He didn't enjoy being a drag. It wasn't like him.

His general state of mind was mild optimism. But there was something . . .

Dillon asked, "How much cash do we have left?"

"You know perfectly well how much." But he said it anyway. "Seven thousand minus the cost of this meal."

Dillon sighed contentedly. "I am just loving this."

They left the Grill and arrived at the bank where they had their savings accounts in time to deposit the funds. Just drove up to the outside window, and Dillon chatted with the lady while Sean filled out the deposit form. Like they were two normal people with a normal wad of cash that came from a normal kind of job.

Dillon asked what Sean wanted to do, and when he didn't answer, Dillon turned them back down Hillsborough. The five-lane road divided the shopping district known as Cameron Village from the thirty-two thousand students of NC State. Hillsborough was a main artery that defined much of what was Old Raleigh, the good and the bad. They headed east toward the state capitol, passed the Y and the Candlelight Inn, toured the blocks of head shops and bakeries and pizza joints and T-shirt factories, before meeting up with the stone canyons of downtown. Then Dillon wheeled them around and started back. Keeping their speed down, just out for a sunset cruise. Sean should have been thrilled with everything. Instead of acting like he was a card-carrying member of the dark-cloud set.

The Charger came with an automatic regulator that reduced the engine's power to just four cylinders when idling or driving at low revs. The switch was remarkably smooth, and the motor still gave off a throaty rumble even when geared down. The noise filled the car with a sense of easy anticipation. Dillon had the radio turned to some HD rock station, which Sean could take or leave. Normally he would have insisted on equal time being given to his jazz, which Dillon absolutely hated. But Sean was still filtering everything through his glum lens. Even the bass line strong enough to thump the car like a metal drum couldn't touch him.

As Dillon slid into the turn lane and rumbled past the old bell tower that marked State's main entrance, Sean tried to argue his way out from under his dark cloud. Gone was any concern over pocket money or summer jobs or SATs or even which college might find room for them both. All of it. Vanished forever. If only they could keep passing those tests. As they rumbled along the university's tree-lined streets, Sean knew he should have been basking in the dual glows of ready cash and a new car.

Which was when the girls flagged them down.

Three female students stood by one of the many glass-covered bus alcoves that serviced the main campus. Dillon swung the car to the curb like he was always getting signals from a trio of beauties. Which these ladies most certainly were. Two blondes and a brunette. All dressed in mini shorts that fit them like bikini bottoms. Small ones. And tank tops that looked spray-painted into position.

The lone brunette leaned into Dillon's open window and gave them a smile Sean felt in his toes. "You guys going to the party?"

"We are now," Dillon replied.

"Can we get a lift?"

Sean already had his door open. "Ladies."

The brunette chose to sit up front with Dillon. Which meant Sean was crammed into a blonde sandwich. Not that he was complaining.

After all, these were *college girls*.

Going to a *party*.

Every single fantasy his seventeen-year-old mind had ever dreamed up instantly grew wings and did a fluttery bat thing around the car's interior.

Thankfully, his inability to respond was masked by the brunette declaring, "I love this song." Then she cranked the stereo up to a volume that could only have been described as headbanging.

And suddenly Sean was in between two girls who actually managed to dance in that small backseat.

Again, no complaints.

The brunette directed Dillon to their destination by means of sign language. And smiles.

NC State still had a number of freshmen dorms inside the main campus. But the vast majority of student housing was now outside the Beltway. The university had bought entire apartment developments, over four thousand units, and were building still more. They set up free dedicated bus service that ran 24-7.

The brunette directed them across the Beltway and into the confusion of countryside being transformed into mini campuses. They passed one cul-de-sac after another, taking a sunset ride through the growing collegiate sprawl.

They pulled into a half-finished complex, where the buildings were surrounded by raw earth and roads going nowhere. A party filled the avenue and spilled into the weed-strewn meadow. Young people danced and drank and shouted and flowed around bars and buffet tables and . . .

Cars.

The center of the lane held every dream car Sean and Dillon had ever drooled over.

Including a new seven-series BMW. The color was Sean's favorite, a sophisticated blend of café au lait and silver. Twenty-inch Michelins with racing treads. The most beautiful machine on the planet.

The blonde next to him said, "Want to drive it?"

The other blonde said, "What is this, *drive*? I bet he wants to *race* it."

The brunette turned down the music and said to Dillon, "Forget those foreign heaps. Let's go drag this baby."

Sean was already preparing the standard backseat warning. It was an instinctive response, because if anyone had asked he would have said that he and Dillon had left their thinking brains back at the bus stop where they found the ladies.

But Dillon said, "Not tonight."

The brunette revealed the most amazing pout. "Not even if I ask nice?"

Dillon said, "Not even for seven thousand dollars."

Which made no sense to anyone but them, but it was good for a real smile. Sean was about to ask the brunette to let them out so they could go join the party.

Which was when he heard the scream.

There was something about the sound. As though Sean had heard it before. Or maybe it resonated inside him. Like the scream vibrated at the same frequency as his bones.

Dillon stabbed the front windshield. "There!"

Sean saw it too. A Nissan low rider streaked up and halted directly in line with them. Eric sat behind the wheel. He leered through his open window, like the sole reason for him being there was to mock them. Like this was what he lived for.

He draped one hand on the wheel. The other was clenched around Carey's neck.

She fought Eric's grip with frantic futility. She looked straight at them and shrieked, "Help me!"

Eric shook her like a misbehaving doll. Carey's hair caught the sunset in a ruby blush. Then Eric goosed the engine and burned rubber in a high-pitched farewell. Dust lingered with the smoke.

Dillon mashed the stereo's off button. In the sudden quiet Sean heard his brother growl deep in his throat.

Brunette complained, "I liked that song."

The words jarred inside Sean's brain. He wanted to ask how she could be so unconcerned about another woman's distress. But Dillon slammed the car into drive and mashed the accelerator.

The Charger responded like it had waited all its short life for this moment.

Up to that point, the engine's noise had been both beautiful and muted. Now it was all bellowing menace. The tires burned with the same rage that flooded Sean and flamed in Dillon's pinched features. Dillon fought the wheel, oversteered momentarily, then took aim for where the Nissan swiftly disappeared. The crowd formed a channel of cheering salutes to their departure.

The blonde to Sean's left kissed his neck and shouted into his ear, her words as hot as her lips, "Isn't this *fun*?"

The lure was too perfect. That was the thought that slapped Sean awake. He tore his gaze off the road ahead and stared at the girl. She met him with an inviting smile. As though this was exactly what she wanted. Him, the race, the danger high. All of it. Perfect.

Yet there was something else now. Perhaps it had always been there. But the roaring engine and the racing acceleration and the adrenaline rush all formed a piercing clarity. And Sean saw beyond the woman's beauty. Into her gaze.

And he realized that *this wasn't real*.

Logic was no more important now than when he was walking through walls. Despite everything his eyes saw, he was certain the spark in the woman's gaze was alien. He could not say why he knew. Only that he was certain.

This was a setup.

He tore his eyes away. He could not let her see that he knew. So when she leaned in close and breathed fire on his ear, he did not respond as he wanted, which was to jerk and shudder with revulsion.

She shouted, "Don't you just *love* this?"

Sean felt his lips pull back from his teeth and hoped she did not catch the lie in his expression or his reply. "This is amazing!"

Only it wasn't. It was terrifying. Because as he saw the road race up toward them, he became instantly, utterly certain of one thing.

They were going to die.

The Charger ate up the straight-line road. The red Carolina clay exposed by the building sites rushed past on both sides, blurring with their acceleration until they tore down a street lined with dried blood.

They gradually caught up with the Nissan. But Sean wasn't watching the car now. He knew that wasn't real either. He had no idea what Eric drove, but he was positive it wasn't this. The thoughts punched his brain faster than the Charger's forward momentum. They were trapped, and this was why the women were here. Or whatever they were. Their job was to get them into this position. So that they could be . . .

Murdered.

The instant he made this connection, the Nissan up ahead of them disintegrated. One moment the four exhaust pipes were flashing flames with each gear change. Then the car was no longer a car at all. Only smoke. A single puff of reddish-silver exhaust. And the Charger punched through.

Directly at the trees.

The road jinked to the right. The curve was too sharp for their speed. They were milliseconds from a strike and their deaths.

And the women shrieked their triumphant laughter.

The Charger struck the curb and was catapulted up. The nose dragged the earth, the car now at a ninety-degree angle.

And still the women laughed.

A tree limb was aimed straight at the front windscreen. Another second and it would become a lance through Sean's heart.

Sean did not think. There was no time for deliberation. He acted.

He shook off the women's hold, then enveloped himself and Dillon in a single protective shield. Sean then used the car's motion to lunge him and Dillon forward.

And transited them through the portal he had fashioned.

He and Dillon tumbled across the polished stone flooring of the massive train station.

People shouted and leapt aside. Sean took down seven people. Dillon collided with an even dozen as he slid a hundred feet or so and came up hard against a massive electronic sign. One of the metal posts crumpled, but the sign remained upright.

Dillon did not get up.

Sean rose, ignoring the angry protests, and raced over.

Dillon's hands were bloody. He gripped a shard of tree limb that stuck out of his side, just above his belt. But the pain on his features had nothing to do with his injury. He looked up at Sean and cried, "I killed them!"

"They weren't real," Sean replied. But his brother probably didn't hear. Because Dillon's eyes rolled back in his head and he passed out.

14

Sean pretty much ignored the firestorm their arrival created. The people they had decked picked themselves up and shook their fists and shouted. The complaints grew louder still when the uniforms arrived. Sean did not understand a word of what was said, not by the passengers and not by the cops. Their uniforms were dark grey and their belts did not carry anything that resembled a gun. But their stern expressions were exactly what he'd have expected from cops back home.

The two cops called emergency services. Sean knew this because soon a young woman rushed through the onlookers carrying what at first glance appeared to be a long white pole, but she flipped it open to form a stretcher. She then knelt over Dillon and checked him carefully. She spoke Serenese and finally got Sean to release his hold, shift over, and help them lift Dillon. But as he started to argue over being allowed to carry one end of the stretcher, the woman muttered to him, "Limp."

At least, that's what Sean thought she said.

He glanced at the cops, saw how they looked at him, and figured they were planning to drop off his brother, then go find a cramped little room with bars where they could lock Sean up. So he did what the woman said and limped. It didn't hurt that he was stained from knees to elbows with his brother's blood.

It turned out the station had its own emergency clinic. And the woman was a doctor who waited until the station's uproar was dimmed by the glass portal to ask, "What happened to you?"

"We were attacked. Or trapped. I don't know how to describe . . ."

"Don't describe," the doctor told him. "Just tell."

Sean gave it to her in words minced by adrenaline and shock. The women, the party, the scream, the chase, and the realization. What he said was enough to cause the doctor to flinch. Like Sean had struck her. Or scared her witless. But the woman recovered swiftly, and when one of the cops barked a question, she replied with a blank professionalism and a few calm words.

The doctor went back to working on Dillon. When she spoke, it was in a voice bland as yogurt. "You are recruits?"

"Yes."

The doctor placed patches over Dillon's temples and heart. A screen appeared in the wall above his head, showing his vital rhythms. She spoke a word and a drawer slipped from the featureless wall beside her. She applied another patch to Dillon's arm, and his vitals slid into the smooth waves of deep sleep. "What planet?"

"Earth?" Sean made his response a question because he assumed from what Carver had told them that the place would be unknown. So he added, "An outpost world."

The doctor translated the cop's next question. "Why did you bring your trouble here?"

"This is the only transit point we know."

The doctor looked at him. And then she smiled. "Really?"

"We have this station on the wall of our bedroom. We've been working on it since we were seven years old."

The cop demanded something, probably wanting to hear her translation. She refitted her blank expression and waved casually, like the whole exchange was unimportant. She checked Dillon's vitals once more, then stepped over to where Sean was holding up the side wall. "Is any of the blood you wear yours?"

"No."

She gave him a careful going-over. The doctor was in her late thirties, dark-haired and cute in a highly intelligent and focused manner. The difference between her and the ethereal beauties who almost took them out could not have been greater.

She turned her attention back to Dillon. "I suppose I should welcome you, but that might be out of order just now. What is your brother's name?"

"Dillon. Will he be all right?"

"Dillon has been wounded and has experienced a severe

shock. But unless there are injuries I have not yet identified, he should make a full recovery."

Sean looked at the branch still poking from his brother's side. "How can you be sure?"

"Perhaps it is because our medicine has advanced beyond that of your outpost world. Your brother is breathing. His heart rate is strong."

"Does your medicine work? For Earth people, I mean."

She seemed to like that. "I am happy to report that all your brother's organs appear to be in their proper places."

The cop broke in at that point, halting their momentary calm with a bark of cop speech, and the doctor translated, "He wants to know who attacked you. But I am reluctant to repeat what you said. Your explanation carries . . ."

"Baggage."

She liked that enough for her eyes to spark. But she kept her expression bland. "Precisely. So may I suggest your official answer be about women and an accident?"

"No problem." And it wasn't, since that was exactly what happened. As he gave a simplified version of events, Sean struggled to make sense in his own head of what had really happened.

The cops made notes on a translucent panel, then held it up and took several shots of both Sean and Dillon.

Sean asked quietly, "Why shouldn't they know—"

"Later, yes? How far along are you in your training?"

"Four days. Unless it's after midnight. Then five."

The cops interrupted her response by reaching for Sean. When the doctor protested, one of them actually snarled at

her. Sean was tempted to snarl back, but the doctor responded
with a sharp retort of her own. When the cop tried to argue,
she became more forceful still and pointed them from the
room.

Whatever she said was enough to turn the cop's face beet-
red. He snarled a final time, then took plastic cuffs from his
belt pouch and reached for Sean's wrist. The doctor objected,
which seemed to please the cop. He cuffed Sean to a wall
hook he had not noticed until that moment. In truth, Sean
did not mind. He was with his brother. The doctor was an
ally. There was a chair within reach, where he could settle
when his knees turned liquid. Which happened the minute the cops left and the doctor started working out the
branch.

The room was long and angled and narrow and completely
white. The front section held a white desk and a padded
white chair and nothing else. The desk's surface was utterly
clear. Sean's chair was white, as was the bed where Dillon
lay, jutting like a white tongue from the opposite wall. The
room was illuminated by glowing strips set in the walls and
ceiling. The doctor spoke a word, and the light angled more
intensely over Dillon's wound. She touched a glowing pad
on the side wall, and an electronic curtain slipped across the
space between them and the front reception area. Instantly
all remaining noise from the station was silenced.

She worked the wooden spike from Dillon's flesh, spoke
another word, waited for another invisible drawer to appear, took out several instruments, gave the wound a careful
inspection, and studied the second screen that now glowed

on the wall. She must have liked what she saw, because she nodded and spoke words Sean didn't need to understand before settling the instruments back in their station. Then she rose and walked over to him.

She frowned over Sean being cuffed and hooked to the wall, but all she said was, "You have had a major shock as well. I want you to rest."

Only then did he notice the patch she held. "Later."

"Now." Her song speech carried the authority of a woman who knew she was right. "Two things. First, your brother will be fine. I am good at my job."

"I believe you," Sean said, liking her immensely.

"And second, the officer will soon return. I suspect he is obtaining orders to move you. You understand the word *cell*? If you are unconscious, I can insist you must remain under my care."

She hummed the words with such friendly intimacy Sean said, "Go ahead, then. Knock me out."

"Knock out. That is a new one." She peeled the back off the pad and applied it to Sean's wrist. "It implies violence when there is none."

"My world is a pretty violent place."

She glanced at the blood caking his form. "So I gather."

He felt the warm tendrils of a drugged sleep begin to filter along his arm and into his body. "Why are you doing this?"

"I told you. I take my professional duty very seriously."

"No, I mean, being so nice."

Her smile transformed her from a very intense young woman into a rare beauty. "What have they told you of the significance behind the image you and your brother designed, and how this is your first transit point?"

"Only that it's part of why we're being given this chance."

"It indicates a deep psychic bond with my world. My hope is to become a field doctor for transiters. First I must complete my duty here at the clinic. All doctors are obliged to serve two years at a posting that our government designates. When this is done, I intend to specialize. I want to make a life's study of the gifted ones."

His tongue felt thick, the words slow to emerge. "I've never been called that before. Gifted."

"Studies have suggested that transiters such as you actually have two home planets. Where you were born, and where you envision your first transit. This initial transit point is known as your twin world." She took his pulse in the traditional manner. "I have faced so many difficulties in my research. My world does not welcome transiters, which is why the station guards are so upset. I will have to transfer to another planet to do my work. My family is very much against this. But if I am offered a place, I am going."

Sean wanted to ask what the name of this planet was. What lay beyond the station. Where all those travelers were going. What the doctor's name was. How she could be so smart and so friendly and . . .

But the lights were fading, and soon went out entirely.

15

When Sean next opened his eyes, he found himself in the same narrow alcove, but back in the chamber's far end, stretched out on a second bed. He pushed himself to a sitting position and looked down to where Dillon still slept.

The doctor greeted him with, "Your brother is resting comfortably and will make a full recovery."

Sean found a unique comfort in hearing the news sung to him. Everything he heard spoken in Serenese carried a sense of directness and honesty. He checked his wrist and was intensely glad to discover he was no longer cuffed. "Can I ask your name?"

"Sandrine. And you are Sean, yes? Did you enjoy being knocked out?"

He liked her smile and the easy way she claimed friendship. "At least the cops left me alone."

"Only because your friend arrived. The Praetorian officer, Colonel Carver." She motioned him over and touched a glowing pad, and the supposedly solid wall behind her slid back to reveal a washroom. "He and two others are waiting to speak with you. But first you should wash."

"Who are they?"

"You will see. Ready yourself."

The mirror above the sink revealed a face still stained by Dillon's blood. Sean winced at the sight, mostly because it brought back the previous terror-stricken events. He then realized he had not contacted his parents. He opened the door and asked, "How long have I been out?"

"My world's time-measurement system would mean nothing to you. You have rested well. That is enough."

"Can I make a phone call?"

"To your outpost world?" Sandrine seemed to like that a lot. "Unfortunately that is beyond this clinic's capacity. Now you must hurry. These are not people you want to keep waiting."

He showered, rubbed his cheeks, and decided to use the razor left out on the sink. There were clothes on a shelf—a T-shirt and drawstring pants and slip-on cloth shoes. The shirt was slightly oversized and the shoes a half size too small, but Sean did not complain. His reflection held him as he brushed his hair, for the eyes staring back at him remained stained by shadows that no shower could wash away.

Sandrine nodded approval and said, "Good luck."

It was all the warning Sean required.

Sandrine touched another pad and the wall behind her became a curtain that drew back, revealing three people in heated discussion. Carver was there, and Examiner Tirian. And a third person. She was taller than both men, an angular woman with silver-grey hair and the sternest face Sean had ever seen. Her elegant appearance jarred with the surroundings, as though she was dressed for a palace instead of a clinic's waiting room. All three people turned at his appearance. Carver was the only person who seemed glad to see him.

His instructor asked, "How do you feel?"

"Okay. But I need to get in touch with my parents."

"I have already been in contact. You are on a school trip. And your school has been informed that you and Dillon both have colds."

The stern woman demanded, "What does that signify?"

"I have no idea," Carver replied. "It was noted in their world's regulations manual as a common ailment. And the school authorities accepted it."

Those few words were enough for Sean to realize who the elegant woman was. "You're Tatyana. Our language teacher."

She looked very pleased. "You recognize my voice. How remarkable."

The Examiner asked, "Counselor, you have been instructing this one?"

"Him and his brother." She continued to inspect Sean. She wore trousers beneath a long overmantle, both a grey so pale they were almost silver. The clothes matched her hair and her eyes, which were the most remarkable thing about her. That and the bejeweled clasp over her heart, an emblem of some sort, shaped from emeralds and sapphires. "I inserted myself into their language program."

The same emblem was sewn into the collar of the Examiner's jacket. "May I ask why?"

Her response was cut off by a feeble cry from the other room. Sean excused himself and rushed back to find Dillon struggling weakly against the doctor. "Stay where you are, man."

Dillon's features were stricken by a fear as real as pain. "Did I kill them?"

Sean had never touched his brother much. Their family wasn't one for hugs. But it came natural now. To lean over his twin, set hands on both shoulders, and say, "They didn't exist."

"How do you know?"

"Because I saw them start to turn into smoke." Sean saw the doctor flash the same fear as the day before. "Just like the car we were chasing."

"I thought I saw . . ." Dillon's fear was replaced by a wince of real pain. "What happened to my side?"

"Later. Now lay down. Let me introduce you to Sandrine, the train station's very own idea of a guardian angel."

"No need." Dillon allowed himself to be settled back. He switched to Serenese and continued, "The doc and I are already talking about where we're going on our first date. Isn't that right, Doc?"

"Most certainly not."

Sean felt his own band of distress let go of his chest. If Dillon was able to flirt, he was definitely on the mend.

Dillon pointed to the trio who had entered the chamber and now stood behind Sean. "Who's the one who looks like a queen?"

"Her name is Tatyana. She's our language prof. Among

other things." Sean watched the doctor retreat to the side wall as Counselor Tatyana drew the two men forward.

When they stood by Dillon's bedside, the Examiner said, "Really, Counselor, I must protest."

Tatyana replied, "Explain your objection."

"They are twin menaces," Tirian declared. "I have no doubt whatsoever that they brought all this on themselves. Certainly there is nothing sufficiently remarkable about these two to alert our foes."

Carver froze the twins with a look. "You are missing the point," he said. "Sean shielded both of them. After four days of training, he transported himself and another individual. Something that only a handful of highly skilled—"

"He *panicked*. You know as well as I that even raw recruits can accomplish rare feats when terrified."

"Not like this," Carver replied. "Not in centuries."

The Examiner sniffed and turned back to Tatyana. "What the colonel refuses to see is how these ruffians perpetuate everything that has happened."

"Ruffians," Tatyana repeated.

"According to what they told the station guards, the pair stopped to pick up strange women, thus setting the disaster in motion. This happened less than four hours after they assaulted an innocent bystander."

"The student known as Eric was most definitely not innocent," Carver said. "And you know of this only because I entered it into their official record. As testimony of how they made proper use—"

"You only have their word on this. Which I heartily discount."

"They saved a young woman from assault."

"Again, hearsay." The Examiner's bald head gleamed like a polished black globe. "I hereby fail both of them."

Sean's gut took a plunge down to the polished floor. The room became encased in a silence so intense that whatever Carver said next became tiny wisps of protest against a fate he knew they both deserved. Everything the Examiner said was true. The facts left Sean struggling to breathe. He and his brother were responsible. They were guilty. They were doomed. He heard Dillon groan and knew he had no comfort to offer.

Carver was saying, "These two have passed every test with flying colors. They have made great strides in learning Serenese. They have—"

"Failing them is within my charter!"

"With each external challenge they have enlarged their powers, and yet they have used them only to protect themselves and others."

"They are irresponsible in the extreme. They are not fit to wield powers of any kind, much less join our ranks."

Carver turned to the silent woman. "Counselor, you can't allow this travesty—"

"She is not responsible for these recruits. I hold the authority to determine whether they pass their exams. I deem them unworthy. I fail them."

Tatyana's voice was as flat and hard as her gaze. "Duly noted."

Carver showed a fury as intense as his distress. "Counselor, I protest in the strongest possible terms."

"Also noted. Gentlemen, this matter is concluded." She silenced Carver's next objection with a single look. "Examiner Tirian, you are dismissed."

"But . . . their mind-wipes are now my purview."

"I shall see to all that is required. Your duties regarding these two young men are hereby concluded. Good day, Tirian."

The Examiner cast the twins a single look, dark and contemptuous and dismissive. Sean let Dillon growl for both of them. Tirian wheeled about, took a half step, and vanished.

As the elegant woman turned back to them, Sean's brain locked on a single thought, as though simple observation was all he could manage just then. Taking an easy breath was certainly beyond his reach. The thought was, *This is what judgment looks like.* For there in those light grey eyes was the implacable force of an individual who had cast verdicts on entire races. The force and the burdens and the merciless determination were all there. Aimed straight at him.

Carver's voice sounded as strangled as Sean felt. "Counselor, I beseech—"

"I have no intention of erasing one iota of their potential."

Sean felt so wrenched by the moment he almost missed Carver saying, "I'm sorry, what?"

"You tried to warn me about Tirian. His school has become a focal point for arguments over our training system. I assumed this was nothing more than a clash over methods." To the twins she explained, "Tirian's system is based upon identifying potential recruits at the youngest possible age, then sheltering them in a school that is isolated from all outside stimuli. He seeks to invoke his concept as a model for the entire system of identifying and training transiters. Your instructor disagrees with this method."

"Not with Tirian's school, Counselor. But to apply Tirian's methods to the entire system would be disastrous." Carver spoke more slowly. Carefully measuring each word. "A few of Tirian's students have asked to become Praetorians. He urges his students to become Messengers or go into government. So there are not many. I only became aware of his school when I met these students at the academy. None have successfully completed academy training."

"Fascinating." She crossed her arms. "Tell me why."

"They are very precise. Exactitude defines them. So long as they face situations that are covered in the manuals, they are the head of the class. But when their training shifts to real-life crises, anything outside the boundaries of logic or the rule book, they fall apart."

"So the introduction of battlefield chaos . . ."

"Terrifies them," Carver finished. "They cannot handle it."

"Most interesting. So the Examiner is developing a cadre of like-minded recruits who are deeply loyal to . . ."

"Loyalty. That is what concerns me most of all."

Tatyana nodded. "I have the authority to bring recruits directly under my personal supervision. Which I choose to do in these two cases. You agree to remain as their tutor?"

"I . . . Of course."

"Tirian and everyone else should be allowed to assume

these twins have been eliminated. He has allies among our power structure. I have no interest in further arguments regarding them and their studies."

Carver said, "I assume you'll want me to establish a protective perimeter."

She dismissed that. "There is no such need."

This time, however, Carver remained firm. "Counselor, there is the chance, however slim, that something or someone did in fact attack them."

Tatyana looked ready to argue, but conceded, "Do so in absolute secrecy. As far as the Examiner and his allies are concerned, they have been dismissed. You may set one team of Watchers in place. Just one, and you must keep them well removed from the twins. Clear?"

Carver obviously did not like it, but all he said was, "Understood, ma'am."

Sean interrupted with, "I've got some questions."

"That makes two of us," Dillon said.

But the lady was clearly not interested. "Carver will do his best to answer them."

Sean decided one couldn't wait. "So, this mind-wipe thing . . ."

"That level of your training is now completed." Tatyana offered them a general's frosty smile. "Welcome to our ranks, gentlemen. You will not always find it a comfortable place to reside. But hopefully the rewards will prove to be well worth the sacrifice." She then turned to where Sandrine stood by the rear wall. "Doctor, I assume you understand what I am doing?"

Sandrine appeared as shaken by the events as everyone else. "Not entirely, Counselor. But I am happy to follow your orders regarding confidentiality."

"Excellent." She addressed the twins. "Now I want your report. Everything you told the authorities upon your arrival, and everything you have so far failed to discuss."

Before Sean was halfway through his description, the Counselor was shaking her head in dismissal. "Impossible."

Carver seemed conflicted, as though he agreed with the Counselor, but still asked, "Shouldn't we hear them out?"

"You may do that on your own time. I for one am assuming some influence was formed upon their abilities to perceive their physical environment, or perhaps shock has impacted their memories."

"But what Sean describes is in keeping—"

"Really, Colonel. Do you truly believe they would launch such an overt assault against two raw recruits?" She gave her fingers a backward flick, as though brushing the concept from the air. "We have never known an outpost world to be the focus of such an attack. Plus there is the one overriding factor, the one issue we know to be true above all others."

"We are off cycle," Carver muttered.

"Precisely." Tatyana turned to the doctor. "Again, madam, I require your absolute discretion."

"Granted, Counselor. You have my word."

"Thank you."

Sean had not followed most of what had just been said. But still he protested, "What I told you was the truth."

"As you perceived it," the Counselor said. "One thing

more. You are forbidden to ever come back here. The station security has orders to arrest you on sight."

Sean glanced at his brother and saw a mirror of his own pain in Dillon's eyes. "That's not fair!"

"Perhaps not. But you did bring minor havoc to the station. And this world is no friend to our kind." She must have seen the arguments burning in their faces, for she continued, "Were you to disobey a Counselor's direct order and become arrested by this planet's security system, we would see no reason to work for your release. And I assure you, their prison system is far from pleasant. Not to mention how you would face further punishment. From me."

Dillon gave her a sullen, "We got the message."

"See that you obey." Her gaze was severe but not un-friendly. "The Colonel tells me you both show great promise. Complete your preliminary training. We will meet again."

She turned, and was gone.

16

The doctor inspected Dillon's wound and declared he was healing well enough to depart. Sean did his best to put some real gratitude into his farewell, but the Counselor's rejection of their experience plus being banned from the station left him hollow.

The twins and Carver then transited back to Carver's so-called home. The odd kitchen, with the sales tags still on the dishwasher and fridge, was somehow welcoming. Sean supported some of Dillon's weight, but already his brother was showing signs of his old stubborn strength.

Sean was still figuring out which protest to level first at Carver when Dillon offered weakly, "Sean knew this was coming. He was worried all day about something bad going down."

"I remember," Carver said. "But a dozen transits in one day would unsettle the most seasoned Messenger. Foul moods and misrememberings are standard fare. Which is why it is included in your instruction. We must be certain your internal state remains stable."

"No," Dillon said. "Sean doesn't have moods."

"I hear your objections, and they change nothing. The Counselor has passed judgment. This debate is finished." Carver walked them back through the living room, where probably no one had ever sat, out to the front porch. Where they jerked to a halt.

The Charger sat in the front drive. Silver. Gleaming. Unmarked.

The twins said in unison, "Spooky."

"The car was here as you see it when I arrived," Carver said. "The police report no traffic accident involving such a car."

"It happened like we said," Dillon insisted. His tone had gone sullen, the child not being heard by the adult. "We didn't lie."

"And we have moved beyond that. Listen carefully. You both are very fortunate. The Counselor responsible for this sector has taken a personal interest in you. This means far more than just being saved from Examiner Tirian's downcheck. Heed her warning. Stay away from the station. And be ready to return to your studies tomorrow."

Dillon said, "So we're supposed to just go home and pretend nothing's changed?"

"No," Carver replied. "Everything has changed. Just not on the surface."

Sean asked, "No more Examiner, though, right?"

"Correct. Tirian is no longer your concern."

Dillon asked, "And the mind-wipe business, that's all over and done?"

"Unless you are convicted of abusing your powers." The

jagged edge returned to their instructor's voice. "Which would include returning to that transit point."

"But—"

Carver held up his hand, arresting further protests, then pointed them across the lawn. Past the gleaming silver car. Into the waiting house. "Have a good night. I will see you tomorrow after school."

But it was hard to go home.

Their mother asked how the trip had been. Then she seemed to tune out halfway through Dillon's lame response. Ninety minutes later they were enduring another silence at the dinner table, punctuated by their parents' sighs and unfinished sentences. All through the meal Sean felt like the TV talk show audience was laughing at him from the other room.

Upstairs Sean played on his computer while night settled in beyond his window. He heard Dillon's muffled laugh through the closed door and assumed his brother was chatting with Carey. The e-games and the internet just couldn't hold him. Which was hardly a surprise. Regardless of what the Counselor and Carver thought, they had just survived an attack from something that wasn't really alive. Not to mention transiting halfway across the galaxy, then facing down an Examiner with the power to wipe his memory. Sean found it hard to go back to the same-old.

As he powered down the computer, Dillon knocked on his door. Which was odd. Normally his brother just barreled in regardless.

Dillon poked his head in and asked, "Mind some company?"

"I was waiting for you to get off the phone so I could come ask you the same thing."

Dillon dumped Sean's clothes on the floor and eased himself into the room's other chair. "I called Carey."

"I figured that's who it was."

"She's really nice."

"I noticed."

Dillon's gaze turned to the wall between Sean's and their parents' bedrooms. "Did you also notice how the folks didn't even ask what we've been doing?"

"They asked if we had a good time."

Dillon just stared at the wall.

"Yeah," Sean replied. "I noticed."

Dillon lifted his shirt. "Check this out."

The scar was still visible. But barely. Sean leaned in closer. No stitches. No sign of his brother almost bleeding out. "Okay. That's cool."

"I still feel some stiffness. But the pain's gone. I asked Sandrine when I could go back to hitting people. Know what she said? I should focus more on not getting hit back."

"She was something else."

"Yeah, maybe I should talk with Carver about some dough I can spend on the other side of the galaxy."

"In case you've forgotten, we can't go back. Even if the doc would give you the time of day."

Dillon sighed. "I can't believe they're banning us from the place we've dreamed about all our lives."

But Sean didn't want to think on that. It hurt too much.

17

He and Dillon stayed polite to each other through the bedtime routine, almost being formal about it. Sean wondered if Dillon felt the same way. Like all their old habits had to be re-formed around the simple fact that their lives weren't the same, and would never be again.

Afterward they both left their doors open. Sean lay in the dark and listened to his brother settle into bed with a groan. He asked softly, "That hurt?"

"I told you. Not really. More like stiffness right at the edge of pain."

Sean stared at the moon beyond his window and said, "Everything's changed."

"What do you mean?"

He had no idea how to express what he felt, so he just said, "That's the first time I've ever heard you admit to hurting."

A blue jay started going crazy outside Sean's window.

Bright moonlight, early summer night, some bird just waking up. Sean listened to it for a while, drifting into sleep.

Then it felt as though the night coalesced.

Sean jerked back to full wakefulness. An eerie tension had invaded his room. The stillness had an edge now, like an unseen threat from some horror movie had just invaded their space. "Dillon."

"What?" The word was half formed, like he'd been pulled back from near sleep.

Sean didn't know if what he felt was even anchored in reality. For all he knew, he was just reliving terror from the attack. So all he said was, "Maybe we should shield ourselves before we sleep."

When Dillon spoke, he sounded fully awake. "We should shield Mom and Dad too."

Sean didn't see any need to say he'd already done it. "Probably crazy, though."

"Yeah. But when we get up at night, we reinforce the shields."

"Both of us," Sean agreed. "Every time."

"Totally nuts, right?"

"Let's hope so."

***

Sean had been asleep several hours when yet another shift in the night woke him. He opened his eyes, blinked in the dark, and listened. He could not hear anything except his brother's soft snores from the next room. But the longer he lay there, the more certain he grew that something was wrong.

He rose from his bed and walked through the bathroom

and crossed his brother's room. Dillon's window overlooked the front lawn and the street. Sean stood by the window and searched.

He did not realize his brother was awake until Dillon asked, "You got those heebie-jeebies again?"

"I don't know. Maybe." Sean turned around. "You think I could come sleep on your floor?"

He expected some snappish comment from his brother. Instead, Dillon rose to his feet. "You want the bed?"

"No, man. You're the one who got speared."

Dillon padded across the carpeted floor to stand beside him. "You see anything?"

"Nada." Sean walked back into his room, stripped his bed, and returned to the front bedroom. He made up a pallet on the floor by the window, something he hadn't done in years. "It's probably nothing."

Dillon remained by the window. "I've got something crazy to say."

"You mean, crazier than me worried about an empty night?"

"Oh yeah." He turned around. "It hit me when I woke up. That maybe I can hunt."

"I don't follow."

"Hunt," Dillon said. "Go out looking for the bad guys. Why sit around waiting and worrying if I can check things out?"

Sean tucked his knees under him, yogi-like. "You mean, like, transit around?"

"Not exactly." Dillon waved his hands, a habit he probably wasn't even aware of. He always fought the air when the words didn't come. "A hunter is somebody who can track the prey, right?"

"Carver called you a warrior."

"Yeah, I got that. But this idea, I don't know."

Sean said, "That's usually my department. Ideas."

"Tell me about it. But when I sat up it was there waiting for me. Not words. But these impressions flashed in my head, one after the other, fast as bullets." He punched the air, then winced when it pulled at his scar. "This is nuts."

"No, no, let's hear it."

"Okay. So I lie back down. And I go for a walk-around."

Sean got it. "Without your body."

"I guess. And you have to be here. With me."

Sean was following him now. "Like your anchor."

"That's it. Yeah." Dillon sounded ashamed. "Will you hold my hand?"

...

It made Sean intensely uncomfortable to sit beside Dillon's bed. He fashioned the same safety belt they used in transits, then sat there in the dark, holding Dillon's hand. Limp and hot. He thought about getting up and pretending to need to go to the bathroom so he could wash his hands and end this craziness.

Then it happened.

The night went utterly quiet.

The absence of sound was as intense as anything he had ever experienced. There were always some noises in the house. The AC blew a soft rush, the fridge thunked from downstairs when it turned on, the floor creaked if his dad got up, Dillon snored, something.

Not now.

Sean sat with his back against his brother's bed, his eyes wide open, listening to the absence of *everything*. He decided this was how a vacuum must be like.

Or death.

Strangely, he was not afraid. The heat from his brother's hand was now accompanied by a current, strong as an electric spark. He knew something was happening. What, he had no idea. But he was comfortable not knowing. He had no idea how long he sat there, encased in a stillness that went much further than just silence.

Finally Dillon released his hand, sat up, and calmly announced, "It's coming."

"What is?"

"The enemy." His brother was intense and serene at the same time. "Shield the folks."

"I've been doing that."

"You feel it too, don't you?"

"I feel something. I have no idea what it is." He watched Dillon ease himself down to the floor. "What just happened?"

"I shut my eyes and I rose up and I went out into the yard. And I hunted."

Every single word his brother spoke left a charred remnant, like cinders that only needed the slightest spark to ignite. Sean pushed aside all the questions except one. "Should we transit?"

Dillon squinted at the wall by the window, like he could

still pierce the night. "I don't . . . What about Mom and Dad?"

"I know what you mean." Sean had been worrying about the same thing. "Like, we transit, and the shields leave with us."

"I can't risk doing that."

"No. Me neither. So you go. You're the one who's hurt."

"Don't even start. Look, shield the folks again, and then try to extend one around the house."

"Good idea," Sean agreed. When he was done, he asked, "What did you see?"

"There are four of them. All look like the Examiner."

"But . . . four?"

"They're not real. Just like the girls. It's like . . ."

"Tell me."

"Like they want the Examiner to be seen."

"But why—"

The question went unfinished. All the others remained unspoken. Because that was when the world exploded.

The sound was muted at first, as though it fought through a barrier of some kind. Even in its muffled state, the noise was fierce. The flames struck in a constant rush and careened out, like a hose blasting against curved glass. The colors were as magnificent as they were deadly. The night and their home were brilliantly illuminated by an electric green fire. Sean felt Dillon move up beside him as the first rift became visible in the shield around their home. It was like watching a fire eat through plastic, burning a tiny pinprick, then dozens, all melting back, growing into flowers of destruction.

Dillon shouted, "Here it comes!"

Sean crouched down, then reinforced the four shields one more time. The roar grew and grew until it formed a furnace blast. The light and the noise surrounded them. Sean stayed focused on the shields, him and Dillon and their parents. He gave it everything he had.

And then he felt like maybe he could give it more.

After all, he was surrounded by energy at its rawest and most ferocious.

So why not take the energy and shoot it *back*?

It was amazing that he could think at all in the middle of that racket. But there it was. Carver's words droned at him. *Shield and attack. Shield and—*

Then Dillon spoke the exact same words Sean was thinking. "Attack! Let's turn this sucker around!"

"It's worth a shot, right?" It was impossible to hear *anything*. But Sean did, just the same. "I don't know where to shoot."

"I do!"

"So you shoot, I'll load."

Which made no sense at all. But Dillon was already standing, the shield around the two of them elongating so as to keep him sheltered. The incoming fire was a great glowing wash, so intense Sean's eyes streamed with tears. He didn't know what he was doing. But he did it anyway. He reached out one hand so that it touched his shield, then drew the energy so that it focused and flowed together, streaming over toward where Dillon's own hands extended out to touch the shield. He watched Dillon heave in a gigantic breath, and the energy formed two great swirling masses around his outstretched hands.

Dillon roared like some feral beast, or at least that was how it seemed to Sean. And the roar was a blast that shot out in four different directions.

The house groaned like a giant in agony. Sean groaned in mortal harmony, a great silent heave of distress. He felt as though he was being split in two. He drew the incoming fire like a magnet and passed it over to Dillon. At the same time he constantly fed energy to the four shields, him and Dillon and their parents.

Then the floor beneath them gave way. The shields held as they fell through what had formerly been their living room. All the while, Dillon kept drawing the incoming force from Sean and jetting it back out. A massive, streaming blast . . .

The flames vanished. Completely and utterly finished. In one brief instant, faster than a single heartbeat, just *gone*.

They found themselves in what had formerly been their cellar. Sean rose slowly from his crouch. Dillon lowered his hands, unarched his back, took a great satisfied breath. Their parents were coiled in two bleary-eyed bundles, still clutching what was left of their covers up to their chins.

Dillon grinned at him. "That is definitely one for the books."

19

The police kept them until almost dawn. The four of them wore EMS blankets over their bedclothes, until neighbors brought over sweats and hot cocoa. The street was crowded with flashing lights and onlookers. Their home and Carver's were both completely destroyed. Ash and cinder formed dark imprints over the cellars. The Charger was a total wreck. Again. Firemen swarmed through the smoldering debris. Over and over they heard the same words. How amazing it was that they survived. How no one could explain them walking away from this alive, much less without a scratch.

There was no sign of Carver. Sean gave the police the number Carver had supplied and shared a worried glance with Dillon. They had to assume the guy had already left for wherever home was. But still, not knowing whether their one connection to the new life had survived was almost as troubling as the attack itself.

The police drove them to a local Homewood Suites. The cops must have called ahead, because the night manager met them at the door and took them straight to adjoining apartments. Sean and Dillon bedded down without a single spoken word. Only when the lights were out did Dillon ask, "Shields up?"

"You bet."

"Heebie-jeebies?"

Sean took a good long look. "Not a peep."

"Good." A few breaths, then Dillon finally got around to saying what Sean had been worrying over since they scrambled from the basement. "In the middle of all that, I thought I heard you."

"I know."

"But you didn't speak, did you?"

"No. I didn't."

"Did you hear me back?"

"Loud and clear."

Dillon breathed long and low, and Sean's chest pumped in tandem. Dillon asked, "Can you hear me now?"

"No. But maybe it's on account of how you don't usually have a single interesting thought."

"Oh. Look at the funny man. Okay, I'm going to concentrate really hard."

"Don't blow a fuse."

"Quiet." A pause. "Anything?"

"Nothing. Let me try."

Then, "My brother, the blank wall."

"Good." Sean half meant it. "Stay out of my dreams."

Dillon rolled over. "Like I would ever want to go there."

They arrived downstairs for breakfast to find Carver and Counselor Tatyana already seated at a table together with their parents. Carver wore dress slacks and a polo shirt, their parents were still dressed in loaned sweats. Tatyana wore a business suit of muted blue. Sean's folks looked red-eyed and severely shaken, and they listened in silence as the Counselor offered professional condolences. Sean and Dillon grabbed some food and took up station at the next table.

The Counselor was saying, "My company can't be certain, but we fear that we may be at fault. There was apparently a leak in an old gas line. If so, we are to blame."

"But we don't have gas," Sean's mother protested.

"Even if you did, it would have come from a different line. The pipe in question was set in place back in the forties. It doesn't appear on any current survey maps. But we fear we're responsible."

Sean's father rubbed his face. "I'd expect you guys to show up with an army of lawyers and a hundred different excuses."

"Quite frankly, Mr. Kirrel, we've decided to leave that option for our phase two. Which would only come into play if we can't settle this with you here and now."

Carver played the role of aggrieved homeowner. "You just want to make all this go away?"

"As quietly and quickly as possible," Tatyana said. "Where were you last night, by the way?"

"Visiting relatives," Carver replied.

Sean's mother asked, "What about all our things?"

Tatyana said, "If you are willing to settle today, my company will write you a check this morning for five times the value of your homes and all your contents."

Carver said, "I accept your offer."

Sean's dad said, "We need a minute."

Their mother protested, "Five times the house's value? What's to discuss? That's more money—"

"We need to talk this through," Sean's dad insisted.

She gave her all-too-familiar sigh and turned away.

Carver rose from the table and jerked his chin toward the motel entrance. The twins rose with him. Sean said, "We'll just be outside."

The day was fresh, the wind welcome, the sky clear. Carver walked them midway across the parking lot and said, "Give me your report."

Sean let Dillon talk. His twin tended to punch words in the wrong spots, emphasizing what should have gone smoothly, dropping in phrases that did not build a solid picture. But he thought Carver's frown was more to do with what had happened than Dillon's manner of speech. Dillon was still trying to describe how it felt to turn the flames around when the motel's glass doors slid back and Tatyana appeared.

Carver motioned for her to join them and said to Dillon, "Start over."

Her high heels made a crisp accent to her impatient walk. "Really, Carver, there are far more important issues than the growing talents—"

Carver held up his hand, then said to Dillon, "From the beginning."

Sean thought his brother did an even worse job the second time around. But the response of the two adults was surprising. Carver continued his frowning inspection of the surrounding trees. But Tatyana offered a patronizing smile. Her disbelief was so evident, Dillon fumbled through the end and finished, "I know it sounds crazy."

"That is not the word I would use." Her reply carried a surprising gentleness. "Do you remember what the Examiner said when we met in the clinic?"

Dillon kicked at a stone and did not reply, so Sean said, "About recruits and stress."

"What you are describing, the passing of thoughts from one individual to another, is a feat we have aimed for but cannot achieve with any regularity or clarity."

"But these are twins," Carver said, his gaze still on the weaving pines.

"It means nothing." She looked from one to the other. "Repeat the process now."

"We can't."

"As I thought. Shields can serve as amplifying chambers for those encased in their force. You spoke, you might even have whispered. The murmur carried."

"This is a common battle tactic," Carver said. "Linking shields, passing messages in the din of combat."

"Now, as to the other issues." Tatyana counted them on her fingers. "The extension of your awareness. Hunting, you called it. This is a highly defined tactic of those individuals we refer to as Watchers."

"We had a team of two Watchers in place," Carver said.

"Their report is that Tirian initiated the attack. The female Watcher is both a pro and a friend. She is highly trained. She says there is no question."

"But it wasn't him," Dillon said. "There were four of them."

"The Watcher says otherwise," Tatyana replied.

Sean demanded, "What about Dillon turning the flames around?"

"Impossible," the Counselor declared. "With time and extensive training, perhaps this may be utilized. But at this stage . . ."

"Battle stress can make for some very bizarre experiences," Carver said.

"You young men have survived by shielding yourselves and your parents," Tatyana said. "That in and of itself is unheard of for recruits with only a few weeks of training."

"A few days," Carver corrected.

"Truly astonishing," Tatyana said. But already her attention was back on the couple in the motel lobby. "Now I must ask for your assistance. We need to clean this up quickly and quietly. No press, no complaints, no lawyers."

Sean didn't want to let it go, but he could tell now was not the time to press their case. "We could go talk with them."

Tatyana told Carver, "Go with them. We can offer more. Whatever it takes."

Sean was heading for the motel's entrance when he saw how Dillon's head was planted straight down. It took him back to the early days, the hard times when they both first realized things weren't right in their family. That it wasn't just how their dad never played with them, or how their mom never laughed, or how the television was used to puncture the home's silence. Around their seventh year, Dillon took to hiding himself away at home. Whenever he had to be around his parents, he lowered his face so his hair created a veil between him and the world that hurt him.

It twisted Sean's gut to see his brother respond to Tatyana and Carver that way. People they *liked*. People they *trusted*.

It gave Sean the strength to swing back around and say, "We've spent our whole lives waiting for this one chance. We figured it would never come. We thought we'd grow up and get fitted for our Armani prison suits and take our place in line. So you need to understand, what you've given us is the most important thing ever. But with this attack, no matter what you say or think, you're *wrong*."

They took their time responding, long enough for Dillon to lift his head and give Sean a look that eased the wrench in his gut.

Carver said, "If you can repeat the occurrence, we will talk."

"The hunt or the chat or the fighting technique?" Dillon asked.

"Any or all of them. Until then, I agree with the Counselor's assessment. On all counts. Including the culprit we must now track down."

Tatyana added, "The Examiner has vanished. What innocent person disappears before being questioned?"

"Someone who knows they are being set up," Sean said.

She sniffed.

"All those things happened. And if Dillon says it wasn't the Examiner, you better listen."

"Watchers are trained to see beyond the physical," Carver replied, his tone both gruff and gentle. "Even if your brother managed to extend himself, which is a senior-level talent, he is not trained to see *beyond*."

"He did it," Sean maintained. "He saw."

Dillon said, "You're going after the wrong man."

Tatyana waved that away. "Enough. We must resolve the crisis with your parents. And then we must determine where you will go for further training."

"What about Carver?"

"I've been assigned to hunt down the Examiner," Carver said. He smiled at their disappointment. "We can still communicate occasionally, if you like."

"We like," Dillon said. "A lot."

The idea came to Sean with such clarity it was like somebody whispered the idea into his head. "I know where we can go. Send us to the Examiner's school."

Dillon gaped at him. "Are you serious?"

"Totally." He found it easier to focus on his brother. "Look. Carver's headed off into the wild blue. We've got to go somewhere. And they've already said they're not going to check this out."

"Your job is to learn," Carver said. "Not play investigator."

"I'm not aiming to *play* at anything," Sean shot back.

Dillon said, "Sign me up."

Tatyana replied, "Carver and I must discuss this. Go and see if you can convince your parents to accept our offer."

20

Their parents weren't concerned about the money. Well, they were. A lot, actually. But that wasn't the topic of discussion. What they wanted to talk about was getting a divorce. The loss of their home and the sudden insertion of money meant that something they had both thought about for years had suddenly become the logical next step.

Twenty minutes later the twins emerged, and their place at the lobby's square breakfast table was taken by Tatyana. Twenty minutes after that, their parents settled on six times the home-and-contents valuation, the check was written, and the papers were signed. One life ended. Another began. All it took was a blast of flame, a near-death experience, and a vanished Examiner that neither Dillon nor Sean would ever miss. Innocent or not.

Drivers were arranged and they went shopping. The twins took one car, their parents two others. All four were given credit cards, compliments of Tatyana's mythical company.

Before they departed, Carver said Sean's idea for where they should go for training was still under discussion. When Sean tried to offer more reasons for why it was a good idea, Carver shook his head and said they were way beyond arguments. The important thing was for them to reinsert themselves into normal life. They needed to remain anchored in sight of the outside world. They were recruits now. There was a meticulous process to be followed. As far as their home civilization was concerned, they needed to remain in clearly defined roles.

Dillon waited until they were in the Hollister shop to ask, "What about all this is normal?"

"Home civilization," Sean repeated, trying to work his mind around the concepts. "Clearly defined roles."

A couple of weeks earlier, the whole deal would have been part of some fantasyland, being given their very own credit cards and told to go spend. But after an hour the whole process was flat. Boring. An endless array of stacked clothes and canned music and happy-sappy salespeople. They ate in the mall's food court, making lists of stuff they couldn't put off until another day.

They were buying a couple of new phones when a familiar voice said, "I should have known to check here first."

Carey waited while they finished paying, took hold of some of their packages, and walked them out before demanding, "Did Eric do this?"

The question caught them both completely by surprise. Dillon was the one she was watching, and he replied, "No. No way."

"Are you sure? Because I've got to tell you, it is just like him. He always said it wasn't who got hit but who was standing at the end of the game."

"Carey, look . . ."

"He loved trolling the dark side of the internet." She wore the same sort of pinched expression as she had the other day. "He and his buddies could spend hours talking about how to make a bomb."

"It wasn't Eric," Dillon repeated.

"How do you know?"

"Because it wasn't a bomb," Sean said.

"Gas leak," Dillon said.

She looked from one to the other. "Really?"

"We've already met with the company," Sean said.

"They signed a check and everything," Dillon confirmed.

She released some of her tension in a single long breath. Sean loved how he could stand up close to her and look, absorb her beauty. Her hair was not red and it was not blonde. It was both. Same with the eyes, not grey, not green, but some amazing mix. On her, the freckles that swept across the upper part of her cheeks and nose were perfect. Like her lips. There was just one problem with the whole mix.

She only had eyes for Dillon.

She asked, "So where will you live?"

"Excellent question," Sean replied.

"Our parents are getting a divorce," Dillon announced.

Her empathy was so genuine, tears formed. "You poor guys."

Dillon shrugged both handfuls of shopping bags. "It's not really a surprise."

"Well, it is and it isn't," Sean said.

"It's not like they fought or anything," his brother agreed.

"But things haven't been great for a long time."

They walked back out to the car, where the driver helped them deposit the bags in the trunk, then they returned to the mall. They took turns trying to describe what it was like around their home. Or rather, former home. Carey was amazingly easy to talk with. And her concentration was total. When a trio of school friends called to her, she either didn't hear or chose to ignore them entirely. The girls laughed in that mocking way that normally would have left Sean's face burning. But today it was just part of the background noise.

They entered a café and ordered, and Carey excused herself, saying she needed to call her father. They took a table by the front window and checked off all the items they had bought.

Carey returned to the table, saw what they were doing, and said, "I hate shopping worse than anything."

"You can't," Dillon replied. "You're a girl. You're beautiful. Shopping is part of your genetic makeup."

"I hate makeup more than shopping."

"Careful," Dillon said. "The mall patrol is going to swoop down and lock you up."

"My dad's best friend teaches business law. He'll get me out."

"They'll put you on mall probation. Make you go to night school. How to become a cosmetic whatever."

"Cosmetician," she supplied. "Double yuck."

Sean listened to the exchange, then watched them back

off and dive into their respective cups. Like they needed a breather. He sipped at his own drink, which had gone cold, and tasted nothing. In the space of that exchange, he had become the outsider.

Carey asked, "Are you guys okay?"

"Define okay," Dillon said.

"Where are you staying?"

"Homewood Suites. We're supposed to meet the folks this evening, decide where we're going to live. You know, who with." Dillon glanced at Sean. "I guess we better talk that one through."

Sean just nodded. There was a sullen lump in his chest. He was jealous and there was nothing he could do about it. Carey was becoming Dillon's girl. It was only a matter of time.

Dillon turned back to Carey and asked, "How do you tell us apart?"

She blinked. "What?"

"You always knew who was who. From the very first time we met. Almost nobody can. I was just wondering."

"I don't . . . You're very different people."

"That's right. We are," Dillon said. "That's the amazing thing about you. You *see* people. You notice things."

Carey wore her hair back behind her ears, but one strand had worked out of the clip and wandered loose over her left eye. Sean wanted to reach out and brush it away, get in close enough to breathe her clean scent. But he couldn't. That was Dillon's job now.

He was brought back around by Carey saying, "Maybe you could come live with us."

Dillon's mouth opened and shut, but all he managed was, "What?"

"Four years ago, Dad's brother went through a bad breakup. My aunt . . ." She waved that away. Another time. "He came to live with us. He and my dad fixed up the garage loft into this really cool place. Last fall he took a job in Seattle. The loft has been empty ever since."

"What about your dad?"

"He never liked Eric. Not even a little bit. I guess in a way he was waiting for the bad thing to happen. When he heard what you did, he . . ."

"What?" Dillon pressed.

She showed them a beautiful crimson blush. "He said it was nice to know there were still some white knights in this crazy world."

Dillon looked at Sean. As if he would ever object to this. When Sean did not say anything, Dillon said, "So your dad is okay with two strangers moving in."

"You're not strangers. He said to tell you that you'd be welcome." She looked from one to the other. Appearing anxious now in a completely new way. "That is, if you want."

21

School the next day held a surreal quality. The principal insisted on meeting with them and spent twenty minutes basically saying nothing of any importance. They were passed on to the counselor, who danced around the unspoken question, which was, were they in some form of well-hidden shock? They listened to both of the women invite them to skip the final few days of school. But Carver's instructions had been very clear. They were to find a new normal and stick to it.

The other students didn't help, the way they kept coming up between classes and surrounding them with comments meant to claim the events as their own.

"My folks drove us past the place yesterday. We were amazed you walked away."

"I looked at that, and it was like, which terrorist did you get mixed up with."

"I was so scared. I mean, this is little Raleigh."

"My dad said it looked like Beirut."

"It was wild, looking down into your cellar. I thought, it had to be a bomb, right . . ."

The comments swiftly grew old.

They had to endure a second session with the counselor and principal after their last class. Neither Sean nor Dillon said much, basically because they had no idea what would get them out of the offices faster than silence. When they emerged that afternoon, Carver was there standing beside a white Malibu that shouted rental. He wore a buttoned-down version of civilian gear—navy jacket and summer-weight grey trousers and blue shirt and striped tie. The second sleeve was filled and the scar was gone.

Carey's home was between the Oberlin Road shopping district and the main NCSU campus. The one-story ranch was set a full two hundred feet from the road, surrounded by pines that whispered a soft welcome. Two massive oaks rose from the backyard, like they were peering over the roof, wanting to have a good look at these newcomers.

When they pulled into the curved drive and rose from the car, Sean realized that the home hid a unique beauty in plain sight. The whole place had a slightly Oriental cast. The cedar-shingle roof was peaked at both ends and ended in stubby carved arms that curved up slightly. The windows were oversized and topped by little copies of the cedar roof. The doorway was peaked and the door bound by ornately carved iron. The drive curved around and ended by a shield of huge magnolias that welcomed them with the fragrance of late spring blossoms. The front walk was slightly raised and shaped from raw planks that grew into a broad open patio, framed by the same carved wood as the roof. A second walk connected to the garage, which had been built to model the home. The walks and the patio were bordered by bonsai gardens and lights shaped like Japanese lanterns.

Carey crossed the patio accompanied by her father, whom she introduced by his first name. John Havilland looked every inch a professor, from his scattered and unruly thatch of grey hair right down to his blue socks and open-toed sandals. He was tall like his daughter and would probably have been handsome, except for how he carried himself in a slight stoop. Sean thought his face had been permanently creased through the effort of bearing his loss.

Professor Havilland shook their hands and said, "Carey tells me I owe you a very great debt."

Dillon had never handled praise well, and today he played the mute. So Sean said, "We're just glad we were there, sir."

"As am I. Believe you me." The professor gave their car a pointed look. "Your parents aren't with you?"

Carey protested quietly, "Dad."

Sean knew Dillon wouldn't say the words, so he did. "Things around our home haven't been great for a while."

"Longer," Dillon said to the ground at his feet.

"Losing the house basically gave them a reason to get a divorce. When we told them we wanted to find a place of our own, they seemed to expect it."

There followed an awkward silence, until Carver said, "I understand you recently lost your wife. Please accept my sincere condolences."

"Mom was an art historian," Carey said. "Her specialty was the Orient. We see her everywhere, so we'll never move. Right, Pop?"

Professor Havilland nodded and asked, "What brings you here, Colonel?"

"These young men will be serving as my research assistants this summer. We have also become friends. I thought it would be appropriate if we met."

Whatever the professor was about to ask next was cut off by his daughter asking, "Dillon, what's wrong?" When Dillon remained silent, she pressed, "Won't you tell me?"

But Dillon just kicked the earth at his feet. So Sean said, "We're surrounded by everything we've never had."

It just tore Sean up inside, saying those words. He was so ashamed. But then Dillon lifted his head and shot him a look of pure gratitude. And he knew he had done the right thing.

Carey looked confused. "I don't understand."

"It's not the place," Sean said.

"Well, it is in a way," Dillon corrected.

"Sure. But what I mean is . . . your family made this a home. You stay here because your mom's still here."

"We've never had that," Dillon said, still kicking at a root. "Not one single day."

The moment was captured by Carver settling his hand on Dillon's shoulder. "This is your life now. Do you understand what I'm saying? It's not about where you sleep. It's about the life you build for yourself. It's the perspective you take on tomorrow."

Sean felt like he was both deeply involved and able to take a mental step back, far enough to see the professor smile softly and Carey reach for her father's hand. They stood like that for a timeless moment, the wind humming through the pines overhead, the tall cane chattering a soft agreement.

Then the professor said, "Why don't we show you your new home."

...

The loft was one grand room, emphasis on the word *grand*. The cathedral ceiling was blond cedar planks, same as the floor, all tongue and groove and hand-finished, or so John Havilland explained to Carver. The twin beds were sectioned off by painted screens that slid shut or could be shunted over to one side. The living area ran into the kitchen, which opened onto a rear balcony. Sean and Dillon did a gingerly walk-around, having trouble taking in the fact that this might be theirs. Their *home*. All the while, the professor continued his gentle probing of Carver.

"What is the subject matter of your study, Colonel?"

"Special forces."

"You were involved in this branch?"

"I still am, to an extent. I serve as consultant on military matters to several groups."

"Including the government?"

Carver did not respond.

"I see. Well. May I ask why you selected these two young men?"

"In my initial meeting with them, I perceived a special aptitude." Carver chose his words very carefully. "I gave them a chance, and they excelled. Their work to date has been of exceptional quality. They show great potential."

Sean watched as Carey glowed with pride over Dillon being praised. Her father saw it too. Sean knew the professor was aware of Carey's feelings for his brother. And the man wasn't certain how he felt about it. But all he said was, "Boys, do your plans include careers in the military?"

"I'm more interested in investigative sciences," Dillon replied.

Professor Havilland was clearly not expecting that sort of precise response from a seventeen-year-old. He took a moment for that, then asked Sean, "What about you?"

"I'm thinking more of a role in government," Sean replied.

"Like your father, then."

"Definitely not," Sean said.

Carey's father just nodded, like Sean's response made all the sense in the world.

Dillon was still zoned out, so Sean decided it was his role to say, "We want to pay rent for this."

"I appreciate the thought, boys, but it's not necessary."

"Sir, we're getting money from the company as well as our folks." They had worked out the strategy with Carver on the way over. "We want a place we can call home. Not just for a couple of weeks. For good."

The declaration caught the professor off guard, particularly when he saw the glow to his daughter's features. "What about your parents?"

Dillon repeated Sean's words, more forceful this time. "We want a place we can call home."

"I see. Or rather, I think I do." He met his daughter's gaze, saw the entreaty, and said, "Tell you what. Let's give it a month's trial run, then we'll have this discussion for real. All right?"

Moving in took all of ten minutes. Carver, Carey, and her father helped. They shook hands all around, then the Havillands returned to their home with the professor's arm around his daughter's shoulders.

Carver announced, "I've rented a place nearby that you can use for transiting. If you do it here, vanishing when people expect you to be home, it could raise questions we don't want."

Dillon was still watching the space that Carey had last occupied. His voice was not dreamy, but it came close. "What kinds of questions?" Which earned him exasperated looks from both Sean and Carver. Dillon blushed. "Oh. Right."

"Pay attention," Carver said. "This is the only time I will be around to show you."

When Carver started toward the stairs, Sean said to his brother, "Yeah, pay attention, why don't you."

"I'm good."

"You're so not good," Sean countered. "This is important, Dillon."

...

They drove past the shopping area and entered the district known as Cameron Village. The rental car smelled of stale perfume and somebody else's sweat. But Sean didn't miss the Charger at all.

The Cameron Apartments were square, red-brick structures dating from the fifties, four dwellings to each building. The units were rented mostly to young families and grad students and newly singles and hourly wagers who worked in local stores and didn't want a long commute. Most of the cars were either Korean or older models with big snouts and fading paint jobs. The streets were a maze that forced the traffic down to a crawl.

They parked in front of a building that was showing its age. Carver removed a For Rent sign from a ground-floor screen door and let them inside. "If anyone asks, you know the drill. The phone number for me will continue to work. But call only if the need is critical."

The living room held three desks, chairs, laptops, and a half-dozen shelves with books on military stuff. Enough to satisfy a casual visitor. The kitchen had the same new IKEA basics. The lone bedroom held a futon and dresser. As empty as a theater stage and just as welcoming. The AC in the living room window gave off a constant metallic cough.

Carver said, "You need to buy bicycles. Come here, transit

out. That's the norm. But we'll practice transits to and from your loft as well."

Dillon broke in with, "Are Carey and her father safe?"

"Yes. They are."

"I need to know you're not blowing smoke here."

Carver was clearly not accustomed to being questioned by his recruits. "Blowing smoke?"

"Some little song and dance you're giving us. A few words to fill the moment." Dillon sounded as hard as Sean had ever heard. "I'm not accepting a level of safety like how we were supposed to be safe before. I don't want to wake up some morning and see a hole in the ground where their home was."

"There are Watchers on duty around the clock," Carver said. "A squad of Praetorians on full alert."

"For how long?"

"As long as I say. Probably until we locate the Examiner."

"And if it isn't the Examiner who's behind this?"

Carver did not reply. Sean found himself unable to say who had the harder gaze, his brother or their instructor.

Dillon finally said, "I guess that's okay."

Carver remained as he was, focused fully on his brother. "You care for her. This young woman."

"Carey," Dillon replied. "Her name is Carey."

"What have you told her?"

"Nothing. Yet. Why, is that good for a mind-wipe?"

"I told you. That phase of training is over."

"So what are the rules on telling somebody?"

"The rules are . . . vague."

"Then I can do it?"

"In theory, it is your decision. You should have my approval. But it is not absolutely necessary . . . Will you tell me?"

"Okay."

"*Before* you tell her?"

"I'll think about it." Dillon waved aside Carver's protest, the gesture right from their instructor's book. "Enough. Let's get started here."

...

The practice session took them well past midnight. Carver shunted them around, their instructor in full military mode. Intent on bringing them to a point where the actions came without thought. When they stopped for infrequent breaks, he hammered on the same core themes. They were moving from what came natural. They were no longer heading out to a place they had chosen during childhood. This was a crucial juncture, being able to transit to destinations that were assigned to them. This was the first step to becoming Messengers. And Messengers formed the backbone of the service . . .

On and on it went. They transited together, alone, roped, unlinked, loft to this apartment, loft to the Examiner's school, school to the loft, over and over until they could do it in their sleep, and almost did. All they saw of the school was a windowless transit chamber painted matte grey with some monochrome symbol on one wall, about as interesting as the principal's waiting room. Sean grew so exhausted he forgot to ask what Carver and the Counselor thought of their joining the Examiner's school. And by the time they called it quits, he no longer cared.

The next morning they rode their new bikes over to the apartment complex and found Tatyana waiting with Carver, deep in discussion over some chart they rolled up and stowed away. Tatyana gave Sean a ten-second blast from those imperious eyes, then said, "Your task is to learn. Not investigate. Do you hear me?"

Maybe it was how Dillon had stood up to Carver the day before. Or maybe it was just how exhausted Sean still felt. Whatever the reason, he wasn't interested in taking more of her orders. "It would be a lot easier to agree if you took Dillon's information seriously."

"We've been through this before. I have the word of senior Watchers who say otherwise."

"Oh. Right. The same guys who sat back and watched us get toasted. You're talking about them?"

She clearly disliked that. "I don't have time for this."

Carver said, "You are still in the earliest stage of your training, and not in any position—"

"If Dillon says it wasn't the Examiner who blasted us, you need to *listen*."

Tatyana said to Carver, "Perhaps this is not a good idea, sending them to the Examiner's school."

"We have to shift them somewhere," Carver said.

"How was their transit?"

"They performed faultlessly."

Sean persisted, "You promised us answers. I'm still waiting to hear who it was that tried to take us out in the Charger."

Tatyana swatted at the words. "You will remember your stations and you will *obey*."

Sean smoldered. Dillon muttered, "Just like a principal."

"The proper response," Carver snapped, "is 'Yes, Counselor.'"

They fumed in silence.

Carver commanded, "Say it."

They did. Sort of.

Tatyana said, "Let's get this over with."

The chief instructor at the Examiner's school was named Josef. The only thing Josef had in common with Carver was that he was probably human. It was hard to tell, though, behind all that hair.

Josef was a soft-spoken, fumbling, benevolent giant. He topped eight feet by a couple of inches. He welcomed them with a warmth that shone through his shock of grey-blond hair and beard. He bowed to the Counselor and Carver, then swallowed Sean's hand with his. By the first day's end, Sean wondered if perhaps Josef was actually shy and loathed towering over everyone, so he twisted his massive trunk whenever addressing a group. Trying to bring himself down as close to everyone else's level as he could manage. It was clear that the students adored him. And for good reason. Josef did not possess a single negative element in his four-hundred-pound frame. He was not actually fat. More like almost everything about him was huge—bones, head, beard, limbs, heart—

everything but his manner and his voice, which were gentle as a baby bird's.

Josef handed them another diadem to wear that night. Their dream-time lessons were shifted from Serenese to Lothian, the dominant language of the world where the Examiner's school was located. The new speech was nothing like the old. Gone was the sibilant music. In came a guttural drumbeat. It seemed to Sean that every consonant was formed at the back of his throat.

He was repeating some of the words to the mirror the next morning when Dillon appeared in the doorway and said, "It makes my throat hurt."

"If Arabic married German," Sean agreed, "their kid would speak Lothian."

The transit chamber opened into a pair of locker rooms. Around the school, students wore navy sweats made from some fabric that actually felt great. Dillon groused that they all looked like magnets for interstellar bullies. But they had not met any yet, so Sean didn't mind.

As they were dressing the second day, Dillon muttered, "Your idea about attending here was a good one. It really comes down to us."

Sean glanced around. The school's two hundred students came from a dozen and more worlds. Classes ran pretty much around the clock, so students came and went at all times. The shouts and laughter in many languages formed a wash that enveloped them in a private bubble. "I thought maybe you were going to let this go. You know, because of Carey."

"That doesn't change anything." Dillon gave that a beat, then amended, "And it changes a lot."

"When are you going to tell her?"

"Later," Dillon said. "Right now it's already more than I can handle."

...

Josef appeared to Sean like a man who never got angry. Stern, certainly. When their class went into a kid-style riot, his worst mood was a very slow burn. Even so, he kept the class in absolute order. He'd show that smoldering disappointment and the most unruly student was brought into line.

Initially Josef placed them with the newest recruits, the oldest of whom was eleven. This lasted all of two days. When Josef was certain they could do what Tatyana and Carver had claimed, he shifted them into the class of their own age. And Josef shifted with them. The instructors must have been used to being swung around, for they moved without a peep. The students, however, knew something was up. The only thing that saved Sean and Dillon from more serious trouble was everybody in the older class was delighted with Josef's unexpected arrival.

A few of the students lived at the school. Most departed at the end of class. For the first two weeks, everybody left Sean and Dillon in their very own isolation bubble. It bothered Sean, but not as much as he might have expected. Basically he was too tired to care. Classes ran ten hours straight. This was followed by the nightly dream routine. Spoken Lothian was combined with the written language. Sean often woke up feeling more tired than when he went to bed.

By the end of the third week, Sean had defined a new normal. Up at six. Threaten his brother with a kitchen pot of water to get him moving. Dillon was out late every night with Carey, mostly just sitting on the patio, their laughter filtering through the loft's balcony doors. Quick breakfast at the kitchen counter. Bike to the apartment Carver rented. Transit to class. Sit through a lecture that defined boring. At least nothing had changed there. Then begin another day of learning new destinations.

The problem was, all these new destinations were nothing more than names. Ditto for the school itself.

The school had no windows. It also had no doors linking them to the outside world. They came, they studied, they went home. There were a lot of reasons for this isolation. But it all added up to one thing, as far as Sean was concerned. The guys in charge had spent four thousand years straining away every ounce of adventure. Leave it to the adults to turn the galaxy's most thrilling ride into a class on tedium. If he hadn't spent his entire life wanting what he couldn't name, Sean would have done his own version of the roadrunner. Adios, baby. Off to see what's out there beyond the monotony.

Twenty days in, they got their first free time. They didn't even know it was happening until they showed up and the school was empty save for a lone instructor who smiled and told them to go play. They would have, definitely, except for how they were both totally beat. They went home and collapsed, for once without the language police invading their dreams. When they woke up they biked over and saw their folks, who were living in apartments a mile or so apart. They listened as first their mother and then their father tried to convince themselves their separation and eventual divorce was best for everyone. Then they went home and spent their first free afternoon of the summer elbows-deep in the adventure of laundry.

Sean was sorting socks when Carey called up the stairs. He greeted her with, "Dillon's wandered off somewhere. My brother's always been afraid of soap."

Carey smiled at his feeble attempt at a joke and said, "He's over talking with Dad."

"What about?"

"Me, probably." She shrugged that away. "I wanted to speak with you."

"I'm all ears."

She made a process of slipping up onto the kitchen counter. "I'm really interested in your brother."

"I know. And he's the same. Only about a billion times stronger."

"I doubt that." Then she must have realized what she'd said and blushed.

Her beauty and her vulnerability and her heartfelt eagerness left Sean swallowing against a sudden hollow feeling. It wasn't so much that he was jealous. It was just, well, he could use a little of the same for himself.

Carey asked, "Are you okay with this?" When Sean did not answer, she pressed, "I mean, you're his twin and all. I just—"

"I know what you mean. And it's great."

"Really?"

"It's better than that." He struggled to say what he had never spoken about to anyone. Thought about, sure. But never said aloud. "Things around our house have never been good. Dillon has spent his entire life looking for someone to give him what he never had. Only he didn't know it."

Carey nodded, and then the motion grew until it took in her entire body. Swinging back and forth on the kitchen counter beside the washing machine, watching Sean fold his laundry, her gaze distant and unfocused. Sean liked being this close to her, looking at her beauty, and knowing she was as much in love as Dillon.

Carey said, "Dillon is sure lucky to have you."

For some reason the words brought a lump to his throat. Sean pounded a fist into the soft fabric and said, "I just wish there were two of you."

Carey slid off the counter so she could hug him. She smelled of vanilla and a spice he could not name. "That would be so cool."

...

After Carey left, Sean phoned Carver. He'd been doing this every few days, just checking in. When the colonel called back, he was his normal clipped, direct self, only with an edge of barely repressed impatience. Sean gave the sort of terse report Carver seemed to expect, then finished as usual with, "Is there anything to report about the attack?"

Carver replied as always before. "Your task is to study, learn, progress."

"I want to know."

"The investigation is none of your concern at present."

"Except for how we were the target," Sean shot back.

"The Counselor specifically ordered you to let this go."

"Whether or not you tell us isn't going to change anything. This is our lives we're talking about. We were the ones who were attacked."

Carver was silent long enough for Sean to fear he wasn't going to answer. Then, "There is no progress on any front. We have found no trace of your attacker."

"What about the Examiner?"

"I just told you."

"And I'm saying the Examiner isn't your guy."

They'd had this same conversation before, and Carver had commended Sean for backing his brother. Even though Carver remained certain they were both wrong. Today, however, Carver asked, "If that is so, why did the Examiner flee?"

Sean had been thinking about that. "Maybe he didn't. Maybe he was captured by the spookies."

"What is this 'spookies,' please?"

"My word for the ladies in the first attack. Have you considered that?"

"There are issues which I cannot discuss with a raw recruit," Carver replied flatly. "Once again, you are hereby ordered to leave this in the hands of your superiors."

Their first tutorial with Josef took place the next day. Sean felt totally unprepared for the transformation their instructor revealed. Gone was the shy, bumbling giant. In his place was a man of blazing intent. He shut the door, slipped behind his oversized desk, and in that instant the outside world was gone. Dillon and Sean and their conversation were it. They were *on*.

Josef began with, "Tell me what you are thinking."

"About what?"

"Anything. Only let us speak Serenese, yes? I need to observe your ability with the Assembly's official language." Josef spread his massive hands. "Let us talk on whatever you like. There are no limits."

Sean exchanged a look with his brother. Uncertain how to take the words.

"By the time I normally start this tier of a recruit's training," Josef went on, "I know my students intimately. I know their strengths, their weaknesses. I know what they want to do professionally. And usually I know what they should not attempt. You see? With you two, I know nothing at all. So I ask you to spend this time talking with me."

Sean glanced over a second time. Dillon nodded once. *Go.*

"You want us to be honest," Sean said.

"If this tutorial is to be of any benefit, our words must be truthful," Josef agreed.

"Which is why we're speaking Serenese. So you can hear more than just what I say."

Josef smiled approval. "The Counselor claimed you were gifted. I have seen confirmation of this in the class. Now I am pleased to know it is not simply a matter of applying your power." When they remained silent, Josef pressed, "Come, come, gentlemen. Tell me this. What is your clearest impression of our school and what we do here?"

Sean replied, "Same-old, same-old."

"What means this, please?"

"We swing back and forth to different places, and we don't see a thing. One windowless room to another. We've learned transits to what, sixteen worlds?"

"Seventeen," Dillon corrected. "Seventeen boring windowless rooms."

"Boring," Sean said. "That's the word."

Josef's eyes were crystal green, a laser intent upon probing deep. "Most of the students here have great difficulty focusing on the transit itself. They need this sameness. It helps them maintain proper aim. Ninety percent of all recruits become Messengers. They are required to learn a minimum of—"

"Forty transit points to graduate. We've heard all that." Sean was glad to finally have a chance to speak his mind. "We're not most students."

Josef continued, "Forty transit points. Correct. This is all they want. This is why they come. They travel, they perform an important role. They graduate and they step from the chambers into new and exciting tasks. They deliver their message, they have a nice meal, they stay in a nice hotel, they return home. They have rank. They are respected."

"You've just painted the life we *don't* want," Sean said.

"Messengers play a vital role within our community of planets," Josef replied.

"Right. Just like galactic cell phones."

"Please?"

"Never mind."

"Plus there is the issue of age. Our students are normally between nine and fourteen Lothian years old when they arrive."

The Lothian year was about three-fourths the length of an Earth year. "So?"

"Their maturity is not at a level where we can permit them to interact with the outside world. Already there are many people, on many worlds, who resent us and suspect our intentions."

"But why? You just said they play an important role."

"There have been problems. Serious ones. But that is for another time, yes? Right now what you need to understand is this. Our isolation is in place for important reasons."

Dillon complained, "But we've never even seen anything

of any other planet. Including this one. Just weeks of blank-walled classrooms."

Josef kept his gaze on Sean as he replied, "In seventeen days, Lothia celebrates the summer equinox. It is a great festival, and you will have an opportunity to see some of this world. But never mind that for the moment. Listen carefully, my two young adventurous gentlemen. A tutorial is meant to delve beyond the boundaries of ability. To stretch the student, to help them redefine the possible. But so far, all I know is what you *don't* want. So before we speak of your professional aims, I must know the *person*. You understand? Yes, I see you do. Excellent. So here is what I ask. Tell me of the secret Sean and the secret Dillon. Tell me what is on your heart. Learn to trust me. You will find me a strong and willing ally."

This time when Sean hesitated, Dillon spoke to him in English. "You're up, bro."

"You think?"

"I know."

"But what if he's the Examiner's pet?"

"You been listening? We're talking Serenese and the guy is coming across straight as a bullet."

"True, true."

"So let's give this a shot. We've been here three weeks and done nothing. It's time to do more than walk through walls."

Sean turned back, took a breath, and launched straight in.

■■■

Sean didn't hold anything back. Including his and Dillon's mutual loathing for the Examiner. And vice versa.

Midway through the description of the Charger attack, Josef rose from his chair and turned toward the floor-to-ceiling bookshelves running along the right-hand wall. The professor was so large he seemed to push most of the air from the room. When Sean hesitated, Josef rolled one finger without turning around. *Continue.*

When Sean finished describing the assault that destroyed their home, Josef remained as he was, frowning and blindly perusing titles before his nose.

Sean turned to his silent brother and said in English, "You've been a big help."

"Hey, you were on a roll there."

Josef halted Sean's retort with, "It is customary in tutorials to speak only the languages that all present understand."

"Sorry."

"No, no, it is I who must apologize." He turned around and gave them a portly bow. "On behalf of my dear friend Tirian, I sincerely regret everything you have endured because of his prejudice."

Sean was taken aback by the words, such that Dillon was the one who said, "Apology accepted."

"Tirian is my oldest friend. I love him like a brother. And he can be the most exasperating, judgmental . . ."

"Bullheaded," Sean offered. "Totally blind."

"A royal pain," Dillon said.

"Just plain nasty," Sean agreed.

Josef pulled at his beard, doing his best to hide a smile. "I should mention that what is said inside tutorials is never discussed beyond this portal."

"Works for me," Dillon said.

"Now then, as to the next step. Counselor Tatyana was most explicit in her instructions. You may not under any circumstances return to your original transit point. You are to study and you are to learn. Nothing more. And yet I myself am facing a number of unanswered questions . . ."

Josef slipped back into his oversized chair. He stroked his beard in silence, one massive hand gathering it together, stroking down, tugging, again. It actually left Sean feeling calmer. He watched the giant and decided that here was a man who took them seriously. For the moment, it was great just not being put down.

Finally Josef continued, "As I said, a successful tutorial will force the student to delve beyond the boundaries of the comfortable. Normally that means the student must grow in unexpected directions. But in your case . . ."

They were content to sit and wait while the instructor dialogued with himself. Time was set aside, as were the worry and the unknown. Here was safety. Here was an ally.

Josef turned and planted his hands on the desk. "Very well. This is what I think. Let us make an agreement. Speak to one another without words a second time, and I in return will do two things. First, I will go against the orders of a Counselor. I will help you in solving this mystery. Because I too fear that Colonel Carver and his team are looking in the wrong direction."

"That's great," Sean said.

Dillon corrected, "It's great only if we can make it work."

"But we will."

"I'm glad to hear you say that," Dillon shot back. "Let me know when you work that out."

Josef held up his hand. *Wait.* "But we must agree among ourselves that this will be our secret. We will do this thing, and we will move in the shadows. Because I for one do not wish to anger this particular Counselor. Already she views Tirian's school with suspicion. If she suspects any wrongdoing on our part, she would shut us down in an instant. I tell you this because I want you to understand that I take a very great risk, even speaking of this in the confidentiality of the tutorial."

"We understand," Sean said. "We won't say a word."

"We really appreciate this," Dillon added.

"You mentioned giving us a second thing if we talk without words."

"When." Dillon grinned at him. "It's just a matter of time, right?"

"The second promise." Josef leaned closer still. Suddenly he was not the gentle, caring professor. Gone were the smile and the shyness. In their place was a warrior's implacable force. "Do this thing, and I will reveal to you the mysteries of higher combat."

Josef did give them one boon immediately, which was an occasional extra day off. There were a number of the older students who were held to a less rigid schedule. They were given personal assignments that were often intended to lead into either their professional lives or higher training. Carey and her father adapted to their schedule and invited the twins to join them for dinners. Professor Havilland began these meals with a few questions about their work, but when they gave half-finished sentences that really didn't say much at all, he let the matter drop.

Another two weeks passed, and their progress on the mind speech remained at ground zero. They basically stopped trying. Nothing they came up with made any difference. So the off days were spent lounging poolside, watching kids their age be, well, kids. All the things that framed the conversations that once were so vital had been stripped away. School, university applications, parents, jobs, girls, parties, cars . . . Sean and Dillon pretended to listen and kept their traps shut.

Carey's job at the school had another three weeks to run, and there was a chance it would be extended through the rest of the summer. When she had a day off, she packed a lunch and took Dillon on long rides. The guy always returned wearing a smile that could only be described as goofy. Sean did not dislike those days. He did not resent his brother's happiness. He did not feel angry at Carey for choosing his twin. But there were some hard times just the same, especially in the small hours when he was trapped alone on the balcony, without a thing to do but think of what he didn't have.

Which was why, on one of those lonely afternoons when he saw the professor working over papers on the front patio, he wandered over. He brought a book he'd been trying to read for months, just in case he needed an excuse. But before he'd made it halfway down the walk, the professor had shifted his papers over to one side. "I must assume you're Sean, since I would hate to think the wrong twin had slipped away with my daughter."

"No, that would definitely be Dillon."

"Come make yourself comfortable. Would you like a Coke?"

"Sure, thanks." When the professor returned carrying two glasses, Sean said, "I was wondering if I could ask you something."

"Of course. You know how I can tell you two apart? I say to myself, 'Sean is the thinker. In ten years, he's the one whose forehead will be creased from hours of concentration.'"

Sean sipped his drink and wondered if he'd also be the guy who was alone. "We need to check something out, and we don't know how." He had struggled to find some way to approach the impossible on the way over. "There's a chance the blast that left us homeless wasn't a gas pipe."

If the professor saw anything odd in the admission, he did not show it. "Have you spoken with the police?"

"Sort of."

"I take it they were not interested."

"They said it wasn't any of our concern."

"Do you think you and Dillon were a target?"

Sean answered as honestly as he could. "I can't figure out why that might be the case."

"If you were," Professor Havilland persisted, "are Carey and I in danger?"

"We have been assured over and over that there's absolutely no risk."

The professor accepted that with a slow nod. "So what makes you think there might be a culprit?"

"Dillon saw something. But the . . . police don't believe him. I didn't see it. But I felt . . . I guess . . . a wrongness." Sean waited for the standard adult dismissal, even offered the guy a way out. "I know that doesn't make any sense."

"Actually, it makes more sense than you will ever know." He turned his chair so he could stretch out his long legs. "Feelings can be great spurs to change. I could name you any number of great discoveries made by thinkers who reached a point where something didn't 'feel' right. My field is cultural anthropology, which is focused on the study of people in their societies. We look at how people interact. How over time they develop their civilization, their art, their music, their value systems, their family structures. For over a century, my field has been divided into two very distinct groups, or perspectives. One side says there are certain underlying values and principles that all human civilizations employ or contain. Or, in some cases, these same elements are willfully turned away from. They are called *absolutes*. And the anthropologists who adhere to this are called structuralists, or classicists.

"The second group is known as cultural relativists, and these days they're in the majority. They insist that *nothing* about human civilization is absolute. All ideas and conceptions are valid only so far as one particular group or nation, and time frame, make them so." He grinned over at Sean. "Guess how well these two get along."

"Not at all."

"Correct. So here you have two groups of people who have dedicated their lives to the study of human civilization, and they look at the exact same evidence and come up with two completely different answers."

"You're saying that if it can happen to them, it can happen to anyone."

"It is always a distinct possibility."

"So what questions should I be asking?"

"There are two possible avenues you should consider. Weakness is one, motive the other. Often they prove to be one and the same. An established leader has every reason to protect his or her work from the attacks of others, even when they suspect the new direction is correct. Do you think the police might have a reason to protect a sacred cow?"

"I don't . . ." Sean felt a faint buzz gather force in his brain, like a tiny drill working its way inside, trying hard to plant an idea. "Maybe."

"Power and money can be strong motivations."

"This is definitely not money."

Professor Havilland glanced over, and Sean feared he was going to ask how he could be so certain. But after a moment's inspection all the professor said was, "Power then. If it is power, you need to search for the motive that binds the explosion to some greater issue. But be careful there. People in power tend to get very touchy when they feel their position is threatened."

...

Sean waited until after dinner and they were getting ready for bed to relate his conversation to Dillon. His brother didn't respond until they were in bed and the lights were out. "You think that was wise, talking with the prof?"

"I went over because I was bored. But now . . . Yeah, I think it might have been a good thing."

"He's one smart guy."

"Tell me about it." With the screen flattened against the wall, their beds were separated by the loft's lone dresser that grew two nightstands like stubby arms. Moonlight streamed through the balcony doors and the skylight over the living area, casting the loft in a silver gleam. "What do you think?"

"You're the sage. You tell me."

"You've never called me that before."

"It's how Carey describes you."

"The sage," he said, feeling a warm glow.

"It fits. So?"

"I've come up with two questions we need to figure out. The first is, who or what was behind the Charger attack?" Sean crossed his arms behind his head, angling his gaze so he could study the silver pillar spilling down from the skylight. "But we can't go straight at it. Everybody is doing their best to keep from talking about whatever those ladies really were."

"There's definitely some secret they figure we can't handle," Dillon agreed.

"So what we need to understand is *how* they do this."

"Josef," Dillon said. "Josef is the key."

"Right, but to make that happen we've got to repeat the mind-speech. And I'm trying. Believe me."

Dillon rolled so he could see his brother. "In the meantime we need to figure out why everybody is so scared of us asking this question."

"If we can. Right."

"So what's question two?"

"What's the link between the ladies in the Charger and the blast that leveled our house?"

Dillon agreed. "They're too close together to be a coincidence."

"If we can get a handle on that, maybe we can understand how Tirian was photocopied."

"As if one of the guy wasn't enough."

26

The idea hit Sean hard as a midnight bullet. It threw him out of bed before he was fully aware of his movements. He couldn't be bothered to use words to wake Dillon. This was not a time for arguments. As he walked past his brother's bed he kicked the foot sticking over the edge.

He received a muffled, "What's the big idea?"

Sean moved into the kitchen, poured two glasses of water, walked back, and handed one to Dillon. They both usually woke up parched as Sahara trekkers. "I just figured it out. Maybe."

To his credit, Dillon didn't waste time with stupid questions. He drank his water, dressed, and followed Sean down the stairs and into the night.

Sean told him, "We've been going at this all wrong. We're trying to *think* from one of us to the other."

"Silly me," Dillon retorted. The guy was alert enough to

offer the day's first quip. "All this time that's what I figured we were working on. Thoughts."

"So how hasn't it worked? Because *it's not about thoughts at all.*"

Crickets filled the silence. The moon was a small sliver almost directly overhead, the sky so clear they could see a faint silhouette of the dark side. The air was Carolina cool, the night windless. Somewhere far in the distance a dog barked. Otherwise the night was theirs.

Dillon said, "In a crazy way, that makes perfect sense."

Hearing his brother speak those words got Sean so totally excited he shivered. "So we start from the energy."

Dillon was nodding now. In tandem. "Focus on the force at gut level."

"Build that up. Form a . . . I don't know, a bubble or something."

"Stick the thought inside."

"And pass it to . . ." Sean stopped talking because Dillon was already on the move. His footsteps made a racing patter down the empty street.

Sean shivered again.

Dillon stopped beneath a streetlight a couple hundred yards away. And stood there with hands on hips. Waiting.

It should have come natural by now, forming a bundle of energy in his gut. Especially when he was so tense it felt like his entire body was ready to fold inward around the fist-like clenching. But Sean was so nervous it took forever. Finally he formed a new shield around himself, then pried out a segment. It helped to see it like an old-fashioned cartoon, the bubble taking shape just above his head. He couldn't think of anything more intelligent to say than, *Can you hear me now?* Like they were struggling against a failing cell phone signal.

Then he sent it scooting off to where his brother stood.

It seemed like the instant he made the invisible move, Dillon started dancing.

His brother went crazy. The touchdown dance in the state final was nothing compared to the ridiculous jig going on beneath the yellow streetlight.

Sean would have been embarrassed to have anyone see him just then, because all of a sudden he was laughing so hard he couldn't stop the tears. And then the message came zinging back at him, and it all got worse.

Bro, we've just redefined spooky.

27

When they arrived at school the next morning, Josef was gone. The instructors wouldn't say where he was, just that they needed to come back after school. So they put up with another day of the same-old. Which was an amazing way to look at transiting between planets. But still. All they saw of their destinations was another windowless room, each with a symbol of some sort planted on the wall. Their destination points, the symbols were called. A lot of the class time was given over to memorizing these symbols for various worlds. More was spent on the cultures they didn't get a chance to see, and the laws governing the civilizations they had no contact with.

But that day held a difference. The school was filled with an undercurrent of tension, which Sean at first assumed was just him being excited over what Dillon had started calling spook-speak. But his brother caught him between classes and asked, "What's going on around here?"

"No idea."

"Maybe they're finally getting ready to revolt, break down some walls, and take a good look around."

"Either that or there's a party we haven't been invited to," Sean replied.

Transit practice took up the entire middle of every day. Then it was back to the classroom for the final lecture. Sean was so whipped he fought constantly against a serious case of the nods. A half night lost to sleep, running around in the dark with his brother, shooting off thought bombs, then into class and all the transits . . . His eyelids had fifty-pound weights attached. He was close to dozing off when his brother messaged, *Incoming at two o'clock.*

Dillon was seated to his left. Sean turned and looked at him. Just too weary to fashion a decent thought. He mouthed the word, *What?*

Dillon pointed to Sean's opposite side and shot back, *The class hottie is checking you out.*

There were several girls in their course who were standouts. But the one Sean found most striking was a younger version of Tatyana. Same white-blonde hair, same amazing eyes, same sharp features. Only on her the sternness was not imprinted. Most people probably found her imposing, for the girl normally walked in her very own isolation bubble. Sean thought she was amazing.

When he turned around, he found her staring. At him.

Sean didn't have any trouble staying awake after that.

When class was done, he held back. She leaned across the desk separating them and asked, "Is class really so boring, Sean?"

He took a risk and responded in Serenese. "How do you know my name?"

She rewarded him with the first smile he had seen her give. Her features were not classically beautiful, they were too sharp, too intelligent, too intense. But the smile had a softening effect, almost like she had opened an unseen door and invited him in. "I know because I made it my business to know."

In her mouth, Serenese came into its own, a song meant to be shared by good friends. Sean felt his heart flutter as he slipped into the next desk, closing the distance. "What's going on around here?"

"What do you mean?"

"Everybody is so, I don't know, intense."

"Ah. The summer equinox is tomorrow."

"So?"

"I will tell you if you ask me again, Sean. But I would prefer to . . ." She stopped as Dillon approached. "Yes?"

"Um . . . I need to take off."

Sean didn't look up. "Okay."

"Weren't we going to talk to Josef?"

"Not now."

"Isn't that more important?"

"No."

"So . . . I'll see you back at the place?"

"Sure."

"Right."

When Dillon was gone, she asked, "What is your language called?"

"English."

"Where is this spoken?"

"The United States. Well, a lot of places." Then he realized what she meant. "Oh. I'm from Earth. It's an outpost planet."

"Your world is not joined to the Assembly?"

"Nobody on Earth has any idea that other human civilizations exist. But if they did, it wouldn't make any difference."

"Why do you say that, Sean?"

"Can I ask your name?"

"Of course. I am Elenya."

For some reason, he shivered. "Nice to meet you, Elenya."

"And you, Sean. Will you answer my question?"

There was a formality to the language that left Sean talking in a manner he never had before, and doing so comfortably. As though he always managed to express himself in chants that shared hints of emotions as well as words. And what he felt just then was shame. "I don't know exactly what is required to join the Assembly. But if unity and peace are two conditions, Earth doesn't stand a chance."

"Don't be so sure. There are stories of many planets that have struggled and grown despite themselves."

"Including Serena?"

She smiled a second time. "No. My planet has not known a war in over two thousand years."

"Wow."

"Yes. Some might call that boring."

"Not me. I'd love to see a planet that's forgotten what war is."

She made a strange sort of gesture, like she was opening an invisible portal and bowing, all while seated. "Then you should come. Be my guest."

"Really? We can do that?"

"We must ask Josef. But he says yes. Sometimes." She smiled a third time. "Perhaps you should let me make the request."

"Absolutely."

"I can be very persuasive."

"If you smile like that, I bet you can wrap Josef around your little finger."

Elenya laughed, and the room shivered with him. "That is something I would like to see."

She rose then, and he felt a very deep regret that the moment was over.

They walked down the empty hall toward the transit chamber. When they stepped inside, Elenya said, "Let us meet here tomorrow, yes? Allow me to share with you the reason why all of Lothia is excited."

Sean wasn't normally so glib with girls, especially one so lovely. But the words came almost unbidden, as though he had waited all his life to have the chance to tell her, "I don't know if I can stand much more excitement than being with you again."

She graced him with the finest smile of all, and was gone.

Sean stood there a long moment, looking around the matte-grey walls with the lone symbol and the narrow bench and the bland lighting. The air held a faint trace of some fragrance, gentle as a summer wind. He wanted to lock everything that had just happened down where he would never forget, not a single fragment. He realized that by switching to Serenese he had caught a glimpse of the woman behind the words. And what defined the emotion carried in her words was warmth. Affection. Invitation.

28

The next morning, Josef heard them out in thoughtful silence. Then he told Sean to describe the process a second time. Josef sat in utter stillness. Gone was the jovial giant, the caring teacher. His intensity was so overpowering Sean was left stammering.

Josef opened a drawer and pulled out two pads and pens, handed one of each to Sean, rose to his feet, and said to Dillon, "Come with me." A few minutes later he returned and asked, "Can you read Lothian?"

"I'm learning."

"Then we will use my own home world's language. Give me your pad." Josef wrote swiftly, then showed the page to Sean. "Do you know what this means?"

"No, sir."

"Good. Send it to your brother."

"We've never tried doing an image."

"Even better. Go ahead. Do it now."

Josef had not said to try. *Do.* Sean focused as tight as he knew how. Then he sent.

When he looked up, Josef asked, "Is it finished?"

"I think so."

He left, moving amazingly fast for such a big man. He was gone long enough for Sean to grow more nervous still. He finally shot off to Dillon, *What's going on?*

He's writing. Hang on. There was a pause, then an image flashed in Sean's mind, this one of a script he had never seen before. It looked like cursive hieroglyphics. Sean was afraid he'd lose it, so he bent over the pad and got busy. Josef entered and loomed over him as he worked.

When he was done, Josef frowned over the pad and slipped behind his desk. "Tell your brother to come back in." When Dillon entered, Josef said, "It seems remarkably simple, which some say is the standard for all brilliant ideas. I wish to try this communication. Are you willing?"

"Sure. I mean, yes, sir."

"All right." Josef shut his eyes. Then, "Do you hear me?"

"No, sir." Sean turned to his brother. "Anything?"

"Not a peep."

"Sorry, Professor."

"No, no, this is important. There have only been a few other twins who both became recruits. A significant percentage have proven to be what we refer to as adepts." Josef pondered for a long moment, then sighed and placed his massive hands on the desk. "But that is for later, yes? You did as I asked, and now I must live up to my side of the agreement. Give me a few hours . . . This will be your first Lothian Solstice, yes?"

"We don't even know what it is."

"Then you are in for a treat." Josef tried to offer them an encouraging smile. "Come see me when it is over. I should have made arrangements by then."

29

The rumbling began as they were walking from Josef's office back to the seniors' classroom. It felt like an earthquake that had not quite reached them yet. A student who passed them said to a friend, "Looks like somebody jumped the mark."

Then the claxon sounded, a blast of noise that Sean felt in his bones. If a car was made as big as a city, its horn would have sounded like that. The claxon gave off a long, low blast then went silent, only it now seemed as though the entire world was mimicking the noise with horns of their own. Even the building holding the classroom gave off a booming roar from somewhere overhead. This was the first real evidence they'd had that the building holding the school was actually surrounded by other structures, that they were actually in a city. There were hundreds of horns. Thousands.

Dillon asked a passing student, "What is going on?"

He asked the worst possible guy, a tall Lothian with hair

gelled into angry spikes tipped in silver. Matching black pants and vest with silver spikes up the legs and ringing the shoulders. Eye shadow and rings everywhere—evidently skin art was a galactic event. And the attitude to match. He sneered, "Don't you know anything?"

The girl walking alongside him would have been called Goth back home. She answered, "Apparently not."

"I know enough to not look like a pair of dorks," Dillon said to their backs.

A voice behind them said, "Don't mind them."

Sean turned and felt the same swooping dive as the previous day. He switched to Serenese and said, "It sounds like a city on the move."

"It is, in a way." She turned to Dillon and gave him a solemn look. "Hello, Sean's brother. I am Elenya."

"Dillon. Hi."

"Dillon. It suits you." She did not actually dismiss him. More like her intent was to focus on Sean. Exclusively. The thought was good for the day's first shiver. "I was looking for you. Where have you been?"

"With Josef."

She nodded and held out her hand. "Come."

"Where are we going?"

"To witness the most beautiful moment of this planet's year."

They joined the stream of students passing through a door that before had been permanently locked, up three flights of stairs, and into a room the size of the entire school. One giant high-ceilinged chamber, four hundred feet to a side, filling with more people than Sean had seen before, certainly more than just those attending the school. The space was consumed with excited chatter, a huge sense of electric anticipation.

But the most intense sensation for Sean was the warm hand holding his.

The grinding noise continued to grow until it took hold of the building's foundation. The rumble grew from all sides. The room was rimmed by tall windows. But all they saw beyond the glass was a featureless greyish-black.

Elenya led them over to a spot where they had the railing to themselves. "Yesterday when we spoke. How did you know I was Serenese?"

"Because you look like Tatyana."

"Who is that?"

"My Counselor."

She clearly liked that. "*Your* counselor."

"It's a long story."

"I positively adore long stories. But not now, yes?"

He didn't care about the dark wall grinding along outside the window. Or how other people crowded in around them. All his being was focused on the long-fingered hand that held his. "Whatever you say."

"Are you always this agreeable, Sean?"

He thought about that. "Yes."

"Good. I am glad."

Sean decided Elenya was fully aware of how he was staring and welcomed his attention. The woman was so controlled, so precise. Her white-blonde hair cascaded in a single perfect line down her back, across the blue of her uniform, which on her actually looked stylish.

He asked, "How old are you?"

"In what planet's terms? Here on Lothia I would be almost twenty-one."

He translated that and realized, "We're the same age, more or less."

She turned to him, revealing eyes grey and luminescent. "Pay attention, Sean."

"I am. Believe me."

"This is important." She turned to the window, beyond which the first pale wash of light began to grow. "Here it comes."

The light grew until Sean could see that the building was rising. The *entire building* was moving up. Up, up, and now he realized they were emerging through . . .

He spoke the word as a question. "Ice?"

"Every Lothian building has a shield generator in its roof. Shields can be made to create massive amounts of heat. For this very purpose."

Ice. Blue streaked with white. Ice. Hundreds of feet thick. *Ice.*

Then the city emerged into daylight. After all this time, waiting to see another world, Sean filtered the entire amazing scene through the sensation of the hand holding his.

Elenya was saying, "Lothia is far from what I would call a beautiful world. But this first sight every summer makes up for everything one must endure here. Almost."

"You've lived on Lothia?"

"Off and on for much of my life. Until last year, my father was the planetary Ambassador assigned to this world. What do you know of Lothia?"

"Nothing at all."

She cocked her head and the hair cascaded over one shoulder. "How long have you been a recruit?"

"Forty-five days and counting."

"And yet you are assigned to the senior class. You and your brother must be seen to have the potential of becoming adepts."

"I have no idea what that means."

But whatever she was about to say was cut off by all the Lothians who surrounded them, lifting their hands and chanting in unison. Elenya translated, "They speak a traditional saying from what is now called Old Lothian. 'Another long night has ended. We enter the dawn light with hope for all the new tomorrows.'"

Other buildings continued to sprout slowly from the ice. A dozen, a hundred, a thousand, a vast city rising into the mist and the light. The sky overhead was partly veiled by clouds colored a surreal mix of lavender and grey. Two suns shone through the covering, but light from both was dim enough for Sean to look directly at them. They were joined by a faint ring of pale pink that shimmered like a sunset rainbow.

A ring. Around two suns.

Dillon spoke in English from his other side. "We're not in Kansas anymore, Toto."

"That's for sure."

Elenya asked, "What did your brother say?"

Sean translated, then explained, "It's from a story about a girl who is transported to a distant world in a storm."

"Perhaps the storyteller could transit?"

"Doubtful."

Dillon leaned far enough over to smirk at their two linked hands. He said in English, "Way to rock and roll, bro."

"The two of you, pay attention," Elenya said, punctuating her words by tugging on Sean's hand.

He huffed a silent laugh. Elenya was already laying claim, at least to the moment. And he was just loving it.

Elenya went on, her words aimed at the glass before her face. "My father studied the planet's history before taking this assignment. You know of the Serenese Records?"

"A little."

"There was no mention of Lothia. None. Then the Lothian adept appeared, the first to come from elsewhere, rather than us going first to them."

"Adept means somebody who can establish new transit points?"

"Correct. Among other abilities."

"I'm no adept, Elenya."

She just looked at him. A single glance, one carrying a wealth of the unspoken. Then she turned back to the glass. Sean could feel Dillon close to his other side, wanting to hear. So he pushed down his protests and said, "Tell me what happened."

"The Lothian adept's first words were, 'I bring greetings from the hollow world.' Lothia held many surprises for the empire of man. Nowhere else have humans been planted underground. But what is more, the Lothians knew of our other worlds."

"They knew they had been planted?"

"Correct."

The buildings rose like defiant spears, gleaming symbols of man's presence. Even here.

Sean said, "But I thought the Serenese Records were the first anybody knew about other worlds."

"For all worlds except Lothia, that is correct. But Lothia knew it had been created by others. Who had done this planting, they could not say. Only that they were intended to grow to where they could connect with the humans of other realms. They searched for this method for three thousand years. And arrived just eight centuries after the Serenese Records revealed the transit concept to us."

"Just eight centuries," Dillon said. "Imagine that."

As far as Sean could see in every direction stretched nothing but rock and ice. The suns and the cloud veil painted the vista in a thousand hues of rose and white and silver and palest violet, a landscape of mystical wonder. And of death. For nothing grew here. Not now, not ever. This world of rock and ice was consumed by the feel of lifelessness.

Sean asked, almost to himself, "How did the planters ever come up with this place?"

"It is a marvel, is it not? But they came, and in the giant underground caverns that are warmed by this planet's core, they planted a green realm of animals and plants whose genes come from a dozen worlds. Here too is another wonder. For on no other planet has there been this pollination of beast and plant. Only humans."

They stood there for over an hour, until most of the others had departed and only the Lothians remained. Sean studied them, wondering what it would be like to live underground for eight months at a stretch.

Dillon said, "We ought to go check in with the professor."

"Right." But he was reluctant to let go of Elenya's hand, and it appeared she felt the same. "Josef wanted to speak with us after we saw this. Thanks for making it so special."

She rewarded him with another of those rare smiles. "I was the one honored, Sean. Perhaps we can meet later and you will share with me tales from your outpost world?"

"I'd like that. A lot. We call it Earth."

Dillon warned, "Josef may keep us awhile."

"Tomorrow then." Her gaze was locked on his, laser intent. "Will you show your home to me?"

"Is that allowed?"

"If Josef agrees."

"Maybe you better ask him. We're already pushing the envelope."

When they arrived at Josef's office, the man wore a different sort of sweats, khaki in color, stiffer, and with a lot more pockets. And the biggest pair of boots Sean had ever seen. There was no insignia anywhere, no sign of a weapon, but Sean was pretty sure this was some version of battle gear. Which prompted the question, what had Josef been doing in his previous life? The change they had noticed earlier, the shift away from gentle encouragement, was magnified. Josef was a giant with a warrior's gaze.

He led them to the transit room and reached out both arms. "Take hold."

Sean felt like he had returned to early childhood, when holding an adult's hand only heightened his sense of small-ness. Josef stepped forward and he and Dillon followed suit. There was the familiar tug of forces, and they transited to . . .

The arrival point was so unexpected, the sight so jarring,

Sean's brain refused to compute. He went into a full freeze for a second or two, until his eyes finally locked on the one thing that made any sense. What he had first taken as a weird greyish-green sky overhead was actually the ceiling of a cave. They were *inside.* But the dimensions were all wrong. And it was cold. There was snow on the ground and ice floes forming weird sculptures and snow falling. And clouds drifting high up, between them and the grey-stone ceiling. The walls were lost to mist. They stood on a hill, he could see the endless snow-and-rock vista in every direction, and there were no walls. The only reason he was certain he stood inside a cave was because of the ceiling, which had to be a mile or so high. Then he fastened on the nearest stalactite, a massive blue-grey icicle that hung way, *way* down, like a pillar with the bottom hundred feet or so chopped off.

Josef waited while they turned slowly and gaped. When they finally fastened their attention back on him, he said, "Directly beneath the Lothian surface open many such chambers. Thousands of caverns, some far larger than here. This one has been partly humanized. The air is breathable. The temperature has been raised to human levels."

Dillon's teeth chattered as he said, "This is *warm*?"

"Even in summer, some Lothian nights the surface temperature drops to where iron breaks like candy. This cavern is a training ground for Praetorians and the Lothian military . . . Do you understand when I say 'not pretending'?"

"Live fire," Dillon offered.

"Correct. Today the Lothians celebrate. So we have this to ourselves. To your left is an opening to the outer world.

That is where we will make our live-fire exercise." He held out his hands once more. "Ready?"

They transited to one side of the cavern, up near one ice-clad wall. Sean needed another moment, longer than the first, to come to terms with where he stood.

Josef said, "The Lothians export their shield technology all over the empire. The shield here is semi-porous—you understand what that means? It allows in some of the cold and none of the atmosphere."

Sean tried to listen. He really did. But the entire scope of their position left him catching every third word at most. They stood atop a natural column, maybe sixty feet wide, and so high the mist boiled about them like a cloud bank. The cavern's floor was lost. The sense of impossible height was magnified by the cave mouth, which loomed behind Josef. The opening had to be several miles across. Now and then something touched the energy surface, causing electric spiderwebs to radiate out a ways, then fade back to nothing-ness. Beyond the shield, the Lothian surface gleamed beneath the two dim suns.

Dillon asked, "You okay?"

"I . . . guess."

"You've gone all green."

"I've just discovered I don't like heights."

"Check out the side wall."

Sean looked where Dillon pointed and saw a dark stain with a deep flame-scoured gouge at its heart. Dillon sounded totally matter-of-fact about it all. "Gives a whole new meaning to live fire."

"This doesn't bother you?"

"You kidding? This is the coolest thing since trains riding on the ceiling."

Josef motioned for their attention and said, "I will transit to that second column. When I arrive, I will wave my hand. When you have prepared your shields, you will wave back. At that point I will reveal a battle tactic that feeds upon this world's natural energy. What do you think that might be?"

"Cold and ice," Dillon instantly replied.

"Correct. This is the core component of a recruit's initial training in battle tactics. Use the energy that is available. Here, as you say, it is cold." The giant waited for a moment, then said, "Remember, wave back only when you are shielded."

Josef took a step away and vanished, then reappeared on a second column that Sean only noticed at that moment. Josef's position was midway between where Sean stood and the cave mouth. The transit only heightened his sense of surreal unease. It made no logical sense. He stood in the middle of a huge, flat stone surface, wider than the school's main assembly hall. But he couldn't get over what waited just beyond the distant lip. Like he was being sucked toward it, even without moving, drawn to the point where he flipped over the ledge and fell forever.

Dillon obviously felt none of this. "Hey, I just thought of something. You know how I turned the fire around when the house got toasted? Maybe I could try that with Josef's ice."

"Too late now." Just releasing the words threatened to bring up Sean's last meal.

"No, hang on, I'll go ask."

Before Sean could tell his brother not to transit to an unknown point, he was already over on the other column, standing by Josef. Sean was too far away to see the professor's expression, but something about the way the giant straightened and stepped back made Sean pretty certain Josef was as spooked by Dillon's move as Sean.

Dillon popped back into view and said, "Josef says I should go for it."

"He didn't look happy to have you show up."

"No, he was okay. Surprised. But pleased. Kinda like watching a clown pop from a hole, I guess." Dillon held out his hand. "You think we could connect like last time?"

Actually, it was precisely what Sean wanted to do at that point. Gripping his brother's hand made him fairly certain he would not fall. Which was ridiculous. But still.

Dillon took hold of Sean's hand and said, "You can't be hot."

"In here? Are you nuts?"

"Then why are you sweating?"

"Man, I am about this close to tossing my cookies."

"Well, just be sure and turn downwind."

"I can't get over how calm you are."

"This is *great*. Okay, Josef is waving. Shields up?"

"Yes."

"Cool." Dillon waved. "Remember, feed me the power and let me pull the trigger."

Sean was about to say he had no interest in shooting *anything*. But there wasn't time to reply. Because Josef began his assault.

The giant seemed to grow even bigger, drawing upon the

power. Sean knew this was happening, even though all he saw with his physical eyes was how the professor began waving his hands. Josef looked like a demented conductor, steering the energy into a whirlwind. Sean watched as the drifting mist and the snow and the cold began sucking in, growing into this massive ball that expanded until it was broader than his platform. A circular tornado with Josef at its center, weaving his arms, building, building . . .

Sean had something to focus on now. The dizzy feeling was replaced by genuine fear. The guy was going to shoot that mass at them.

Dillon laughed out loud. "Frosty!"

Sean had never actually hated his brother until that very moment.

"Remember!" Dillon shouted. "Feed me the force!"

Sean decided there was no point in telling Dillon where he'd really like to insert the force. He just squatted down. Clenched the stone base with the hand not holding Dillon's. Almost able to carve his fingernails into solid rock.

Then the force struck. A blast of ice and snow and power, a tumult that Sean actually *heard*. Like they had stepped inside the heart of a frozen waterfall. The roar was flecked with the sounds of stones and ice striking the shield, a tight drumbeat, fast as machine-gun fire.

Dillon shot Sean a thought bullet. *Feed me. Feed me.*

All Sean could think about was where they were and what would hammer him if his shield didn't hold. Even so, he managed to flick a tiny fragment of his attention out to the shield, catch hold of a stream of the torrential energy, and draw it in. It felt like a toffee pull, except made of ice and rock and energy, but still. Even with his fear and his shaken state, Sean was actually able to follow what the first time had been a gut-level act. The toffee line coursed down his arm and through his grip and into Dillon.

Sean formed the thought bubble and sent back, *Go.*

Dillon probably didn't mean to roar like he did. But the force of his rebel yell was enough to shrink Sean down further to the floor.

His brother was actually having a good time.

The onslaught lasted another few seconds. Or hours. Depending on who was asked. Then the assault ended, and the world went quiet.

Josef transited back into view. He was chuckling. "Well, well."

"Man, did you see that? I was *killing* it!" Dillon moon-walked around the platform, punctuated by the giant's bass laughter. He started cocking an imaginary shotgun, swinging the weapon in circles, banging away at moving targets. "Dudes think they're bad news, man, do I have a little surprise in my pocket."

Josef looked down to where Sean was gradually uncoiling from his crouch. "I take it you are ready to transit back to home base."

"You got that right."

Dillon deflated. "Aw, man. Can't we do it one more time?"

Sean rose to as close to full height as he could manage. "Absolutely not." He decided he wasn't even waiting for them. "I am out of here." And he left. Bang and gone.

His brother arrived back an hour or so later, thrilled over what he had accomplished. He woke Sean, who was dozing on the balcony, and announced that Josef wanted to send Dillon up for advanced battle training. As in, ship him off to the Praetorian Academy. The place where every other recruit from the Examiner's school had washed out. Josef was as excited as Dillon, finally having a student who might, just might, make it through.

Sean listened to his brother describe what was in store. Dillon danced through the process of showering and dressing, never stopping his constant chatter, not for an instant. And Sean grew increasingly certain that behind his brother's adrenaline high lurked the same three questions that burrowed deep within him.

What about Carey?

What about their hunt for who was behind the attacks?

What about them?

The third question sat like a lead weight attached to his abdomen. Because one thing Sean knew for certain. Even if the powers that be asked, even if they *begged*, there was no way Sean would ever be going to battle school.

Dillon sang his way down the stairs and whistled across the lawn. Carey answered the door, and his brother said something that made her laugh. The sound was there long after the door shut. Sean sat and watched the dusk gather and knew he had no interest in another night sitting on the balcony. Alone.

He transited back to the school. It was odd, because for the first time ever he actually liked arriving in that featureless grey room. He didn't change into sweats because he wasn't staying. He slipped down the hall and passed through the portal that before had always been locked, and took the stairs up to the glass-walled mega-room.

There were several dozen other people scattered around the vast hall, some stretched out on cushions, others in portable chairs, one group dining at a candlelit table. He walked over to an empty space along the wall that faced the suns and stood there. Unhappy and content at the same time.

"I thought this was where I'd find you."

Sean wheeled about and watched Elenya walk toward him. She wore her own version of at-home casual, or so Sean assumed. A shoulder emerged from a top that was pink and not exactly translucent, but certainly a far cry from the school's staid sweats. She wore shorts or a short dress, accent on the word *short*. He had never seen her legs before, and they were really nice. Her sandals had velvety ribbons that laced up almost to her knees. A matching band held her hair back. She was, in a word, beautiful.

Sean had always assumed the true beauties were out of

his league. And all the responses he had seen from them confirmed this. As Carey grew closer to his brother, Sean had the lurking suspicion there was something about his personality or some hidden trait the beauties could smell or sense, something that just plain turned them off.

So here he was, thirty thousand light-years or so from his home turf, dealing with the mystery of a truly awesome lady who clearly was interested in him.

There was no reason why Elenya's sudden appearance should add to his sense of uneasiness and disquiet. But it did. And he hated it.

Sean asked, "How did you know I was here?"

"You can establish a link, Sean. It sends you an alert whenever the other arrives at the school."

"I didn't know that."

"You miss a few things, climbing through nine years of schooling in a month." She held out her hand. "Shall I teach you what you don't know, Sean?"

The invitation was delivered so calmly, so matter-of-factly, that he had taken hold of her hand and turned back to the frozen double sunset when it hit him. What she said. What she *meant*. Maybe.

He was still trying to work through how to answer when she asked, "How do you see your shield?"

"I don't."

"Of course. I mean . . ."

"What I visualize when I'm making it." He felt slightly embarrassed. "Like a big golden egg."

She nodded slowly. "And your brother?"

"I have no idea. It's never come up."

"You men. You are ashamed of this, perhaps?"

"It just seems kind of personal."

"I will stop." But her voice was even more musical than usual with hidden laughter. "Men are astonishing."

He could not stop the words any more than he could extinguish the flames. "I don't want to be *men*, Elenya. I don't want to be *grouped*."

She sobered. "I have upset you."

"What is it with you?" He could see faces turning his way. There was probably some Lothian protocol about arguing in public. He hated being the center of such unwanted attention. But he could not stop. "How can you be so . . . in total control over everything?"

Her laughter was gone now, her eyes very grave. "What you mean is, how can I be in such control when we are together, yes?"

He gripped the railing with both hands, squeezing the words from his confusion. "We've only just met and you treat me like . . ."

"Like I've known you for years. That is it, yes?"

He bowed over until his head was down below his shoulders, his entire body tense. He was going to blow this. He just knew it.

She touched his shoulder with a pair of fingertips. "I have known about you and watched you since the first day you came to the school. Since the first hour."

Sean remained where he was, bowed over, staring at his feet. But listening.

"I have no interest in most men, Sean. You need to believe me."

He said to the floor, "I believe everything you tell me."

Her grip on his shoulder grew firmer. "I want to become a Counselor. I want a partner who will be with me in this. Most of these students, they are so . . . *limited*."

"You don't know anything about me."

"I know you come from an outpost world. I know you and your twin were discovered by accident. I know most of the older students resent you and fear you. Why? Because you know no limits. None."

Slowly he straightened. But he couldn't bring himself to look at her. The suns hung within their rose-tinted ring of fire, one degree above the horizon, turning the distant mountain range of ice and rock into gemstones and lava. "My brother showed me one of my own limits today."

But she was not done. "My mother has always resented my father's gift. She loves him and he loves her. But this has always stood between them, how he can transit from world to world, and she can only travel when he takes her. It is his power. And she . . ."

Sean spoke to the glass. "She wants what he has."

"I do not know *men*, Sean. It was wrong of me to say what I did. It was an expression I have heard my older sisters use. I only know two lessons about love. One from my mother, who is a biochemist. She uses what is known as a planetary metabolic index in studying the subtle diversities between humans of different planets. Some traits she has found do not change, regardless of how distinct are their mutations.

One such trait is, the female gender matures faster than the male."

He could see her reflection painted upon the dual suns, the beauty and the zeal. One word clung to the glass like it had been etched into the surface. *Love.* Along with the intensity carried by everything she said.

"The other lesson came when I was nine, the same year I entered this school. My oldest sister had joined with a mate, supposedly for life, and less than a year later she was back home again. Crushed and brokenhearted and groping for answers. The same thing happened to my middle sister just a few months ago. The family is still reeling from this, how two beautiful and intelligent young women could both have their lives wrecked by love with the wrong man. My father told them both something that stays with me. He said, 'Love is a ruthless game unless you play it right. And then it is not a game at all.'"

He turned toward her then. And repeated, "You don't know me."

"Nor you me," she agreed. "But do you think perhaps we should seek to gain this knowledge?"

He could not meet her gaze. It was like she could strip him bare, not of clothes but of his flesh and bones, leaving his very soul exposed. He turned back to the window, as conflicted as he had ever been in his entire life. And more scared than he had been on the pillar.

And yet despite how he felt, Sean found himself describing for her what had happened that day. The cavern and the cold and the pillars and his fear. Dillon's excitement. His own terror, gripping the stone, wanting nothing more than for it to be over. Dillon's return and the electric thrill he carried of being invited to battle school. Then Sean tried to describe what it meant to hear his brother so enthusiastic about a step that meant them being separated, probably for good. And his concern over how Dillon might lose the finest love he had ever known. Using that word for the first time ever to describe Dillon and Carey. For Elenya to understand what it meant—Dillon's love and their own relationship—he had to unravel at least a bit of the tangle about their parents.

He started crying.

He had never, not once in his entire life, wept in public. But this was as much beyond his control as everything else about that day. He tried to make it sound like a series of coughs, like he was choking. So ashamed he could have dissolved into the floor.

Elenya maneuvered him by will and motion, drawing him around, not allowing him to hide his face. She held him not just tightly but from sandals to hairline, melted in so close she could almost breathe with him, weep with him. Which was the only thing that allowed him to regain control. He took a pair of shuddering breaths and tried to release himself so he could dry his eyes, but Elenya wasn't having any of that. She pulled his arm back around her, then lifted her free hand and wiped his face herself.

And then she kissed him. Long enough for his heart to stop and then restart.

Sean tasted tears, but he could not tell whether they were his own or hers.

If somebody had asked Sean how he'd feel about meeting a beautiful girl who would see it as her job to chase and land him, Sean would probably have replied that he'd be high as a skyrocket with his tail on fire. That is, if he didn't laugh the questioner into next week. But when Sean returned to the loft that evening, what he felt most of all was confused. Okay, yeah, he could still feel her lips on his, and that was beyond great. But it didn't make all the other stuff just turn to smoke and fade away. Nor did it fill the empty void at the dinner table, where he ate alone. Or how he turned in on his own, then lay there waiting until Dillon showed up sometime after midnight.

Sean slept badly and woke cranky. Dillon didn't look like he had slept at all. They managed the entire morning routine without a word spoken. It was their day off, and Sean wished he had school to fill the empty space. Another first. He shifted to the balcony so he didn't have to sit there pretending to ignore Dillon staring down at his empty cereal bowl, his hair falling to veil his face. If he was waiting for Sean to make things better, he had a long day ahead of him.

Sean had time for a couple of breaths of the good pine-scented air when the loft behind him was rocked by a massive, resonating *bong*.

That was how it seemed. He had no other way to describe the sensation. There was an insistent force to the sound, like the air had been compressed and then sent out in all directions. Not just a sound but a vibratory power intended to cause alarm.

Sean reentered the kitchen and almost timed his words to Dillon's. "What was *that*?"

Then it happened again. Not really a chime, not really a bell, not electronic. But something that carried a sense of all three. Deep and resonating. *Bong.*

Sean was paying careful attention when the *bong* happened the third time. He felt the pressure on his face and hands, saw it ruffle his T-shirt. Like he had been pressed by a sudden breeze.

Then a stranger transited into their loft. He wore the Messenger uniform, fresh and crisp and proud. He was young enough to be one of their classmates, but Sean did not recognize him. The Assembly pin gleamed from his collar. He addressed them in Serenese. "Greetings, citizens. Professor Josef sends his respects. You are summoned."

There was a formality to his tone and manner that left Dillon mute. So Sean asked, "When?"

"Now."

"We're on our way."

The Messenger cast a long glance around him, like he was memorizing this glimpse of an outpost world. Then he was gone.

Sean turned to his brother. "I guess we better—"

"Hang on a sec." Dillon had not moved from his position at the kitchen table. "It's coming to the point when I need to tell Carey about . . . everything."

Until that point, Sean would have said there was nothing that could have slowed their departure. "That's right. You do."

"It's time."

"Right again. Beyond time."

Dillon lowered his face to the table, showing Sean the scared little kid. "I'm afraid I'll blow it."

Sean didn't reply.

"I don't want to go on without Carey. I can't . . ."

"I'll do it."

The silence held. Like Dillon could scarcely bring himself to accept the offer. Even though Sean knew this was why they were talking at all.

Then his brother surprised him. "She's a lot like you. She hears and sees things I don't. I need to ask her advice. I need her to tell me what . . . how . . ."

"You ever thought maybe she already knows?"

Dillon nodded to the tabletop. "She suspects. She's asked some questions I've danced around. Badly."

"We need to tell her father too."

Dillon looked up at that.

"Carey is everything to him. He deserves to know."

"What will Josef and Carver and the Counselor say?"

"This isn't about them," Sean replied. "This is about doing right by two really good people."

Dillon's gaze opened. It was remarkable how he could do that. The warrior-in-training showing genuine fear. "What if she says no? Her father . . . Man, I don't know."

"She loves you. She needs to hear this and make up her mind. Her father is part of this. I don't know how I'm so sure, but I am."

Dillon nodded slowly. "No, no, you're right."

"We're having dinner with them tonight. We'll just lay it all out—" Sean slapped his forehead. "Oh, man."

"What is it?"

"I promised Elenya we'd get together."

Dillon shocked him then. Way beyond surprise. Out there in the realm of blowing Sean into the middle of September. "So invite her."

"You serious?"

"How are we going to make this real, go do our jig through walls? Let them meet someone from out there. It could help."

Sean shrugged. "I'll ask her." Which meant asking Josef how to get word to her. Which meant admitting to their professor what was happening. He added, "If I can."

Dillon rose slowly from the table. "I guess we better go find out what's waiting on the other side of the wall."

•••

They transited and changed and walked to Josef's office. But the door was locked, so they stood cooling their heels in the hall. Which was where Elenya found them. She wore another outfit of pink translucence, same sandals, same hair band, same beauty. She did not quite dance down the hall. But close. Her smile was brilliant, like a jewel that didn't see the light of day very often. She nodded a hello to Dillon, then took Sean's hand and swung it. "I was hoping I wouldn't need to wait until tonight."

She said it in *English*.

Dillon was pushed from his funk enough to say, "Major wow."

"I've only had three night lessons. Am I speaking correctly?" Her accent was musical, like she had been taught how to sing in English, not speak.

Sean said, "This is absolutely amazing."

"You like?"

He told her the truth. "English has never, ever sounded this good."

Her reward was a quick kiss, which brought a flame to both their faces. But it was worth it, because Dillon smiled. Like all the worry and the unknown were just lifted away. "So go ahead, dude. Ask the lady."

Elenya asked, "What is this 'dude'?"

"It is slang for 'friend.'" He watched her taste the word. "We have a problem. Sort of. Dillon needs to tell his girlfriend about what's happening."

She looked from one twin to the other. "She is from your home world?"

"Yes."

Elenya turned to Dillon. "She is the one, this lady?"

Dillon swallowed, then answered with a certainty that touched Sean more deeply than anything that crazy morning. "Yes. She is. If she'll have me."

"Telling her can be difficult."

"We need to tell her father also. Carey lost her mother about two years ago."

Elenya nodded slowly. "Father and daughter have bonded at a special level."

"They are good people and better friends," Sean said.

She looked at him with those amazing eyes. "You want me to be there?"

"If you think—"

"No, this is a good idea. I can represent what from you will be just words. When do we do this?"

"Tonight, our time. We're having dinner at their home."

"I will make a special request . . ." Elenya stopped as the professor's door opened. But it was not Josef who appeared. Rather, Carver stood in the doorway. A different Carver. One dressed in formal military attire. With an expression to match.

Carver's fathomless gaze flickered over the way they still held hands. Sean tried to draw away, but Elenya gripped him tighter still. She lifted her gaze a fraction. The quarter-inch shift was enough to transform her from student to the daughter of a planetary Ambassador.

Sean could not have been prouder if she had grown wings.

Carver showed his laser-fast dimples and said, "It is customary to introduce your friend."

"Elenya, this is Colonel Carver." Then the grey-haired

lady appeared in the doorway behind Carver. "And this is Counselor Tatyana."

"Colonel. Counselor."

Tatyana said, "I know your father. A very fine gentleman."

"Indeed." Elenya turned to Sean. "When should I meet you?"

"In . . . I left my watch in the locker room."

"Six hours by Lothian time," Dillon said. "Less."

"I will be in the transit room in five." She nodded a farewell to the officials and departed. Regal as a queen.

Carver watched her depart, showed another flicker of that almost-humor, then said, "Inside, the both of you."

"We have located Examiner Tirian," Tatyana announced. "He has been arrested."

They were seated in a wide circle with Josef's desk at the center. The professor's features were creased with pain, his gaze shattered. One look in Josef's direction was enough for Sean to forget Dillon's issue, forget his own unease, and just plain burn.

Dillon said, "You've gone after the wrong guy."

"Nothing's changed," Sean agreed. "You're still looking in the wrong direction."

Tatyana studied them both. Back and forth. "I would say," she replied, "that a great deal indeed has changed."

Carver asked, "What is your impression of this school?"

"It all comes down to Josef," Sean replied.

"He's the best," Dillon added.

"Everything about the Examiner and his work is under

official review," Tatyana said. "We have been asked to deliver a verdict on whether the school should be shut down."

"Different question, same answer," Sean replied. "Wrong direction."

"Right," Dillon said. "The school is not the issue."

"Tell us why," Carver said.

"He *listens.*" Sean glared at the Counselor. "Unlike some people."

Dillon said, "He didn't believe the mind-speech thing was possible. But he gave us a chance."

"I invited you to repeat the experience," Tatyana protested.

"So you could dismiss us," Sean shot back. "Tell me I'm wrong."

Tatyana frowned but did not respond. Which was a very telling reply as far as Sean was concerned.

"The mind connection was real," Dillon said. "What if the other stuff is real too?"

"We don't like Tirian any more now than we did before," Sean said. "But the guy is innocent."

Tatyana said, "Because your brother claims he saw what escaped a trained Watcher."

"Tell you what," Sean snapped. "Why don't you drop the *claim* business for a while. See how that fits."

Josef spoke for the first time since they'd entered. "Your tone is not proper for addressing a Counselor."

Sean just sat and fumed.

Dillon asked, "What do you figure was the Examiner's motive for going after us?"

"Fury over being proved wrong," Tatyana replied. "Your

abilities challenge every assumption he made in founding this very school."

"You'd be nuts to shut this place down," Dillon said. "Josef and his team do a great job here."

Carver protested, "You heard what I told the Counselor. Not a single student has ever passed through the Academy."

"Then don't let any more apply," Sean replied. "Make them Messengers. Or bureaucrats. Whatever. Tirian's concept isn't bad. He brings them in young, he trains them, he *protects* them. They're fine for whatever."

Tatyana demanded, "What about their loyalty?"

Because it was the Counselor who asked, Sean wanted to dismiss that as well. But he had to admit, "We haven't been here long enough to know for certain."

"We're the new kids on the block," Dillon agreed. "We're shut out of a lot."

"Ask Elenya about the loyalty issue," Sean said. "She's been here for years."

"Excellent point," Tatyana said. "I will do just that."

"What about the first attack? You're pinning that on the Examiner as well?"

It was Tatyana's turn to hesitate. "If we accept that there was indeed an initial attack—"

"There was," Sean insisted. "It happened."

"We have theories, but no explanation that satisfies. Tirian is being questioned over his role as well." The Counselor rose to her feet. At a motion from Carver, Sean and Dillon followed suit. Tatyana stood there, ignoring the four men, frowning at the side wall. Finally she declared, "I accept the twins' observation, Professor. Your school has a temporary stay."

The giant released a long breath. "Thank you, Counselor."

"New Examiners will be assigned to undertake a full assessment of all students. This is necessary."

"I understand."

She glanced at the twins. "I was wrong to dismiss your claims. I apologize."

Sean wasn't ready to play nice just yet. "You're wrong about Tirian as well."

"Perhaps." Though she clearly did not believe them, at least the dismissal was no longer her standard response. "But the judicial process has now been set in motion. The Judge assigned this case feels Tirian pronounced himself guilty by fleeing."

"What if he was taken?" Sean looked from one adult to the next. "And what if he's been released because you're ready to hang him?"

"We don't hang anyone. What a barbaric thought."

Carver halted Sean's retort with a cautionary squint and said, "The Examiner claims this was precisely what happened. That he was kidnapped."

Sean asked, "Where does he say he was held?"

"He claims to know nothing. He was found wandering about the Serenese capital city in a confused daze."

But the Counselor was back to frowning at the wall. Then, "You proved your abilities to Josef. Do the same regarding your means of identifying who was actually behind the attack."

Sean decided that was as far as Tatyana was going to bend, so all he said was, "Right. Good. Okay."

"Professor, you have my permission to share with them whatever you deem to be in the best interests of truth. Only take care. If the Examiner is indeed innocent, we do not know who was behind the attack. Or whether they might try again."

"Very good, Counselor."

She turned back to the twins, her gaze once again carrying the quality of an executioner's blade. "I suggest the two of you get to work. Tirian's trial starts in four days."

34

After the Counselor and Carver departed, Josef remained seated behind his desk, frowning at the wall. Finally he turned back to them, his gaze shifting back and forth between the twins, as though he had never seen them before. Or was seeing them differently, a change that was not particularly welcome, but one over which he had no control. Finally he rose to his feet, moving with slow, awkward movements, and held out his hands. "There is something you must see."

Sean took hold of one massive hand, as much as he could grasp, and Dillon took the other. They transited. And the vista squeezed a gasp from them both.

"Behold the Academy of the Praetorian Guard," Josef said. He released their hands and took a step back.

They stood upon a broad platform carved from the solid rock of a lone mountain peak. The surface was black and cold and lifeless. Behind them rose a curved arena that could have held several thousand on benches of ancient lava. The speakers' platform where they stood was massive, larger than a tennis court. An empty dais rose like a black thumb at the center.

Beyond the arena stretched a vista of devastation and ruin.

The Academy itself was impressive enough, a silent fortress shaped from the same black lava. The buildings rose like spears behind a tall, dark wall. It shone in grim repose beneath a sky of slate-grey cloud.

Spreading out in every direction was a realm of ancient doom.

Josef said, "This is Hegemony, Tirian's and my home world. And this before you is what we must never be allowed to forget. The war that led up to Hegemony entering the galactic empire almost destroyed our planet."

From their vantage point, Sean could see the ruins of five different cities. They were connected by raised road systems whose remnants clung to the earth in a script of desolation and woe. The cities were crumbling tombstones to a time that was no more.

"There was no shortcut through the horror of war for my planet," Josef said. "No comfort in the time of mayhem. Our world was divided between those who wished to join the Assembly and those who saw it as a threat to their cherished cultures and an end to their grip on power. The war lasted nineteen years. It ended three hundred and seventeen years ago, the last great war our planetary system has experienced. May it be the last we ever know."

A breath of acrid wind flicked dust into Sean's eyes. He wiped his eyes, determined to see everything.

"My world was forced to witness what no civilization should ever glimpse, not even for an instant. We endured the descent into the horror and depravity of the worst that man can do to his own kind. We saw the shadow of our own making. And in the end, we turned away.

"The aftermath was worse than the war in some respects. Generations of broken and bitter folk had no one to blame but themselves. Hatred was the watchword. Life was sold for a penny. For a song." Josef walked forward so he stood within their field of vision. "I am the result of genetic manipulation, when feuding nations sought to build a better warrior. After the war, my kind was hunted and killed like animals. We reminded the survivors of the horrors they had inflicted upon themselves. We represented powers they could never afford to release again. The only reason a remnant survived was because Hegemony voted to join the Assembly of worlds, and the first Counselor and Ambassador ordered that the purge be halted."

Josef turned and pointed over at the Academy. "All incoming and graduating classes are gathered here. The opening ceremonies of each new year are held here. As is the anniversary of my world's granting the Academy this entire province for its training. All take place here. So that we will remember. So that the bitter lessons of Hegemony's tragic past are kept alive for all time."

Josef leaned forward to bring his face within breathing distance of their own. Close enough they could see the tension and the fury and the fear. "I need only stand here to know that Examiner Tirian would never, *never* release the fires of battle on two young men. No matter how much he might despise what you and your outpost world represent—another raw planet full of egotistical leaders who shout of battles yet to be fought, who permit children to suffer and die unnoticed. Tirian would *never* be one to release what has wreaked such havoc upon his home world. The lessons are too great, the wounds still unhealed. Tirian is many things, and his character is one that invites friction. That too is the legacy of my culture. But he would not do this."

Dillon's voice sounded as broken as Sean felt. "It wasn't Tirian who attacked us."

"I know this to be true. I have known this before the Counselor brought you to my school. And for this above all else, I count you as my allies." He held out his hands. "Come."

When they returned to the office, Sean saw the school through different eyes. The absence of windows, the locked portals, the identical uniforms, the rigidity of their training, the absence of any chance to explore the boundaries of what their talent might do. He did not agree with it. He most certainly did not like it. But for the first time ever, it all made sense.

Sean asked, "What do we do now?"

Josef slipped behind his desk. "To try to save Tirian is the basis for your current tutorial. I am expressly ordered not to participate beyond my role as instructor. I have a school to run, and new Examiners arriving who will seek a reason, *any* reason, to shut us down. You understand what I am saying?"

"We are on our own."

"No, no, I am here to give you what I can. But you must see this as an opportunity to explore, to reach, and to grow." He gave that a beat, then added softly, "Go and save my friend. Please. If you possibly can."

When it came time to go meet Elenya, they were no closer to identifying what their next step might possibly be. Dillon's interest gradually waned in the whole process. Sean resisted the urge to snap at his brother, tell him to stop checking his watch and glancing out the open balcony doors, remind him they faced a different ticking clock. Nothing would come from it.

Finally Sean gave up and headed for the shower. When he emerged ten minutes later, Dillon was gone. Sean dressed and tried to pretend that he wasn't nearly as excited as he felt, that his own focus remained at least partly held by the innocent Examiner. But just then, as he prepared to transit back to school, it was hard to think of anything more than seeing Elenya again.

But when he arrived in the school's transit room and saw Elenya seated on the little grey bench, he could not help but blanch.

She rose to her feet in a nervous jerk. "What's the matter?"

"No, it's nothing." He did his best to smile. "Ready to go?"

"No, Sean. Tell me. Is it my clothes?"

Elenya wore an elegant version of what Sean had come to think of as Tatyana's uniform—a high-collared shirt dress with slit sides and matching trousers. Both in a silky material that shimmered like liquid with her every movement. Their pearl-like color formed an elegant backdrop for the matching bracelet and necklace of woven gold with jewel pendants.

Sean replied, "You look nice. Really."

"But it is not suitable."

"These people we're meeting, they're . . ."

"Rustic."

"Don't let Dillon hear you say that, okay? You're right. They are rustic in a way. But coming from you, especially how you're dressed, what he'd probably hear is 'primitive.' And they're not that. At all."

"I did not mean—"

"No, no. I know that." He reached for her hand. "Maybe we should just . . ."

But she was not ready to go anywhere. "What should I be wearing?"

"Exactly what you had on when you met me upstairs."

Elenya blushed a flaming scarlet. "My mother would never permit such a thing. When she saw me return, she was so upset."

Sean smiled. It was not often he saw this lady lose her composure. "I thought you looked great."

"Then I am glad I wore it. Do you know of a place where I might buy suitable clothes?"

"There's a shopping center three blocks from our home. But it's not necessary—"

"Please, Sean. I want to do this. But when dinner is over, can I leave the clothes with you?" Sean's surprise must have shown on his face, because she added, "Have I said something wrong?"

"No, no, it's just, leaving clothes at a guy's place means something in my world."

"Correct. It means I don't need to argue with my mother."

"I've never done this before. Led somebody else through a transit. Well, I did once. But I had no idea what I was doing."

"It is simple. You extend your shield around us both. Then you step, and I step with you." She held out her hand. "Perhaps we should hurry."

...

Elenya marveled at everything. Their loft, cars, trees, sunlight, more cars, stoplights, birds, clouds, pedestrian crosswalks, the people. Sean watched her more than anything else, delighting in her delight. The regal young woman seeing his staid outpost world for the very first time, and just loving it.

He took her to the mall, where the salesgirl was taken with Elenya from first glance. "I love your clothes. Are they Armani?"

"Please?"

Sean broke in. "My friend is foreign. She needs something for a backyard meal."

"Casual chic," the salesgirl offered. "Our specialty."

"Right. And we need her ready in . . ." Sean checked his watch. "Twelve minutes?"

"No problem. Parents involved, right?"

"Sort of. My brother's new girlfriend."

"And her father," Elenya added. "It could be tense."

"We can't be late," Sean said.

"Okay, we're on it." The salesgirl pointed Sean into a chair. "Why don't you sit there and play happy." She led Elenya away. "Who does your hair?"

"My mother."

"No kidding. What is she, like, a major stylist?"

"A molecular biochemist."

"I guess that works. Your accent is wild. Where are you from?"

"Serena. I am Serenese."

"That's like, where, Europe?"

Elenya smiled, clearly having a wonderful time. "Further."

"Cool. What are you, like, a six?"

Precisely eleven minutes later, Elenya reappeared wearing patterned tights and an off-the-shoulder top with a tank top beneath. Everything was a pastel mix of off-white and several shades of pale pink. She was, in a word, stunning.

Sean said, "Wow."

"That's what I like to hear from my guys, you know?" The salesgirl was already ringing them up. "Nothing beats the wow factor in my book."

Sean watched the salesgirl bag four more tops, another pair of leggings, two trousers, a jacket, and two pairs of shoes besides the pink sandals Elenya now wore. "You just set a land-speed record for shopping."

"Your girlfriend is, like, the easiest person to fit I've ever seen." The salesgirl lifted the bag holding Elenya's original outfit. "You want to wear your jewelry?"

"Leave it in there, please."

"You got it." She checked the total and announced, "That comes to eleven hundred and thirty-eight dollars."

Sean tried hard to stifle his wince, but Elenya noticed. As they walked back, she offered, "I can pay for all this."

"No, it's okay." He just needed to alert Dillon so his brother didn't have heart failure when he checked their account.

But his worry must have shown, because when they crossed the main road and entered the residential section, she asked, "You and your brother are of course aware that you receive a salary?"

That definitely rocked him. "What?"

"Ah." She nodded. "As I said, Sean, there are some things you miss in jumping over all those school years. Yes. Speak with Josef. You are paid every ten days."

"How much?"

"By my planet's standards, rather a lot."

"Even as recruits?"

"You are intended to be in a financial position where you are never open to bribery. Why do you smile?"

"I've never had any money."

"Well, Sean, you do now."

He shifted her bags to his other hand, took hold of hers, and said what he'd often thought since that very first day. "I love the way you say my name."

36

When they climbed the stairs and entered the loft, they found Dillon standing in the living area. Sean suspected his brother had been caught in mid-pace. "Ready to go?"

"I guess . . . Maybe we should wait."

"It's time," Sean said gently. "And you know it."

"But you'll tell them?"

"I said I would."

Dillon did not appear the least bit reassured. Then he noticed Elenya. "You look great."

"Thank you, Dillon."

"I can't get over you speaking English."

"Badly," she added. "Speaking English badly."

"Your English isn't the problem tonight. What are all those packages?"

"Later," Sean said. He stowed everything under the bed except for the bag holding Elenya's original gear, which he put on his dressing table. "Let's go."

As they walked the path to the house, Elenya asked, "How should I address them?"

"Professor Havilland and Carey. He'll probably tell you to call him John."

"If he doesn't kick us out," Dillon muttered. "Shout and shove and done."

Elenya said, "I asked my father how he would handle this."

"Her father's the Assembly Ambassador to Lothia," Sean told Dillon.

"He was," she corrected. "Now he is training to become an Assembly Justice."

Dillon stopped beside one of the mock Japanese lanterns. "So what did he tell you?"

"That we should treat this as already accepted," she replied. "This is his favorite tactic when dealing with difficult negotiations." She stumbled over that last word.

"That makes a lot of sense," Sean said slowly.

"I never knew this until today. I was glad to have a reason to ask him. He said be clear on what you want. Begin from the position that they have already agreed to everything. And that your path is already harmonious with theirs. Then you simply help them arrive where they already are at some unseen level." She shook her head. "My father is the smartest man I have ever met, and I was ashamed I needed my first meal on your outpost world to make me understand this about him."

They started on down the path. The dusk was blanketed by heavy clouds. The still summer air was laden with the musk of pine sap and magnolia blossom.

Elenya's eyes shone in the half light, as though illuminated from within. "Your world is very beautiful, Sean."

"Parts of it are."

"Do you have moons?"

"One. We call it Luna."

From ahead of them, Dillon muttered, "Do we have moons. Oh man."

"Lighten up there, bro."

"How about you hold off on those questions tonight, okay?"

"Dillon."

"I'm just saying."

Sean pulled on Elenya's hand, drawing her to a halt. "You go on. We'll catch up."

Carey chose that moment to open the door and call out, "Dillon? Is everything okay?"

Dillon glared at them and replied, "Dandy."

Carey waited until he was climbing the front steps to say, "We're thinking about eating on the front patio, but it'll mean dashing inside if it rains. Is that okay?"

When Dillon slipped past her and entered the house, Elenya asked, "Did I say something wrong?"

"No. Dillon's scared. He's always responded to fear by fighting. Ever since he was a kid."

"I'll be careful, Sean."

"Elenya . . ."

"What is it?"

He was still uncertain about it all, the tumult and the emotions and everything. But just then he was pretty certain that the right thing to do was to kiss her. Which he did.

The patio door slid open and Carey said, "How nice. Come on up when you're done. Dinner is ready."

...

Both John Havilland and his daughter knew something was up. Maybe it was the way Dillon kept shooting tight glances Carey's way. Or how Elenya insisted on looking to Sean for guidance before answering the simplest question. Or how Sean had to offer Elenya a slow-motion guide to knife and fork. Yeah, that one definitely raised the professor's eyebrows a notch.

Midway through the meal, Dillon announced, "I went to see Mom and Dad today."

Sean was surprised on a multitude of levels. First, that his brother had done it on his own. Second, that he'd be so easy talking about it in front of Carey and her father. Third, that Dillon felt now was the time to discuss it. But all he said was, "You did?"

"You're handling so much, I just thought . . ." Dillon shrugged.

"No, no, it's great. I'm glad. How are they?"

"Okay. Well, not okay. But coping. Trying to work things out." Dillon watched as Elenya reached over and took Sean's hand. "She knows?"

"I know a little," Elenya replied. "I am sorry you face this now. With everything else."

John must have taken that as the signal he had been waiting for. "Speaking of which. Will you tell us what is going on?"

"Yes." Sean used his free hand to push his half-finished plate to one side. "I will."

"Does this have anything to do with our discussion the other night?"

"Actually, sir, it does. A lot."

"Are you and Dillon in trouble with the authorities?"

"Absolutely not."

John seemed to take comfort from the solid response. "Will you tell me where your young lady is from?"

Leave it to the professor to get right to the heart of the matter. "That is part of what we need to tell you. Actually, it'll be easier if we just show you." Sean rose to his feet. "Will you come with us to the loft?"

Dillon got that deer-in-the-headlights look again. "Are you sure about this?"

"I think so."

"And I agree with him," Elenya said. "They will need to see this sooner or later. And showing them in the beginning will make everything else move more swiftly."

Father and daughter watched the exchange in silence.

Dillon reached for Carey's hand and said, "I am so in love with you."

"And you are making me so scared."

"I know." He looked at Sean. "Okay. Let's do this."

37

The loft felt crowded with them all standing around. But Sean didn't ask anyone to sit down. John and his daughter looked truly spooked. Which was only going to get worse. Sean had intended to ask Dillon for the first demonstration, but his brother looked so scared he decided to ask Elenya instead. "Will you show them?"

Carey demanded, "Show us what?"

Elenya held to her poise, which was amazing. And despite all the fear in the room, and all the eyes on them both, she lifted up on tiptoes and kissed him.

Then she vanished.

Carey did not squeal and she did not cry out and she did not gasp. She did all three. John made no sound at all.

Elenya returned. Took hold of Sean's hand. And waited as Sean said to Dillon, "Now you."

"Sean . . ."

"Go."

Dillon sighed and went. And returned.

Sean then explained from the beginning. He was terrified of getting it wrong. Not for himself. For Dillon. And at the same time, he held on to Elenya's suggestion like an anchor. Doing so stabilized him against all the unseen turbulence that gripped their loft. Sean did his best to share with people he cared for and who cared for them. People who were ready to understand and accept before he opened his mouth. He hoped. Desperately.

Sean described the childhood design that he and Dillon had made of the train station. The one where people came and went without regard to outside gravity. The crystal tubes and the glass trains. Then Carver's arrival. And the challenge. And the Examiner. And the test. And the argument and the Charger assault and the Counselor and the attack and the school. He talked until his throat went dry, and Elenya poured him a glass of water. He drank that and went on.

Then he reached out his hand for John's. "There's only one way you'll really understand this."

"No," Dillon said. "Wait. You're sure?"

Sean kept his gaze on the professor. "If you want to come and see, I want to take you."

John demanded softly, "You can do this?"

"Yes."

"No, I mean, it's permitted?"

"We asked. They said the rules governing contact with . . ."

"Loved ones and their families," Elenya supplied. "The rules are . . ."

"Vague," Sean said. "Intentionally so."

"But it is vital you understand that you cannot ever speak of this," Elenya added.

"Why is that?"

"Because your Earth is, well . . ."

Dillon said, "An outpost world."

"Our leaders are contacted every decade or so," Sean said. "One of them, at least. And so far they've always said no to joining."

The professor reddened. He wiped his mouth, stifling whatever flamed there in his eyes. Then he turned to his daughter and asked, "Do you want to do this?"

"More than anything."

Dillon made a sound then. It was as close to a sob as he could come without actually breaking down. And it was enough to erase the room's tension. Like it had never actually existed at all.

Carey moved like water, just flowing across the impossible distance and enveloping him in an embrace. "Oh, Dillon."

He spoke to her hair, lost so that his face could not be seen, and the words were so muffled and soft as to be indistinct. But Sean was certain his brother said, "Thank you."

Elenya smiled at them, wiped her eyes, and reached around Sean's waist. Happy and sad at the same time. Just like he felt.

Carey asked, "Does it hurt?"

"Not at all." Sean offered John his hand a second time. "Ready?"

...

As they left the transit station and passed down the long hall, Josef came out of his office and observed them. Carey squeaked at the sight of the grey-blond giant, but that was all. No one else spoke or made any sound. Until they arrived upstairs.

When they emerged in the grand windowed chamber, father and daughter both plopped to the floor. And stayed there for a good half hour. They probably would have remained longer, but Elenya finally announced, "I must go."

"No." John clambered to his feet. "Don't."

"I am already very late. My mother will be upset."

Sean explained, "This was her first time on Earth."

Carey laughed without humor.

John pleaded, "A few questions."

Elenya looked back and forth between them, then said, "One moment."

When she stepped and departed, Dillon asked, "She doesn't need the transit room?"

"Experience, maybe," Sean said. Then to the others, he explained, "She's been doing this all her life."

"Her parents can . . . transit?"

"Her father only. He was the Assembly's Ambassador to this planet."

"Splendid," John replied.

Carey stared at her father. "Did you really just say that?"

"Imagine the discussions!"

Carey sniffed, but her response was cut off by Elenya's return. "I am very sorry, but I must go. My mother . . . I do not want to give her a reason to say I cannot return." She then turned to Sean and continued in Serenese, "My mother is livid."

He slapped his forehead. "Your clothes."

"I forgot as well. She wants to know who this outpost boy is who forces me to dress like a . . ." She stifled the comments. Tried for a smile. "Until very soon, I hope."

"Tell your father thanks."

Dillon added, "From us both. And from the heart."

Elenya kissed Sean and smiled to the others and vanished.

"Astonishing," John murmured.

Carey asked Dillon, "How do you speak her language?"

"It's the language of the Assembly. And the Academy."

"Well, of course it is."

"Carey," her father gently chided.

She colored and eased back. "How did you learn it so fast?"

"They teach us in our sleep."

Josef emerged from the stairway and stared over at where they clustered. His silence was more than enough for Sean to suggest, "Maybe we should continue this discussion back home."

John made a long, slow circle of the room, sighed once, and declared, "A hundred questions. A thousand debates. All answered with one glimpse of our tomorrow."

Sean found himself lingering on the patio that night, and it had nothing to do with Dillon and Carey being in the loft. He could have transited over to the Cameron apartment, new bed, no worries. But John showed no interest in going anywhere. Nor did the professor have any further questions, at least any he was willing to voice. Instead, when the professor finally did speak, it was to ask, "You want to tell me what's on your mind?"

Sean had to laugh. "You mean, other than how Dillon is getting on with Carey?"

"I think they'll work this out just fine."

That startled him. "How can you be so calm?"

"Oh, my world is rocked, all right. But just now all my major worries come down to one thing. Can I trust Dillon to take care of my little girl. And the answer to that seems very clear. Dillon is forthright. It's a word that's gone out of fashion, and more's the pity. But that is the word that describes your brother."

"Yes. It does."

"See?" John spread out his hands. "A simple answer to a complex question. Your brother will do his best to do right by Carey. There will always be transitions. And what I don't want is for my fears, my needs, my loss, to color how they are just now. This is about them, not me."

Sean felt that same burning lump as before. There was no way to completely erase his own yearnings for the chance to rewrite his family history. But what the professor said applied to him as well. Tonight wasn't about him. So he decided to speak about the other thing that weighed heavy on him. "Can I talk with you about another problem?"

"Of course."

He laid it out. The issues they faced and the mystery nobody would talk about with them could not be discussed unless Sean first described how the system worked. He stumbled more over this telling than he had in explaining the new life and worlds they lived in. But it felt good just the same. No clear answers. But here was a mind he could trust.

John heard him out in silence, then went back to studying the night. "So let me get this clear. We have one of those teams—what did you call them?"

"Watchers."

"On duty out there somewhere."

"More than one."

"And we've got a squad of . . ."

"Praetorian Guards."

"On high alert, ready to defend us against an attack."

"Right."

"As of yesterday, your former Examiner is under arrest and facing trial."

"But he's innocent."

"And they won't accept this."

"The physical evidence is all pointed straight at him."

"And because of the strange nature of your and Dillon's new talents, they discount your own findings as unimportant."

"They won't even listen to us."

"But it all comes back to one thing, doesn't it."

Sean nodded, loving this conversation. How they were walking along the same unseen path. Totally in sync. "The attack in the Charger."

"There is something they're not telling you. Why would they prefer to think this was nothing more than your overactive imaginations at work?"

"Either that or blame it on the Examiner."

"Someone in the group must at least be willing to consider that you're giving them a correct account. That you were indeed attacked. In that case, why would this one man put together such an elaborate scheme when he had the power to erase your memories? I don't buy it."

"Tirian called us reckless. He said we were a threat to ourselves and others. They're probably assuming he put this together to show he was right. And keep the blame off himself in the process."

"That makes sense," John murmured. "Perfect, logical, irrefutable sense."

"But there's something else. They won't talk about the *how*. Every time the topic comes up, they shut us down."

"Which leads you to think . . ."

"That it's tied to the *other* thing they won't talk about. The aliens."

Sean expected the professor to come back with some dismissive comment. The sort of thing adults were all too good at doing whenever the conversation strayed into uncomfortable territory. But John studied the cloud-covered sky for a time, then said, "Do you remember what I told you the other night about my field?"

Sean thought hard and replied, "Cultural anthropology is the study of how different civilizations develop distinctive traditions, philosophies, values, and ways of life. And your field has been divided into two groups. I forget what they're called. They look at the same evidence and come up with two different outcomes. And what I need to do is look for a pattern or a motive that might have led to a mistake in judgment."

"Very good. Excellent, in fact. Tonight I give you an A-plus."

"But I've been trying, and I haven't come up with anything that helps."

"*Yet.* You haven't come up with something *yet*. So let's take this one step further." John pushed his chair back from the table and crossed his legs. "To truly understand a culture from within, we must first confront a very basic issue in ourselves. Who are we, this group that *studies* the culture? How do we make sense of something that is totally unfamiliar to us? We run the risk of falling into very real traps. We can rely on our own cultural measuring sticks. We can remain tied at an unconscious level to the bonds of our own upbringing. We can view everything out there through the lens of our own past."

Sean found himself listening on two different levels. He was taking this all in, trying to see how it fit the patterns he had experienced within this mystery of the attacks. But he was also looking at himself. And reflecting on how this was what it was like to be an adult. Sitting together in the night, parsing out the impossibilities they faced, drawing on the wisdom of others, talking as equals. He had once heard that the greatest challenge every teenager faced was realizing they were not actually the center of the universe. Either they grew through this or they failed at life. And tonight, for the first time ever, he felt as though he was given a glimpse of what lay on the other side.

Then something pinged.

It was far below actual thought. More like a new buzzing sensation at some bone-deep level. Sean had no clear idea of what was happening. Only that it was important, and it was tied to what John had just said.

He spoke as much to himself as to the professor. "So Carver and Tatyana could actually be responding to something in their past, and not the attack on us at all."

"Not exactly. Their *analysis* is colored by past experience. You see the difference? They see this event very clearly. But their judgment is tainted by previous incidents that have shaped their vision and their character." John gave him a minute, then went on, "Tell me, what do you think of the atmosphere at your school?"

His response was instantaneous. "Stifling."

"What makes you say that?"

Sean described the windowless transit rooms, the careful discipline of point-to-point transits, the absence of doors to the outside world, the way the school itself did not even have windows overlooking the Lothian caverns.

John did not let him finish. "There may be your answer."

"Sorry, I don't . . ." Again the ping. Again the sensation of something far below conscious thought.

"Let me give you a for instance from my own field. World War I was the most brutal bloodbath mankind had ever inflicted upon itself, at least in this world. Afterward, all the theories governing our study of other cultures were thrown out. It wasn't that new evidence was suddenly discovered. Instead, the *perspective* changed. People of all walks and disciplines were repelled by the error of their ways. Everything that had brought them to this point—culture, civilization, the Western world's air of superiority—all of it was dismissed. Scholars looked at the world through an entirely different lens. One fashioned through the flames of war and brutality and loss."

Suddenly Sean's chair became constrictive. He bounded to his feet and began pacing the patio like it was a wooden cage. Seeking a way out. Hunting. "So you're telling me that some terrible event happened . . ."

"Perhaps, just perhaps, a cataclysmic event has reshaped their perspective. Not just about this attack. On everything you face. The school included."

Sean paced and thought and paced some more. Then he realized the professor had spoken to him awhile back, and he had no idea what the man had said. "Sorry. I missed something."

John actually seemed pleased by being totally ignored. "No, no, it's good to see a mind at work."

"I guess I better get to bed."

"Sean."

"Sir?"

"Thank you. For trusting me as well as Carey. Someday I hope you understand just how much this has meant."

Sean stumbled up the stairs, flung himself onto the bed, and was out. At least, until an idea woke him an hour or so before dawn.

Sean ate breakfast standing at the kitchen counter and left the loft before Dillon was even awake. For once, Sean was actually glad the school was its own enclosed world. He liked being able to transit into a place without doors or windows. It meant a minimum of distractions.

Two hours later, Dillon found him seated on the bench outside Josef's office. "Thanks for the note."

"I didn't . . . Oh. Sorry."

Dillon settled onto the bench next to him. "So what's up?"

"Thinking."

"Don't sprain something. About what?"

But his response was cut off by Josef striding down the hall toward them. The giant moved with remarkable grace for a man his size. "Are you waiting to see me?"

"No, sir. I was just looking for a quiet place."

"Ah." Josef was followed by all the school's instructors. He pointed them into his office, waited until they passed, then asked, "You are working on your latest tutorial assignment?"

"Trying."

"Are you ready to discuss results?"

"They're not results yet."

"I see. Come with me." Josef walked them down the hall away from his office and stopped in front of a portal that Sean had never seen open. Josef set his thumb on the fingerprint reader and the portal slid back. "This is Tirian's office. Some might say it is an appropriate place for you to continue your efforts."

"This is great."

"The new Examiners arrive in an hour. Once that process begins, I am unavailable except in an extreme emergency."

"Understood. And thanks."

"I will inform your instructors that you are working on a special assignment." Josef turned to the door, then offered them a final, "I am counting on you."

When they were alone, Dillon said, "No pressure, right?"

"If you see Elenya, tell her where to find me."

"That sounds to me like a 'get out now.'"

Scan was already moving for the desk. "Shut the door when you leave."

...

Sean regretted Elenya's continued absence. But in a small-hearted way he was also glad. Frustration over his lack of progress grew with each passing hour. He stayed in his isolation chamber all morning. Tirian's office did not give up many clues about the imprisoned Examiner. Even so, Sean was grateful for the chance to share the man's space. It served as a constant reminder to push ahead. The desk, floor, walls, chairs, and shelves were all various shades of bland beige. There were no windows, no plaques, just one wall of photographs of graduating classes. Tirian did not smile in any of the pictures.

When Dillon came to fetch him for lunch, Sean confessed, "I'm seriously worried."

"Outstanding. Long as you're fretting I don't need to." He ducked Sean's slug. "I'm serious. You squeeze and squeeze and then all of a sudden, wham. You come up with the incredible."

"I've wasted an entire morning."

"It's not wasted."

"I've got all these fragments of ideas. But I can't put them together." They entered the lounge used for meals. The tables were silent, the students glum, the instructors not there. "What's going on?"

"The Examiners are going through the records of each student. From day one to now. As in, maybe they don't get to stay, maybe they don't pass, maybe they bring back the mind-wipe. Or so the rumors go."

But Sean was mostly looking for a face that wasn't there. "Have you seen Elenya?"

"She hasn't shown up today. I asked."

Sean got in line for a meal he didn't feel like eating. "Her mom was so mad."

"I can't believe the lady got so bent out of shape over some new clothes."

244

"Oh, really." Sean filled his tray and followed Dillon to an empty table. "You have to admit this doesn't look all that great to Elenya's mom. Her daughter pops out to dinner with a guy she doesn't know. This guy has only been a recruit for, like, a month and a half. And oh, by the way, he's from some outpost free-fire zone nobody's ever heard of. And what happens, this beautiful daughter shows up long after curfew. And hey, look at this, she's wearing different clothes. And somehow she's just plain forgotten that her own clothes and her mother's jewelry are back in the bedroom of Frontier Frank."

"Well, hey, you put it that way . . ."

"If you laugh I will scalp you."

"Check it out, bro. This is me totally not laughing."

Sean returned to Tirian's office and spent another futile few hours scribbling and pacing and worrying. When the walls started closing in he went upstairs to the grand glass-walled chamber, but what he mostly saw was the carpet in front of his next step. When he grew tired of pacing he went back downstairs. Finally he gave up and went home. He took a long bike ride through the hot afternoon. A thunderstorm struck when he was midway back. He cycled through the rain and arrived home drenched. The rumbling din and fractured vision fit his mood entirely.

Dillon showed up soon after and unfroze some dinner Sean didn't taste. His brother spent the meal watching the clearing sky beyond the balcony doors. The sunset was a lot more entertaining than Sean.

As they were clearing up, Sean finally got around to asking, "How are things with Carey?"

"Good. Better than good. I mean, she's shook up, but . . ."

"You two are still an item."

"Believe it or not." Dillon grinned. "She said it'd take more than a galactic transport system to change her mind."

"I'm glad."

"Sean . . . thanks, man."

"Happy to help." Sean fit the dish towel onto the drying rack and stepped over to the balcony's screen doors. He saw Carey and her father going through the same process, clearing up from their own meal, and had an idea. "Why don't you invite her over? I'll make myself scarce, give you guys some room."

"What will you do?"

Sean was already reaching for his backpack. "See if the professor minds some company."

···

John Havilland seemed to find nothing strange in having Sean take over half the dining room table. Night sounds of crickets and dripping rain filtered through the screened patio doors. John made them coffee, and within minutes both of them were surrounded by papers. Sean looked up from time to time, watching the professor write in longhand before entering whatever he worked on into his laptop. They sat at opposite ends of the long table like two friends. *Adult* friends.

At one point Sean glanced through the screen and across the patio, up to where light shone from the loft's balcony. He had the impression that this was where he and Dillon had been headed for years. Struggling to fashion a new relationship around changing worlds. The gift of transit and Carey only sped things up. And Elenya. Thinking of her caused his breath to catch in his throat. He hoped with a desperate longing that she was okay, that *they* were still . . .

Sean forced his mind back to the work at hand. He reviewed all the items he had developed over that long, frustrating day, and everything he had jotted down before. His notes were written on everything from the blank front page of a book he'd never finish to a scrap of grocery store checkout tape to today's lined notepaper. He laid it all out with the precision of a Vegas dealer. Studying each in turn. Switching them around. Trying to make the puzzle fit together.

This time the answer did not come in some sudden burst of insight. He did not find his mind threatened by an explosion of blistering impact. There was no lightning bolt. Instead, it grew from a conversation he'd never actually had.

What he did was start talking in his mind to the man at the other end of the table. Trying to make things clear by explaining each fragment, describing why he felt it could be important. Asking if John thought it might fit together this way, then that.

When suddenly he saw the scraps and splinters coalesce.

He pushed back his chair and took his idea out on the patio. Stared up at the stars. Wondered if one of those blinking silver lights might contain another outpost world like his own, waiting for some kid to wake up and realize he could move between planets.

Sean stayed where he was for almost an hour, giving the new idea space to grow and congeal and take hold. When it was time, he went back inside, but he did not sit down. He stood over the table and stared at the papers as they swirled and re-formed.

Then he looked up and saw that the professor was watching him. He said, "It all comes down to asking the right question."

John nodded approval. "It usually does."

"I need to go now." Sean gathered up his papers. "And thanks for this."

"This has been one of the nicest evenings I've had since . . ." John smiled sadly. "Take care, son."

It was only when he was midway across the lawn that Sean realized what John had said. But when he turned back, the professor was once more intent upon his work.

Sean stopped beneath the balcony and called up, "Yo, Dillon. It's time."

There was a moment's silence, then Dillon appeared. "You got it?"

"Yes."

"No 'I guess.' No 'I think.'" Dillon grinned down at him. "My brother the sage. Give me two minutes, then let's go save the world."

40

The school operated on a twenty-four-hour clock. Or rather, the Lothian equivalent of one. The transit room and lockers were normally filled with people coming and going. But when the twins arrived, the place held the stillness of a disused tomb. Sheets of paper attached to the transit room's side wall stated in several languages that the school had been temporarily closed. Students were urged to study on their own. Officials would be in contact shortly.

Sean stood in front of the wall, inspecting the sheets with the hope that some clue, some hint of a next step, might suddenly arrive. He could only think of one thing. "We've got to wait."

Dillon glanced through the open portal, down the empty hall. "Wait."

"Yes."

They headed for the lounge, their footsteps shuffling along the carpeted expanse. The rear wall was a meal repository, offering a constant variety of food. Most of it was Lothian in origin, with a single section for special requirements and noted only in the language of the recipient. Most of the stuff tasted as bland as the school. They ate whenever possible in the loft. But there was one dessert they had both come to love, layers of something that resembled cake alternating with a toffee-like substance that tasted like dark chocolate. They carried two plates to their customary table, which was weird, since they had the entire place to themselves.

Dillon took a bite, inspected the next one, and said, "I wonder where this stuff comes from."

"Best not to ask."

"Yeah. Droppings of flesh-eating glowworms, probably." He took another bite. "Still tastes great. Even at midnight and counting. Which brings us to the question, what are we doing here?"

"I told you. Waiting."

"Which explains absolutely nothing." He scraped up the last slivers of the goo. "Sure would like to know why I'm missing sleep."

"We need Elenya."

"So we're just going to sit here until she decides to check in?"

"There's some kind of alert system you can sign up for. It lets you know when the other person shows up. She went to Josef and he put it in place."

Dillon grinned. "Elenya went to Josef and asked him to set up a galactic alert whenever you came to school."

"What's so funny?"

"Nothing, bro. Not a single solitary thing. Just admiring your way with the ladies, is all." Dillon easily avoided Sean's swipe across the table. "I'm asking again. Why are we here?"

"This whole plan revolves around us going back to the train station."

Dillon's good humor vanished. "Back to where we've been ordered never to set foot in, ever again."

"That place. Yeah."

Dillon gave that a beat. "You want to explain why you think going to the train station is worth risking a mind-wipe?"

Sean told him. Or tried to. But part of his mind and most of his heart remained caught by the woman who was not there. Added to this was all the pressure and the fear of having gotten things terribly wrong. It was a poor way to relate an unfinished idea, stumbling over all the things he had not yet worked out. But Dillon didn't seem to care. In fact, long before Sean arrived at what he thought was the conclusion, his brother announced, "Okay, I got it."

"I'm not done."

"It doesn't matter. I know enough to know you're handling this."

Sean let his uncertainty show. "Glad you think so."

"What . . ." Dillon stopped because Elenya appeared in the doorway, and Sean's chair held nothing but an empty space.

"Elenya, I'm so sorry." The words were totally inadequate, especially as he saw the shadows in her eyes. But Sean could think of nothing else to say.

"It's not your fault."

"In a way it is. You changed clothes before our dinner because . . ." Then he realized what she carried.

A pair of cases. One in each hand.

Sean watched her settle them by her feet and felt his heart do a swooping dive. "What's going on, Elenya?"

"Can we sit down, please?" There was a new quality to her calm, a gravity he had never seen before. She seated herself, greeted Dillon, and announced, "My mother has forbidden me from ever seeing you again."

The soaring and swooping grew sharper, like his heart and gut were riding a roller coaster, one that did not care at all how the rest of Sean's body remained perfectly still. Frozen, in fact. A rigid human post, squeezed by all the things that could not wait. The conflict and the burden left him incapable of drawing a single decent breath.

She went on, "I tried to convince her that I am not too young, that this is not a whim . . . My mother was not interested in being convinced. She was not interested in listening. Her mind is made up. She claims to know what is best for me. I am the youngest of five daughters. My middle sister has just gone through a terrible breakup. My mother despised the man. I told you of this, yes? And before that my oldest sister also went through a bad end to a bad relationship. My mother assumes I am making the same mistake. It is all she can see, how she will be forced to watch another daughter be crushed by giving her heart to the wrong man."

Sean tried to follow what she was saying. But his brain

kept getting snagged by the two cases waiting there by the door. And everything they signified.

Elenya regarded him with an ancient's solemn gaze. "My mother's outrage grew steadily worse. She refused to hear anything I tried to tell her. The day after our dinner, it became evident that I had no choice. As soon as the Examiners and Counselor Tatyana and Carver finally finished with me, I started making plans. I was so glad when your alert arrived. I'd been hoping that you would come to school looking for me."

"So . . . you've left home."

"Yes. But there is a problem. I have nowhere to stay." She motioned to the empty school. "All the boarders have been sent away."

Dillon offered, "Stay with Carey and her dad."

She offered him a solemn inspection. "Will they agree?"

He was already up and moving. "One way to find out." To Sean, "Don't start with the fireworks until I get back."

When he was gone, Elenya asked, "Fireworks?"

"We need your help with something."

"Is it important?"

"Very. And urgent." Sean knew he should be offering comfort. He knew there were a dozen things a better man would be saying just then. But all he could think of was the ticking clock. How a man's life hung in the balance. How they did not have time for this. Any of it. How what he felt at that very moment, the one thing that was squeezed from his frantically swooping brain was . . .

Helplessness.

She continued to watch him, waiting. When he did not speak, she said, "I need to know this is not a whim, Sean. I need to know you are . . ."

The word sprang to mind. He said it because she waited. "Committed."

"I know it is too early. I wish we had more time. But my mother is very determined. She will find a way to drive a barrier between us. I can't let that happen. Not if you are truly . . ."

He nodded slowly. The only word his mind could shape rang through the empty room. *Committed.*

"I know that we are very young. I know that we may change. But I want to take this risk. If you are . . ."

He had no idea how he felt. But he could not say that. To even *think* this was awful. But it was the truth, and he would not lie to her. Not ever. So he remained there. Nailed to his chair. Squeezed from every side. While his heart and his gut kept up their crazy ride.

Her voice became more solemn still. "By my leaving home, I hope she will understand that I am as determined as she. That she is no longer in a position to dictate my life's course. But this is a very big step, Sean. I do this for you. But only if this is truly what you want. Only if you . . ."

He had to breathe. But unlocking his rigid frame was such a struggle that what he did was shudder. His words emerged in a terribly shaken state. Exactly how he felt. "I can't think about this now."

She did not change one iota. And he sensed that part of her had expected this very response. It was her turn to freeze to her chair.

He pushed out, "Tirian's life depends on my getting this right. It's all I can think of, all I have room . . . They've arrested the Examiner."

She tasted the air, tried to shape some word. But it did not emerge.

"I need your help, Elenya. Desperately. If we have to do this without you, Dillon and I, we . . ."

She trembled, almost like she was trapped and fighting the same forces as him now. "Desperate."

"Tatyana said we could be arrested. Carver threatened us with a mind-wipe. But we have to do this. If I'm right, and the Examiner is punished, and we didn't do anything—"

"Tell me what you want me to do," she whispered.

Dillon chose that moment to come racing into the lounge. He announced triumphantly, "It's all taken care of. The professor and Carey say, 'Welcome home.'"

Elenya shuddered. She tried to smile at Dillon, then she turned back to Sean. And waited. Already convicted by what he could not give her.

He said, "I've got this plan, really just half a—"

"No, Sean. No." Her voice was little more than a broken whisper. "Just tell me what to do."

So he did, though each word he spoke seemed to stab her, causing her to wince with a pain she did not fully suppress. So he kept it as short as possible. Three sentences. No more. When he was done she forced in another shuddering breath, then said, "I will do this."

"That's great, Elenya, I can't thank—"

He stopped. Not because she rose from the table and

excused herself, but because she was crying. And the sight was the worst thing he had ever seen. Just totally, wrenchingly awful.

When she was gone, Dillon leaned across the table and savaged him further by asking, "Bro, what have you gone and done?"

41

Since Elenya had no idea where she was headed, Sean transited with her. He was concerned about her on many levels. Her hand had the limpness of wax. Her eyes were not blank, just hollow. Like she had lost some ability to hide the void she now carried inside.

And it was all his fault.

As soon as they arrived, Elenya took a long look around and declared, "This is the central station on Cyrius."

"You've been here?"

"Never. But the station is famous." Her tone was as hollow as her gaze. "They use it as a selling point for their gravity modulators."

"The doctor's name is Sandrine. Tell her as little or—"

"I know what to do." She started away.

Sean watched as the crowd swallowed her, until not even the white-blonde hair was visible. Then he transited back to the loft.

Sean spent the next hour and a half pacing. Dillon's company was about as welcoming as a Taser. He sat at the dining room table. Every time Sean came into view, Dillon zapped him again. Doing what Elenya wouldn't.

Sean wanted to be there when she returned. But if he stayed around, he and his brother risked another battle, only this time they'd tear apart their only home. So he tumbled down the stairs and out the door and onto the front lawn.

The day was summertime close, hot and so humid the temperature was just a theoretical number. Clouds blanketed the sky and pressed down hard. Thunder rumbled off in the distance, a deeply discontented growl. Even the weather was angry with him.

He came around the edge of the garage, then drew back before he was spotted. John Havilland sat alone at the patio table. Which probably meant it was either Saturday or Sunday, Sean had no idea. He risked another glance. The professor's face was creased with such agony, the sight reached across the distance and squeezed Sean's heart. Carey was nowhere to be seen. John clearly thought he was alone and could release his sorrow, just for an instant. Breathe the loss in and out. The professor's gaze came to rest on one of the cast-iron pots that anchored the patio's corners and held miniature fruit trees. His gasping, shuddering breath was audible across the distance.

Sean did not need to dialogue with the older man. He knew exactly what he was seeing.

Here before him was the price of love.

The risk of getting it wrong was so huge. Sean was definitely too young. The timing was just awful. Events and risks crowded in from every side. He had every reason to do as he had and put her off.

Sean turned and looked down the drive, out to where it connected with the road. And the road to the highway that would take him to the alternative.

His parents moving into separate apartments had not really changed anything. They had been alone for years. That was what scared him the most. How he had been surrounded all his life by wrong moves.

Sean started back up the stairs. He was pressured on all sides by a thousand choices.

But only one of them was right.

As soon as he came into view, Dillon seemed unable to hold it in any longer. He lashed out, "You're *crazy*. She's *beautiful*. She's smarter than you, and you're the smartest guy I've ever known. How could you be such an *idiot*?"

Sean shuddered his own way through a hard breath. Nodded to the floor at his feet.

"How could . . . You let her down! I don't know what you said and I don't *want* to know."

Sean just stood and nodded. Took it because he deserved it.

Dillon sent his chair crashing back. "Are you so desperate you can't wait to wind up like Mom and Dad?"

Sean shook his head. *No.*

"She's come into your life *now*. You need to act *now*."

Sean remained as he was. Beaten into submission by the truth.

The absence of a foe must have defeated Dillon. He headed for the stairs, knocking Sean hard with his shoulder as he passed. He was midway down the stairs when he stopped and said, "You make it up to her. I mean it, Sean. Either you square it with Elenya or . . ."

The truth in his words lingered long after Dillon left. Smoldering hot as guilt.

...

An hour later, Elenya appeared in silence. Her emotions formed a luminescence around her. Perhaps it was just his own internal response, Sean seeing her through the lens of an open heart. But he didn't think so. The aura was too powerful for that. This was part of her, a hint of the same strength that granted her the ability to tell her family no. To declare her affections and intentions. Even when it cost her . . .

Everything.

He stepped in front of her and stood without reaching, though he wanted to. He felt his tone was as formal as a courtier's bow. It was what she deserved. "I was wrong, Elenya. I should have said what you needed to hear. I should have done it without hesitation. I'm sorry."

Elenya released a tear. Another. She wiped her face. "I never cry."

"And I've made you do it twice in one day. My heart is wrenched by the sight. And by the beauty. I am filled with a regret as strong as pain." He was normally not so eloquent. It would be wrong to say Serenese was made for poetic remorse.

But it definitely came easier. "If you will let me, I would like to do now what I should have done this morning. I want to commit, Elenya."

Another tear slipped out and fell, sparkling like a gemstone. "Why didn't you before?"

"I have any number of reasons. But none of them matter. Or rather, none of them matter *enough*."

"Tell me anyway."

"I'm under intense pressure to save the Examiner from a punishment he doesn't deserve. His trial is starting in a couple of days."

"That is one."

"I have no experience at love. Failed love, yes. A hopeless and empty home life, years of that. Dillon and I were raised around two people living unhappy lives together. That's all I knew growing up."

"We can study."

"No, Elenya. You will have to teach me."

She reached one hand out, then retreated. She walked over and seated herself at their little table. Sean hesitated, then joined her. She sat there a moment, looking deep into his gaze. Another tear spilled down her right cheek. Sean feared his heart would break.

Then she set one hand upon the tabletop, palm up. He settled his hand upon hers and found the strength to breathe again. She looked down, and the shift in her gaze released one more tear. "You have small hands."

"Do I?"

"For such a big man. Yes. And a delicate touch." She linked

her fingers through his. "Your hands are a trace smaller than your brother's."

"That's right. They are."

She looked up, though it was hard for him to meet her gaze and see the unshed tears gathered along the rims. "There's a faint hint of gold to your green eyes. Dillon doesn't have that either. His eyes are a shade darker."

"No one has noticed that before."

"Your features are slightly sharper. More carefully defined. His are . . ."

"Stronger."

"Physically, yes."

"He is the warrior."

"The officer," she corrected. "He will never be the common soldier. Not even among the Praetorians."

"He'll love hearing you say that."

She reached out with her free hand and traced a finger along the edge of his chin. "Your face holds a keener intelligence." She moved upward. "Your hair does not grow as far down your temples and forehead. You may go bald."

"I'd hate that."

"Then we will find a way to stop it." She continued her inspection. "You have two lines across your forehead, very faint, but they run the breadth of your eyebrows. They are marks of concentration. And worry. Dillon has none." She touched his lips. "Your smile is slightly canted, pulled to one side just a trace by all you carry."

She let her hand fall to the table. He reached over and took hold of this one as well. He breathed in and out. She breathed with him. They sat there for a few minutes, an eon of healing quiet.

Then Dillon thumped up the stairs and came into view. He inspected them a moment, then said, "So you're good."

Elenya answered quietly, "Yes, Dillon. We are good."

"Did he apologize?"

"He did, yes."

"Because if you want him to say something more, just give me the word. I'll . . ." Dillon stopped as Elenya rose from the table and walked over.

She reached around him and held him tightly. Just for an instant. But long enough for Dillon's face to change. Sean saw the flicker come and go, swift as Carver's smile. Dillon looked across the room at him, the anger gone now. Totally vanished.

Sean said, "I guess we better get to work."

42

Elenya pulled the shopping bags from under Sean's bed and dressed in another of the outfits from the local mall. Then she took them shopping.

Dillon had never been good at this particular job. With the shaky start to the day, he was ready to give in to some serious complaints. Carey was putting in extra hours at the school and so wasn't there to offer encouragement.

But Elenya was firm. "Dr. Sandrine's shift does not begin for another hour. More importantly, you are forbidden from returning to Cyrius, correct?"

"Where?" Dillon asked.

"The train station," Sean said, "is on Cyrius."

"Serious, like, grim?"

Sean spelled it out.

But Dillon was on a roll. "So the Examiner's fate and our own mental futures depend upon a planet called Somber. Stern. Grave." He shook his head. "This just keeps getting better."

Elenya went on, "The authorities will be alerted. You need to blend in. I took note of how Cyrian travelers dressed."

Sean was so content to be there, walking down the street holding her hand, he would have followed her just about anywhere. "So you didn't speak with Sandrine?"

"I did not say that. I said she was not on duty yet. I spoke with her by the clinic's phone. Dr. Sandrine will meet with you." Elenya stopped in front of a store. "This is perfect."

Dillon was aghast. "No way."

"Inside, Dillon." Elenya led them into Brooks Brothers and over to the men's dress section. In twenty minutes she had them both decked out. Dillon wore navy dress pants with a matching cotton sweater that zipped up to the neck. Sean was a study in grey—gabardine slacks, matching summer-weight turtleneck. Black belt and loafers. He got busy writing another check before Dillon could get a look at the total.

When they returned to the loft, the twins took turns changing in the bathroom. Then they took hold of Elenya's hands and with her guidance transited straight into the clinic.

Actually, they transited into the doctor's private office. Elenya touched a door tab, stepped out into the clinic proper, and swiftly returned. "Dr. Sandrine is with a patient."

The office was the same stark white as the clinic, even the desk. Sean pulled the desk chair around and said, "I've been thinking. What if I got this all wrong? What if we do this and nothing happens?"

"And Carver and the Counselor find out," Dillon finished. "We're toast, is what."

Sean was tempted to urge Elenya to take off. Leave them. Figure out another way to . . .

Dillon must have seen the worry in his gaze, because he shot out, "Sean. Drop it. Now."

Elenya was clearly as in tune as Dillon. She reached out her hand. Not to Sean. To Dillon. She said, "I've always wanted a brother."

They sat there in silence for a while, letting the quiet white clinic work on healing them all. Finally Dillon said, "So. You've been thinking."

"Right. What we need is the next big thing. Something that will take their mind off, you know . . ."

"The mind-wipe business," Dillon said, dropping Elenya's hand. "Or jail. Whatever."

"So we talk to Sandrine. We send Dillon out hunting. Elenya goes walkabout. And in between, we work on . . ." Sean stopped because he realized the doctor was standing in the portal, listening in.

She greeted them with, "Talk to Sandrine about what?"

43

The doctor was every inch a professional, whether taking the branch out of the side of a transiter or seated in her office. "Why do you want to discuss the aliens with me?"

Sean leaned against the rear wall, leaving his partners in crime in the chairs that separated him from the lady behind the desk. "We think we might have been attacked by them. Twice."

"And you survived."

"Yes."

"You and your brother. Raw recruits."

Sean sensed she was not nearly as skeptical as she appeared. "When we first showed up, you suspected aliens were behind the assault."

"What makes you say such a thing?"

"When I told you what had happened, you flashed fear. I don't think very much scares you."

"What—" She stopped when a chime sounded. Sandrine

touched a wall panel, which became a screen showing a woman and young child in the clinic's front room. "Wait here."

When she was gone, Sean asked Dillon, "You want to go check things out?"

"Sure thing."

Sean turned to Elenya. "Can I have your chair, please?"

She rose and took Sean's position by the wall. "What are you doing?"

"Dillon is going to go have a look around the station."

Light dawned. "While he is still here?"

"Yes."

Her eyes went completely round. "This is the realm of senior Watchers."

"We know." Sean fashioned the invisible belt, then gripped his brother's hand. "Ready?"

In reply, Dillon shut his eyes, released a long breath, and went still. Five minutes passed. Ten. Then he breathed deep, opened his eyes, and sat staring at nothing.

"You saw something?"

"Not a single solitary thing." His words emerged very slowly. Like his mouth found it difficult to shape the words. "But, I don't know . . ."

"You sensed a wrongness."

"Nothing that strong. Like a taste of something bad. But old, you know?"

"Like they've been here and now they're gone."

Elenya said, "We have to tell someone!"

"They don't believe Dillon can do this. They won't believe

anything he claims to have found." Sean released his brother's hand. "You need something?"

Dillon rose to his feet. Stretched. Yawned. Sat back down. "I'm good."

"You sure?"

"Just give me a minute."

Sandrine chose that moment to return. She took her time crossing the office, avoiding all their eyes in the process. When she was seated behind the desk, she continued where she had left off. "Why are you asking me? What makes you think I have anything to say about aliens?"

"You told me you wanted to make a career in interplanetary medicine."

"Did I?"

"Yes. I doubt you are drawn by the idea of treating transiters with colds."

"Even if that were so, it is in the future. Now . . ." She gestured at the room. "You see the medicine I practice."

Sandrine continued to avoid answering him directly. But she was also speaking Serenese. And the language continued to work its subtle effect, releasing far more than her words. With each comment, Sean grew increasingly certain that not only did Sandrine know, but she was also fascinated. And worried. The odd mixture formed a cauldron that bubbled softly in his gut. As though all his own concerns were slowly coming to a boil.

He asked, "Will you tell us what you know?"

She fiddled with an apparatus Sean assumed was used to record her clinical notes. She inspected a fingernail. Finally she said, "It has been a hundred and forty-one Serenese years since the last attack."

Elenya calculated swiftly. "Ninety-six Earth years."

"There is a very precise cycle. Or rather, there was. Up to that point, the attacks occurred every forty-seven Serenese years. But the last attack was their least successful. Their defeat came within days of their first appearance. For the third time in a row. Then the aliens skipped a cycle altogether. The first time in forty centuries they did not attack some planet where humans live. When the aliens did not appear on schedule, some suggested that they have learned their lesson and will not try again. Now there has been another missed cycle. And people have become very lax."

Dillon's eyes seemed to spark with the same odd mixture as Sean was feeling. "You're saying it's time for another attack?"

"No. The next attack cycle is not due for another Serenese year."

Elenya said, "The governments are very complacent. They think the worst is over."

Sean said to the doctor, "You're not so optimistic."

"We know so little about them. We have no idea where their home planet is, or even if one exists. We don't know why the cycle has continued now for almost four thousand years. We don't know why some assaults are much less focused than others. The last three, for example, have been very minor events. Except for one thing. The one trait that linked them together."

Sean listened with an intensity that seemed to bind him to

the doctor. Grant him the ability to track what she was not saying. "Their attack was focused on transiters."

Sandrine snapped around. Stared at him. Gaped, really. "How did you know?"

"I didn't."

Dillon said, "Sean does that. Jumps ahead of where you want him to be."

Elenya offered, "Sean is an adept."

"No," Sean protested. "You can't—"

Elenya mimicked his brother. "Sean. Stop. Now."

He sighed.

Sandrine clearly approved of this exchange. "The authorities have done their utmost to classify everything about these assaults as confidential. But I have seen medical records. I used them as part of my final thesis. Outside of the invasions themselves, there has never been an actual alien sighting. We do not even know if they exist in what we would class as a physical form. They *take over* people. And yes, in the last three attacks, they targeted transiters."

Elenya said, "Which explains why everything about these attacks has remained classified. Already there are many planets that resent the transiters and seek to limit their reach."

"Including Cyrius," Sandrine confirmed. "A hundred and fifty years ago we were given an official warning and put on planetary watch. It lasted almost twenty years. Our leaders were humiliated. Some of the warring groups banded together and demanded a global referendum, seeking to withdraw from the league. They were defeated. But resentment still lingers."

"And here we show up," Dillon said.

"Flying across the station floor, knocking down over a dozen people, leaving a trail of blood in your wake. People are still upset you weren't thrown in jail."

"There's something else the aliens use in their attacks, isn't there," Sean said, recalling the women involved in the Charger attack. "They make fake humans."

"Human-like drones," Sandrine confirmed. She rose from her chair. The area behind her desk did not offer much room for pacing, but she did her best. "Incredibly real. Sometimes one or two. Other times hundreds."

Sean asked, "Do you know how?"

"Here is where we move into the realm of speculation, but it is where I want to focus my future work. What we think is this." Three paces, her face almost planted on the side wall, swing about, three paces more. Arms linked across her middle. Holding herself tightly as she moved. "They steal a fragment of hair, skin, saliva, something that contains an entire genetic strand. They replicate. And it is from whatever intelligence they gain in the initial takeovers that governs who they replicate. They go after faces and people that the entire world wants to follow. Leaders, stars of entertainment, teachers of note. These are duplicated over and over and over. Armies wearing the planet's most beloved faces."

Dillon asked, "How many planets have been lost?"

"Seven. They attack, and where they win, they destroy everything. Nothing survives. Not a plant, an animal, a fish, a human. All gone."

Sean recalled, "The Counselor said something about our Earth possibly being safe from them."

"Again, we have nothing to go on but their past methods," Sandrine replied. "No outpost world has ever come under attack. Why, we have no idea."

"Do these aliens have another name?"

"They have a hundred names. A thousand. Every world that knows of them has named them. And they all come down to one concept. They are the enemy. Sometimes the assault is small. A probe, they are called. We've had three such probes in a row. All defeated within days. The relatively new class of Praetorian Guards known as Watchers has managed to identify the enemy, even when they transit to different worlds in the bodies of those they have taken over. Then they—"

The wall monitor chimed again. Sandrine keyed the controls, inspected the newcomers, and said, "I must see to this."

When she was gone, Sean said, "Dillon, go take another look around. Then let's see if we can do what she said."

"You want to try and replicate a human?" Elenya looked from one brother to the next. "Why?"

"Because," Dillon said, "our job is to rock their boat."

"This I do not understand," Elenya said. "Not at all."

"We've got to find some way to make them accept our version of events," Sean said. "And that means proving the impossible is real."

44

They spent the rest of the day patrolling the station and trying to put Sandrine's theory into action. And failed miser-
ably on both accounts.

Sean anchored Dillon while he went on regular patrols.
He waited while Elenya did her hourly walkabouts. The
bodiless hunting rendered Dillon increasingly exhausted.
Even so, Sean envied them both for the liberty to escape the
doctor's office, at least partly. Especially after his hours of
effort got him nowhere.

He tried to form a shield around a strand of hair, fill it
with energy, draw it out. Did it holding Elenya's hand. Used
other components. Tried with innate objects long associated
with one person or another. Tried to link his own internal
force with Dillon's. Then again with Sandrine. Nada. Over
and over and over. A totally futile day.

Dillon napped for a while. Elenya returned from one foray
carrying the Cyrian form of vegetarian wraps. The taste was
odd but good. Elenya and Dillon played a hand game from

her childhood. She went out for another walkabout. Dillon hunted. Sean did nothing whatsoever constructive.

When Elènya returned from the next walkabout, she sat down beside him and said, "Maybe you should take a pause."

"I like that idea." Dillon was sprawled on the floor opposite the desk. "Pausing is good."

"Yeah, you're a real pro at that sport," Sean shot back.

"Think about it," Dillon said. "You do your best thinking when you're not thinking at all."

Odd as it sounded, Sean had to admit, "You've got a point."

Dillon raised both hands to his unseen audience. "Dillon Kirrel, problems solved, damsels rescued, dragons slayed. My specialty."

Elenya said, "Teach me how you shoot your energy."

"I don't," Sean said. "Dillon does."

"But you feed him the energy, yes?"

It felt good to struggle over something else. "It's like passing a ball. You get it and you hand it on, quick as it comes. It hardly touches you. You basically just guide it on."

Elenya asked, "Can I try?"

So Dillon and Elenya played at that for a while, while Sean did what Elenya suggested. He propped his feet on the doctor's desk and did his best to keep his mind off the problem and the ticking clock. Elenya came over eventually and settled on the desk so that she could rest one hand on his leg.

Sean asked, "So how do you see your shield?"

"There is a bird on Serena, it drinks nectar from flowers. The bird is so small." She held up her thumb. "Smaller than this."

Sean said, "They beat their wings so fast they look like feathered blurs."

Dillon said, "Hummingbirds."

"Please?"

"That's what we call them," Sean said. "The sound you make when you sing without words. Hum-birds."

She looked from one brother to the other. "Truly, these birds are on your planet?"

"Sure thing," Dillon said.

"It's a beautiful image," Sean said. "You grow hummingbird wings and they form your shield."

But she had already left that behind. "I must tell my father. Other than on Lothia, there is no planetary species that . . ."

Sandrine entered the office and announced, "My shift has ended, and my replacement has arrived. It is no longer safe for you to remain."

■■■

When they transited back to the loft, Sean was ready to give in to the exhaustion of a futile day. His shoulders and neck ached from carrying a burden he couldn't shake, the fear that he had made a terrible mistake. That the whole exercise was not just pointless but suicidal. Every wasted hour taking them one step closer to a face-off with the Counselor.

Then Dillon noticed the yellow sheet of paper folded tent-like on their table. He picked it up, read it, and blanched. "Carey came over because she heard voices. Looks like Tatyana and Carver showed up."

The electric terror was enough to erase every shred of his exhaustion. "Where are they now?"

"Over with her and the prof." He dropped his hand, like the note weighed a hundred pounds. "They brought company. A man. Carey says he's very distinguished looking and he's dressed like Elenya."

Sean watched as Elenya paled to the color of old parchment.

...

Tatyana greeted them with, "You're under arrest."

Dillon just plopped down in the nearest chair. Like a doll with the stuffing jerked out.

Carey did not comprehend the Serenese, but she clearly understood the result. She moved swiftly, draped a protective arm around Dillon's shoulders, and stood between the attackers and her man. She demanded, "What's going on here?"

Sean had never liked her more than at that moment. Even when he didn't have the strength to reply.

Carver stood at parade rest behind the sofa holding the professor. His gaze scalded Sean, a silent communication of disappointment and concern and frustration. A senior officer brought low by the deeds of people in whom he had placed his trust.

John Havilland had clearly been informed of the situation's gravity, for his features were stained with very real concern. His gaze swiveled around the room, always returning to his daughter.

The Counselor went on, "You were expressly forbidden from ever setting foot on Cyrius. And yet off you went. Failing to notify anyone of your actions. Involving a third party in this latest escapade. Can I at least assume you did not drag Elenya there against her will, that she went of her own volition?"

Sean found himself disappearing inside himself. As though he had been looking all day for this very level of pressure. To squeeze and compress him until he arrived at the point where he was looking at the world from beyond. The region where logic held no place. Where his thoughts could scramble in their fear and their adrenaline rush. Out where the impossible became real.

Tatyana sniffed her disdain at their silence. "Did you even bother to inform the young lady of the edict in place against your returning to Cyrius?"

Elenya remained planted in the center of the room. The point at which no one would look directly. Oddly enough, she did not seem the least bit vulnerable to Sean. She remained where she was by choice. Waiting. For what, Sean had no idea.

"It's not enough that you must now endure the mind-wipe." Tatyana motioned to Carey and her father. "You also involved non-transiters. Who now must undergo the same treatment as you. I am only sorry you will fail to live with the guilt you deserve—"

Elenya broke in. "What about me, Father? Are you going to erase my mind as well?"

The Ambassador was not a cruel man. Elenya's own nature testified to this fact. Instead, he had been distilled down to a deep and almost primitive core. The essential nature that defined Tatyana and Carver was revealed here, a man sculpted by the whirlwind force of planetary politics. His silver-white mane was swept back from craven features, like some Plains Indian from a time before time. His gaze was as fierce as a hawk's. How Elenya withstood his glare without flinching, Sean had no idea.

The Ambassador replied, "You were an unwilling participant. You—"

"Oh, but I *wanted* to participate. I readily admit my guilt. I was the one who insisted they return to Cyrius."

The three officials winced in unison. Sean wished he could do something to support her. And yet, even the wash of pride left him somehow untouched. He felt as though he watched his beloved taunt a lion, but viewed through a telescope. He was that removed from the unfolding scene.

Elenya went on, "It was all my idea. So what now, Father?"

The Ambassador rumbled, "That is not true."

"Perhaps not," she shot back. "But I will insist upon claiming this responsibility in an interplanetary court. You taught me that. It is my right."

"Stop it."

Mentally and emotionally Sean drew farther away. Not just from the wrath on display. From the day's failures. He looked at this from a totally new perspective. One he had not even considered until that moment.

Elenya retorted, "Or what, Father? What will you do? Drag me back home? For how long? Do you think I will stay for—"

"This is neither the time nor the place, Elenya."

"This is *precisely* the time. This is *exactly* the place. How *dare* you hide behind this Counselor's skirts? Do you think for an instant I would not recognize your hand at work?"

Sean heard what was beyond Elenya's words. Serenese was an open language, even when communicating fury. Which Elenya most certainly was. A cold, implacable force that shocked her father.

And which pushed Sean yet another step away.

Back to where he could finally glimpse the answer.

The aliens did not exercise two attack modes—infiltrating some humans, genetically duplicating others. They did not penetrate living people and take them over temporarily, and then biologically make copies of others.

The force the aliens used in both forms of their attacks was one and the same.

What granted them entry into an individual also fueled their duplication process.

Sean sensed a transition within Elenya. Or guessed it was happening. In this realm where logic had no place, he could not isolate his guesswork. He simply knew that Elenya's icy rage created a vulnerability. One that he could now use.

No matter how great or powerful an individual's shielding abilities, Sean realized, nothing could withstand such negative forces. Fear, terror, rage, consuming desire. All became an acidic force that ate away the transiter's natural protection. Which meant they became defenseless. They were exposed. The aliens could re-form these negative emotions into entry points. Turning human life into instruments of self-destruction.

"Let me tell you what will happen, Father," Elenya said. "After your puppets have punished these two innocent young men."

Tatyana protested, "I am most certainly not anyone's puppet—"

"*INNOCENT!*" Elenya shrieked the word so high and so powerfully it pierced them all. She stood there, poised on her toes, hands clenched by her sides.

Wisely, Tatyana did not rise to the challenge.

Sean reached into Elenya. What he was about to attempt scared him as badly as Tatyana's threat of punishment. But he did it anyway. In a semi-perverse sort of way, it felt natural. Like Elenya was not actually growing angry with her father because of this outside event. Instead, the whole deal was set in motion so he could . . .

Do what aliens do.

"Innocent," Elenya repeated, softly now. "Let me assure you, Father. I am lost to you. I am gone. I denounce you. I disown you. My departure is only the signature on the document you yourself have written."

First Sean formed a shield bubble separate from himself. Then he took aim at the human race's Achilles tendon. The rage, the fear, the ugly hidden forces that ate at an individual's natural shield. He drew it away from Elenya. And fed into this all the similar forces that rocked this room. All the wrongness. Sean sucked it in and passed it on, leaving him tainted. Weak. And determined.

The Ambassador protested, "Elenya, do not speak words you will soon—"

"Look carefully, Father. Because this is the last glimpse you will ever have of your youngest . . ."

She stopped talking because she was no longer standing there alone.

Now there were four of her.

Elenya turned and gaped with the others at the new trio. All dressed as she was. But immobile. Silent. Until Sean gave them the words to speak.

Sean formed the words, and the trio of Elenyas said, "The aliens went after Sean and Dillon for the crime of showing up at the wrong place at the wrong time. Same as Tirian. He went to the train station as Examiner. And as a result, he became just another target."

Carver was the first to find his voice. "So the aliens . . ."

"Are readying their next attack," the three mock Elenyas confirmed. "And it will be centered on the Cyrian central station."

45

The experience left Elenya very fatigued. Which was hardly a surprise, since Sean had worked like an emotional parasite and drawn from her enough energy to form three duplicates.

Sean thought everyone seemed the worse for wear, as he had pulled on the emotional force emanating from everyone. Except for himself. Despite being wearied by the experience, Sean felt great. Proving his theory left him feeling like he had swallowed about a gallon of galactic energy drink.

They returned to the loft, where Elenya stretched out on the sofa. Sean warned her that he couldn't wait for her to wake up, but he wasn't sure she even heard, she was gone that fast. Carey refused to leave Dillon's side, even when it meant enduring Tatyana's protest and the Ambassador's glare. But by then all three of the officials had lost a good deal of their starch, such that when the professor said he deserved to be included as well, they hardly kicked up a fuss.

But no one expected Sean's next step, which was to ask for a meeting with Tirian.

He explained what he thought might be the key, giving them enough to justify his request. Not saying what he really felt needed to be stated. That it was time to release an innocent man. They would have to come to that conclusion on their own.

At a word from the Ambassador, Carver and Tatyana left for the courts. Sean and Carey and Dillon and John returned to the house to make sandwiches. The Ambassador agreed to transit to Cyrius and inform the authorities that an attack *might* be incoming.

As they crossed the lawn, Sean said, "I guess I should be happier that things are finally in motion."

"All I can think of right now is that we're not getting wiped," Dillon replied.

John said, "That's some lady you've got there, Sean."

"I don't have any idea what Elenya told them," Carey said. "But it was still as strong as a punch to the heart."

The words warmed him through the impromptu meal and the planning and the return of the three officials. And the confirmation that a meeting had been arranged with Tirian. One that the Chief Justice assigned to the case would attend. Dillon left with Carey for the Cyrian clinic, this time with the Ambassador's consent. When Sean asked whether Dillon could check things out when Sean wasn't there to anchor him, his brother stated with absolute confidence that Carey's grip would prove as solid as Sean's.

The Ambassador had yet to speak a word directly to Sean.

Sean returned to the loft to find Elenya up and waiting for him. She listened to his summary of everything that was happening in silence, then asked, "Has my father behaved?"

A voice from the bottom of the stairs replied, "He most certainly has."

Elenya stopped him in mid-climb by saying, "Stay there, Father. We're coming down."

Sean nodded his agreement. The man might not be his enemy, but Sean had no interest in the Ambassador entering his private space.

Elenya planted a hand on Sean's chest, then kissed him. She must have liked the flavor, for she smiled and kissed him again. Then she took his hand and led him downstairs. "Father, I would like to introduce Sean. Sean, this is my father, Anyon."

Sean was not going to lie and say it was nice to meet the guy. So he simply said, "How do you do."

Anyon grimaced over everything unspoken yet revealed by his native Serenese. "Still coming to terms with your discovery, is how I am."

"Start by accepting that Sean is an adept, Father." Elenya squeezed Sean's hand hard enough to halt his protest before it emerged. "That will make everything else much easier."

Anyon mulled it over, his gaze on their entwined hands. "Shall we join the others?"

They returned to the home, where Elenya hummed her pleasure over John's tomato and basil and mozzarella sandwich. Then they all transited together. John joined hands with Carver, who offered to serve as translator.

They arrived at a standard transit room, but one that smelled somewhat musty and held a symbol Sean recognized from class. "This is . . ."

"Serena," Elenya confirmed. "Home to the planetary government and the main prison."

Sean didn't say anything. But what he thought was, this would definitely not count as his first visit to Elenya's home world.

They exited the transit room into an unadorned prison chamber, where more security and several officers greeted them. Everyone gave Sean a good look as they went upstairs, through electronic doors, and met more officials, and then Sean was left in a room alone. Everyone else crowded into the chamber next door, watching through the blank mirrored surface to Sean's right, and probably through unseen cameras as well. The silence was intense.

Tirian was led in by two security. The guards seated the former Examiner at the central table and hooked his wrist to a hold on the tabletop. Then they backed up and planted themselves by the rear wall.

Tirian's attitude had not been improved by prison. "Come to gloat?"

"We don't have time for that." Sean seated himself and said, "The clock is ticking."

"What do you want?"

"Confirmation," Sean replied. "That this whole deal was a case of wrong place, wrong time."

The room was a muted ivory, same as Tirian's prison garb. The visitation room was impeccably clean, the air almost sterile, void of all sound and smell. But one look at the shrunken man across from him told Sean everything he ever needed to know about the interplanetary prison system. Tatyana's cold voice echoed through the chamber. *You're under arrest.*

Tirian drew him back by glaring at the mirror taking up much of the side wall and demanding, "Who is in the next room?"

"Carver. Tatyana. The Judge assigned to your case. The former emissary to Lothia."

"Ambassador Anyon?" Tirian's stark black features were made to sneer. "For an outworlder, you certainly haven't wasted any time."

Sean felt so disassociated from the man's scorn he could easily brush aside the comment. "Let's review what we now know. The Cyrians dislike us. They have done everything but ban our presence."

"*Our* presence," Tirian repeated. "So now you count yourself among us."

"They resent authority being imposed from beyond their own world." Sean found it remarkably easy to ignore the dark scowl, the suspicious gaze, the unseen observers beyond the one-way glass. "But the Cyrians need us to export their technology. They may also use us as a stick to keep their leaders in line. But they detest us for what we represent. The unspoken evidence that their strand of humanity is not unique. That they are not the sole human race. That they are not superior beings."

"Who told you that?"

Sean chose to ignore the question. "Which brings us to the aliens. And we now enter into the realm of speculation.

But this is necessary to understand why we are seated here. May I continue?"

Sean could see that Tirian wanted to refuse. The young man seated opposite him was stark evidence of his own failure as an Examiner. The fact that his freedom rested in Sean's hands was almost too much to bear. He fluttered his cheeks with a harsh breath, one that almost shaped a word.

Sean took that as the only green light this constipated soul would offer. "The aliens have been defeated all but seven times. Now that they've missed cycles, many want to believe the threat is gone. That they won't return at all. But you think differently. All you need to do is look at the legacy of your own world and the wasteland now used by the Academy. You knew the threat of war wouldn't just fade away. You suspected it was only a matter of time. So you set up your school. You started choosing your students while they were still very young. You wanted to control them, guide them, shield them from the threat of being attacked in the next cycle like transiters had been three times in a row. And you remained certain another invasion was coming."

Tirian did not meet his eye. But the man was listening intently now, his breath catching with each exhale.

Sean went on, "You figured the previous three attacks were just probes. Your concern was that the aliens might now be returning in a new guise. That they were readying a different method of assault. You had no idea what it was going to be. But you were determined to protect your students. The aliens were not ever going to have access to those placed in your care. Even if it meant turning your school into a windowless prison, one that only opened to the outside world on the solstice, when every door and window on Lothia was ordered to be opened."

"Pure conjecture," Tirian muttered.

Sean ignored the interruption. "You suspected the next attack would come on a world like mine. An outpost world. One where the empire had almost no presence. You had no idea that the Assembly feared the exact same thing. Or that Watchers and Counselors had been assigned to monitor any suspect activity."

He snapped around. "How do you know this?"

"I told you. It's all conjecture. But it makes sense, doesn't it. There is no way a Counselor responsible for several outpost words would take such an interest in two raw recruits. Or planetary Watchers would be set on constant alert, or Praetorian Guards readied for attack. They wouldn't do this for new recruits. They wouldn't keep us in place. They would ship us off to a school like yours, where we could be monitored and protected. But they didn't. And I can only think of one reason to keep us there, out in the open."

Sean turned to the mirror. Glared beyond the glass. And finished, "They used us as bait."

When he turned back, Tirian's scowl was twisted by a fascination he no longer tried to hide. The former Examiner chewed on something, but all he said was, "The aliens."

"Right. Once this is over I want to research how the three alien attacks that focused on transiters might be linked. But here's what I think. The aliens almost succeeded. It was only by chance they were halted. It's why the authorities let you make your school so confined. It's why they don't allow recruits to extend their abilities. It's why the instruction is so *boring*. Because everyone is terrified the aliens will use any new experiments as a conduit to enter and take over and attack."

"They're right to be afraid," Tirian said.

"This fear restricts our understanding of their tactics," Sean shot back.

Tirian's sneer took hold once more. "Forty centuries of fighting an unseen foe, and here you come. Less than two months of training and you have all the answers."

"Just one," Sean replied. "More like half an idea. Which is why I'm here. I need you to tell me what happened before you were taken."

46

Tirian froze. His mouth worked. He needed several tries to reply, "I don't remember anything." But the truth was evident in his flickering gaze and the tension that stretched his dark features tight as a drumhead.

Sean replied, "I know you do."

"You know nothing." But Tirian could not draw up any scorn. Not now. "You're accusing me of lying?"

"I know there was an instant between your normal life and your period of being under the aliens' power. I know this because we were almost taken as well. I need to know what happened next. What we did not experience."

But Tirian was not listening. He twisted his wrist against the plasti-steel bracelet clenching him to the table. "I am ready to return to my cell."

"The aliens could be attacking Cyrius next. It's crucial that I—"

"Guards!" He struggled harder. "You can't deny me my rights under the planetary convention!"

But as the prison security stepped forward, a disembodied voice said, "Hold as you are."

"This is outrageous," Tirian said, but his snarl was toothless.

The door opened behind Sean. Carver and Ambassador Anyon entered, accompanied by a stout woman with features flat as a cooking pan and eyes hard as agate. The woman said, "As Justice assigned your case, I hold the power to release you to house arrest while your fate is determined."

"I'm innocent," Tirian said. "I've done nothing to deserve—"

"But first you must answer the young man's question," the Justice said. "That is your choice."

"Take me back," Tirian insisted weakly.

"You are so eager to face further imprisonment? Even when the court recognizes you may have done nothing more than be used by our enemy?" She pointed to Sean. "Answer his questions and return home. Refuse again and go back to your cell. That is your choice."

When Tirian remained silent, Sean softly repeated, "I need to know what happened in the moment of your capture."

Tirian's head went down, his features slack. He kept tugging against his restraint, but it was the feeble efforts of a defeated man.

Sean could taste the man's fear. "They lured you in."

Tirian muttered, "You know nothing."

"Actually, I do," Sean replied. "They did the same to us.

And now you know I'm speaking the truth. The attack at the Charger was real. It almost succeeded." He leaned across the table. "Tell me what I need to know."

The act of drawing his next breath caused Tirian's body to spasm. Then he confessed.

...

It was a sordid and shameful tale.

"I . . . met a woman," he began.

The image of the three beautiful college girls waving at them from the bus stop caused Sean to shudder.

Tirian must have taken Sean's movement as assent, for he went on, "She was young. Beautiful. Vibrant."

Sean knew a bitter shame at having undergone the same temptation. He did not like the former Examiner any more now. But he felt for him. Deeply.

"She had such a delicious laugh." Tirian's hand trembled as he wiped his mouth. "I can still hear it. She . . ."

"Wanted you," Sean said softly. Remembering.

"She drove me mad. The more I had of her, the more I wanted. Only it left me hollow and wasted."

Sean studied the man seated opposite him. Tirian's empty flesh was nothing more than a dull wrapping that encased old rage and bitterness at the core of his being.

"She consumed *everything*." The tremors fractured Tirian's words. "When I finally accepted what was happening, she lost her physical form and swept into me. I know that sounds impossible."

"No," Sean said. "It doesn't."

"I was utterly helpless. She *devoured* me." Tirian became wracked with shudders so tight his words became almost unintelligible. "She feasted on my life with a delicate bliss. And I could do nothing but watch."

Sean gave him a minute to recover, then asked, "What happened next?"

"When she had gorged on me, when I was truly empty, she reached out," Tirian replied. His eyes carried the feverish quality of returning to that dark hour. "It felt like she touched a switch. And I lost consciousness. The next thing I knew, I was being arrested and brought here."

Sean turned to the Ambassador and said, "I have what I need."

Anyon was clearly a man coming to terms with the restructuring of his family's core. He viewed Sean through this dual lens, a young man who possibly held the key to the empire's safety, and yet the same man threatened to steal his youngest daughter.

Every eye in the room save Tirian's shifted to Anyon, and still he struggled to fashion the simplest question. "Will you tell us what is happening?"

Sean replied, "We need to get back to the station and start putting things in motion."

Tatyana protested, "First we must have a clearer sense—"

"The aliens are coming," Sean replied. "Right now that's all you need to know."

47

Sean wished he could lose himself in the act of just walking around the station. Reveling in the place they had dreamed about for ten years and counting. Carey smiled as she watched Dillon and Sean turn in a slow circle. The two of them. Out in the open. Free to do whatever they wanted. Which for the moment was try to take it all in. Watching the people on the moving walkways that curled up the sides and across the distant ceiling. They observed glass trains that swooshed in and out of the long glass tubes. Riding into a world that beckoned.

Dillon's yearning and excitement were clear in his gaze. Sean knew what his brother was thinking. They could take their seats and fly off to some unknown city. They now had passes to the planet's entire rail system. And a payment chip, good for whatever, embedded in thin gold bracelets the four of them wore on their left wrists. Sean especially liked how Carver had supplied one for Carey. He knew it was the adults' way of clearing the decks, not going so far as an official statement of regret, but saying in more than words that he and Dillon were now part of the team.

Dillon lifted his arm and let the bracelet sparkle in the surrounding lights. "We could have it all wrong. Maybe the aliens came for the veggie wraps."

Elenya clearly did not feel this was a time for jokes. She gave that gentle pressure to Sean's hand, her own manner of silent speech. When he looked at her, she whispered in time to the whoosh of a departing train, "Soon."

He nodded, grateful that she understood. Wherever they went, the trip needed to hold that special sense of fulfilling a lifelong dream. And he did not want to rush that.

Plus there was the small issue of not knowing when the aliens were going to show up. All they could say was, Dillon's last sweep had turned up nothing new.

Of course, this was assuming that they had it right. That they hadn't blown the whistle for nothing. That the invasion was real.

But something else had come to Sean as they were leaving the prison. An experience so powerful he had asked for this moment before they started on the next step. Because there was every possibility that it would be his only chance to revel in this place. His and Dillon's very own twin world.

The experience had occurred as he'd returned to the prison's transit room. In that grim and charmless tomb, Sean had received an idea from somewhere beyond himself.

Only it was not just an idea.

The event had been amped a thousand degrees. It had

not been just one concept. Instead, a myriad of images had flooded him, swirling through his brain with the brilliance of a lightning barrage at ground zero. But without the noise, the charge, or even the shock.

Sean had been frozen to the spot, for how long he had no idea. But when it was over and he managed to refocus on the prison's transit room, the adults were still clustered, talking over what steps to take and when.

In that instant, Sean knew what it was he had to do. Even though he probably wouldn't survive.

...

Sean made a final slow circuit of the Cyrian train station. He took it all in deep. He was swamped by an abiding sense of sorrow over how this could be as far as he ever went on Cyrius.

Dillon asked, "Something wrong?"

Sean saw the uncertainties on the faces that watched him. And the trust. And that gave him the strength to hide away what he could not reveal, the plan that was his alone. For the moment.

He said, "I guess we better get to work."

...

Station security operated from a warren of offices located a third of the way around the central belt from the clinic. Glass portals opened into a large front chamber with counters running down both sides. Electronic screens flashed and voices called. More and more people crowded into the vast space, their faces grim, their attitudes pompous.

Sean came here because he needed to confirm what he had suspected would happen, which was, the adults would mess things up.

He didn't need to understand the language to know a lot of egos were jostling for position. The glances cast their way were swift and dismissive. He sensed Elenya's disquiet and Dillon's irritation. But this was exactly what Sean had hoped to find.

He spotted Carver deep in discussion with Tatyana, Ambassador Anyon, and a number of other officials he didn't ever need to meet. He walked over and stood where Carver could use him as an excuse to break away.

Sean spoke in English so Carey would be included. "We need to change the way things are getting done."

"In case you hadn't noticed, that is what we—"

"Not them. Us. And we have just one chance to get this right."

Carver had a military officer's ability to pare away the noise and the confusion and focus on the essential. He focused that laser gaze on Sean now. "Explain."

Sean summarized his reasoning. When he was finished, the best thing he could say about Carver's response was, the officer did not dismiss him outright.

Carver asked, "How long do you think we have?"

"I can't . . . Hours, maybe. Or minutes. But we need to get started."

Tatyana heard his tone, glanced over, frowned, and went back to her serious conversation with the officials. Adult to adult. Carving out turf. Wasting time.

Carver said, "Tell me how you can be so certain about this

change in direction. I'm asking because your idea is going to set off a firestorm."

Sean motioned to the various clusters of adults. "They're putting in place the same old guidelines that missed everything that's happened so far. The aliens have changed tactics. We need to do the same or we'll miss this chance."

Carver asked Dillon, "You sense this also?"

"I know they've been here. To this station. Small ins and outs. I can't say more than that. Sean's the one who fits together the pieces of invisible puzzles. That's his specialty."

"You need to listen to him," Elenya urged.

Dillon said, "Remember how you missed the signals Sean picked up before the Charger attack? If he says jump, you've gotten your orders."

Ambassador Anyon chose that moment to break off his conversation and walk over. "Is there something I need to be aware of?"

Sean saw Tatyana frown at the interruption, but she joined them as well. Sean felt Elenya's rising ire like heat off a stove. But he felt this conversation was inevitable. It had to be dealt with. Now rather than later.

Tatyana asked, "What's going on here?"

Anyon replied, "I was hoping to find that out."

Sean could tell Elenya wanted to snap at them. Again. But he took her hand, squeezed, and released. A quick jolt. Enough to stifle her comment. Carver caught the motion and offered Sean his trademark half-hidden humor.

Sean said, "We need to move everything that's happening here outside the station."

"We are organizing a central power structure and setting up a defense perimeter," Tatyana stated.

"You should be pleased," Anyon said. "An interplanetary response is being readied, all on the basis of your intelligence."

Words, Sean thought. *Adult gobbledygook.* But what he said was, "That's great. But it's not what I'm talking about. You need to think of us as an early-warning system. And for this to work, we need to get everything we're doing and all these people outside the alien attack zone."

Dillon halted in his murmured translation for Carey long enough to add, "Like you said, you're here because of our intel. You need to accept we have ideas all our own."

Sean almost smiled. That was as close to diplomatic as Dillon would probably ever come.

Carver interrupted the Ambassador's retort with, "What do you need?"

"Keep all your transiters off-world," Sean replied. "Especially any other Watchers. Bring us the two who were on duty the night they blasted our home. Give us the clinic. We'll bring you confirmation."

Tatyana protested, "What you're suggesting will undo everything we're trying to put in place."

"You're missing the point," Dillon said.

Sean said, "The aliens have moved on. You need to do the same."

"Sean isn't talking turf," Dillon added. "He's talking strategy. And you need to do what he says."

Sean went on, "The last three times, the aliens used a different system of attack. They went after transiters. They tried to hit one point, then spread."

Carver muttered, "The station."

"Same concept, different planet," Sean confirmed. "They failed going head-on against the Guard. So now they're hitting a world and a travel point where the Guard aren't welcome. And these forays are their method of making sure we're not around."

Carver was with them now, nodding in time to Sean's words. "Which is why they masked the attacks on you and Tirian."

"They went after us because we were here on Cyrius," Sean said. "Transiters suddenly arrived at their next target. They saw us as a threat to their plans. We had to be taken out."

Anyon asked, "What do you suggest?"

"Like I said, get everybody here outside the station. Nothing that might alert the aliens when they show up next. Then bring us the Watchers. I need to ask them a question, and they need to give you official confirmation this thing is real. Once that happens, we'll also need our own space beyond the station perimeter."

Carver offered, "I'll go fetch the Watchers."

"And one more thing," Sean said. "Everyone who enters our space comes under our command. No arguments, no back talk."

"This is going to be our ops center," Dillon said.

Elenya saw her father's resistance and added, "And no exceptions."

"We need to get started," Sean finished. "We don't have much time."

The four of them plus Carver went back to the clinic. Thankfully, Sandrine was on duty and did not protest when Carver insisted they were temporarily taking over the space. The colonel then departed to fetch the Watchers. Sandrine moved back and leaned on one of the beds and played willing observer. Dillon paced, halting now and then to reach for Carey's hand. Elenya gave it a few minutes, then took her impatience back to where she could pressure her father and the others to act. And *now*. Sean watched her depart, grateful that she was on his side.

From time to time Sean stepped back into the station proper and looked over to the security headquarters, which grew increasingly crowded with people used to holding power. He watched the energy being spent on things that didn't matter, and in the wrong place, and knew he had been right to insist. He'd just as soon send the whole pack of them off to the Cyrian equivalent of the North Pole. But he couldn't. They would fight the battle. That was not his job.

He was after something else entirely.

Carver returned with the Watchers in tow. Elenya popped back a few seconds later. Sean asked Carver, "Any progress on shifting the power crew outside the station?"

"First they want to hear from people inside their system that this is a real threat." When Dillon huffed a humorless laugh, Carver added, "At least they have resisted bringing in Watcher teams of their own. And the Guards deployment is happening off planet. For now."

Sean accepted this because he had to. "I need you to do something else."

If Carver found anything odd about taking orders from his newest recruit, he hid it well. "Name it."

"Go ask Josef and Tirian to join us."

Dillon stared at him. "The professor I can understand. But Tirian? Really?"

"He needs to be here," Sean insisted.

Dillon snorted. "What, you don't think the day already has enough trouble?"

"He's under house arrest," Carver pointed out.

"Which is a perfect reason to leave him out," Dillon said.

Sean told his brother, "We were inches away from landing in the exact same place."

"What place is that?" Dillon shot back. "Perpetually angry? Nasty by nature?"

Sean shook his head. "Broken."

Dillon's features showed intense disapproval, but he bit down on any further protest.

Sean turned to Carver and said, "We need them. But only if they agree to work under our orders."

"Under *your* command," Elenya corrected.

Carver offered his flash of approval or humor, or perhaps both. "Understood."

"Hurry," Sean said, but he was already talking to empty air.

···

The two Watchers Carver brought in were as unmatched a pair as Sean had ever met. Chenel was a solid brick, her voice deep and rough, the sound of a three-pack-a-day fanatic. She was probably young, probably tough, probably a lot of things. But one aspect was very definite indeed. Intelligence burned in her gaze, strong as wrath. By contrast, Baran was a tiny wisp and tended to cringe every time anyone looked his way. The woman was his friend, or so Sean assumed, because she stood where he could slip behind her whenever required. Sean liked them both on sight.

He asked, "You were watching our home the night it got destroyed?"

"We did our duty," Chenel said. The woman was taut and shielded against the attack she assumed was incoming. Sean knew she spoke to all the unseen authorities stacked on the station's other side. "We did it right."

"This isn't about blame," Sean said. "This is about getting ready for the invasion."

Dillon left the translating for Carey to Elenya and stepped up beside his brother. He pointed out beyond the clinic's perimeter and said, "We're here because they don't trust us and they don't especially like us. Which suits us just fine. We're all about working outside the box."

"They've spent four thousand years cramming the whole transit thing in a tight little package," Sean said. "It's partly political, and it's partly ego and partly necessity. Some worlds don't like us. They send in bureaucrats who make sure to strip away every ounce of fun and adventure from the process. They've wrapped the whole thing in bureaucratic tape, and they call it safety measures."

"Or expediency," Dillon said. "We get that one a lot in our world. It usually means the adults are getting ready to mess things up big-time."

Slowly, a half step at a time, the skinny guy emerged into the open. Chenel pointed to where Elenya stood beside Carey, translating softly. "Who are they?"

"Allies and friends," Sean replied. "Elenya's father is over there leading the bureaucrats. Now, back to the night they blew up our home."

Chenel's question lacked its earlier heat. "What is so important about that now?"

"It's what he does," Dillon replied. "Sean takes bits and pieces from different puzzles and somehow makes the things all come together."

Elenya added, "Sean is an adept."

Baran's voice was delicate, like he wanted to speak without actually disturbing the air. "Can I ask something first?"

"Anything."

"Carver says you claimed to have done an external observation."

"If that means hunting beyond the physical body, it isn't a claim. And it wasn't me, it was my brother."

Dillon added, "Carver doubting it happened is a major reason why we're here on our own."

"Their doubt and their insistence that we work inside their comfort zone is a major pain," Sean agreed.

Carver chose that moment to return, the two men in tow. "I heard that."

Sean gave a moment for the introductions. Josef's presence was a relief, even if the giant did push too much air from the room. Tirian scowled at all in turn and said nothing. Sean didn't care. So long as the former Examiner followed orders, he could stay as nasty as he liked.

Sean turned back to the Watchers and took up where he had left off. "The night of the attack, I sensed something. Things felt wrong, like my bones were vibrating to a bad tune. Five minutes later, Dillon had this idea. He wanted me to hold his hand, strengthen his shield with mine, so he could go out. Walk around. Without feet. See what he could see."

The two Watchers exchanged a glance. "What did he find?"

"Four Tirians, spaced around the compass. All four attacked. What I'm thinking is this. They *wanted* you to see that."

From behind him, Carver said, "There is debate whether the aliens even have a thought process."

"And that's the problem," Sean said. "If you'd stop worrying so much about keeping the lid on transit powers and started looking at what is possible, you might actually learn something."

Baran stepped a fraction farther out into his own space. Chenel actually smiled. Tight, but approving. Sean smiled in response and went on, "Maybe when the aliens take over a human, they are able to do more than just control and duplicate. I'm thinking absorb. They study us from the inside."

"Then they reshape their tactics according to what they discover," Elenya said.

Carver said, "Permission to ask one question. Why did they let the Examiner go?"

Sean had been spending a lot of time on that one. "My guess is, they treated Tirian as a diversion from the beginning. He was sent back to be the guilty guy. Give the bureaucrats a reason to ignore the other evidence."

"Which you all did," Dillon said. "Which you all *wanted* to do."

Chenel said, "To answer your question, we didn't see anything before the blast."

"Why not?"

"Watchers cannot be on constant patrol. We would burn out in a matter of days. What your brother sensed is our standard mode of operation. One anchors, the others patrol."

"Sniper-spotter," Dillon said.

Sean waved that away. "Go on."

"We patrol, reach the limit, return, switch, go back."

That was what he was after. "The switch. How long does that take?"

"Theoretically, no time at all. But as I said, there are limits."

He could feel it all coming together. Finally. "These limits. Tell me about them."

"You understand the standard time measurement, yes? We are out for two standard units, we return for ten."

"Ten minutes on, fifty off," Elenya translated.

Chenel added, "Halved by two Watchers sharing duty."

Sean nodded his understanding. "So there are five units every cycle when there is no Watcher watching."

"Of course, that is assuming we don't eat or sleep. Which is why there are normally a minimum of six Watchers to a team," Chenel said, burning Carver with her own ire.

"The Counselor did not wish to give me any Watchers at all," Carver pointed out. "I worked with what I had."

"Sure. You guys did great." Dillon glared at Carver. "Thanks for nothing."

"Dillon."

"I'm just saying . . ." He huffed and went quiet.

Sean said to the Watchers, "So you weren't scoping when the attack happened."

"Baran went out just as your home was blasted. He saw that one." Chenel indicated Tirian.

"Because he was there," Dillon said. "All four of him."

"Baran didn't identify but one."

"Because they did not stay around and let you." Sean felt light as air, his mind dancing through the crystal clarity of seeing the scene as a unified whole. "They are aware of your presence. They know when you are watching. Which is why they come here, to Cyrius. Because transiters aren't welcome. And they've been checking on this place. Tight little Watcher forays all their own. Dillon's caught their scent."

Carver said, "I don't . . ."

Sean wasn't interested in getting the adults up to speed. There wasn't time for that anymore. He said to Carver, "Go to the security office and bring back Tatyana and Anyon."

"I'll go," Elenya said.

"No, let Carver. You and I need to talk."

When Carver left, Dillon asked, "So what do you have in mind?"

"Ambush," Sean replied.

Dillon grinned his approval. "Cowboys and Indians. I love it."

Elenya asked, "What does this mean?"

"Later," Sean replied, reaching for her hand. "Come with me."

As he drew Elenya back into the rear office, Dillon called after them, "You want me to take these two out on a circuit?"

"No, stay where you are."

"But—"

"Dillon, stay." Like he was talking to a stubborn dog.

The instant Sean shut the door, Elenya flowed into his arms. "You are an excellent leader."

He wanted to show his fear. His uncertainty. All the things he had to hide down deep in front of the others. But there wasn't time. The clock ticked as loud as his hammering heart. He kissed her, he breathed in her scent, then he released her and stepped back and said, "I need to tell you what I'm planning."

He led her over to a chair, moved his in close enough for their knees to touch, gripped both her hands with his. Trying to make a connection strong enough to let him communicate through osmosis. But he failed.

A half-dozen words were enough to strip away every vestige of happiness. She stared at him in horror. "This is suicide. It is madness!"

"I don't think so."

"You are willing to risk your life for this? You are willing to risk *us*?"

Sean watched her leap up and readied himself for the same onslaught she had directed at her father. She stood over him, breathing hard, eyes filled with tears. But she remained silent. So he asked, "Will you let me explain why this has to happen?"

Her nod was scarcely more than a shudder, just enough motion to dislodge a tear.

"Everything you say is true. I know that. I'm not going to pretend. The risk is real. But you know this needs doing, because it's the only reason you're letting me talk at all." He felt as though every word he spoke was another nail in his own coffin. But it had to be said. It had to be *done*.

Elenya replied, "Someone else can do this." The words were not loud, they were not angry. They were a musical moan. The Serenese chant was laced with the agony of a woman torn in two. "Someone better trained. Someone more experienced."

Sean did not reply.

"I want to *love* you. I want to *live* with you. I want *tomorrows* with you."

Sean used both hands to wipe his own face. "If I don't do this, I'll suffer the guilt of turning away from what I know I'm supposed to do. I'll carry that weight for the rest of my life. It would taint everything. Including us."

"You know this? How?"

"The night the aliens attacked us, Dillon had this idea. He said it felt like it had come from outside himself. That's exactly what happened to me with this."

"Describe that moment for me, Sean. When it came to you."

"I was leaving the prison. We were back down inside the transit room. And suddenly . . . it's like I walked into a cloud. A hundred images, all whispering to me at once. It wasn't just *how* I should do this thing. It was *why*."

"How did it feel?"

There was a new tone to her voice. A sense of hearing far more than his words. Sean lifted his head and saw that along with the horror was something new in her gaze. He hoped against hope that it was truly a hint of acceptance. "Like a flood of concepts, each one carrying a unique force, almost like I could taste and smell the images as well as see them. They just *arrived*. Like the whole idea had been waiting for me."

She groped blindly for the chair and slumped down. Sighed. Wiped her face with both hands. "That is how the records were discovered."

"Wait, you mean . . ."

"The story has become a part of my planet's legend. How the first adept realized there was an invisible repository that she could access by taking the impossible step."

Sean leaned back in his chair. Took a breath he feared might not come. Knowing he was not going to face this alone was a pleasure beyond exquisite. "I need your help, Elenya."

Her voice was resigned now, soft with love and defeat. "And I will do what you say."

All he could think to say was, "Thank you."

She reached for both his hands. They sat like that for a

time, linked by far more than flesh. Finally she said, "You have never asked about the planet where I first transited."

Her fingers were still damp, convicting him of the pain he'd caused this beautiful girl. Again. "You're right."

"It is called Helene. I was seven years old. I thought I had gone to paradise. Two of the three suns were above the horizon, one rising, the other setting. I stood on a shore. The sea looked like a liquid jewel." She wiped her face. "I have never told anyone about this before. Promise me we will go there together, Sean."

"As soon as this is done," he vowed, hoping against hope that the day might indeed soon be theirs to claim.

49

When Sean and Elenya emerged, they found Carver in the front room with Tatyana and the Ambassador in tow. One look at his daughter's tear-streaked face was enough to turn Anyon's mood fouler still. But all he said was, "We need to know there is a logical, definable purpose behind your desire for us to weaken our position."

"We're not weakening anything," Dillon retorted. "We're setting a trap."

Sean said, "We don't know when the next attack will come. We don't really know *anything* about them. Our knowledge has been restricted like everything else about the transit powers. The aliens are developing new tactics and we've remained stagnant. And unless we prepare for their new strategy, we risk losing another world."

Elenya's voice revealed her severely shaken state. "Father, he is correct. These are exceptional circumstances. And Sean is the man to work out our solution."

"You know this how?"

"Because he is an adept. He had an idea come to him from beyond. He says that it was as if he walked through a cloud of an idea. Do you remember hearing those words before, Father?"

The Ambassador was silent. Thoughtful. Intent. Behind him, Tatyana and Carver leaned closer, clearly drawn by Elenya's unexpected words. Sean glanced around the room. Baran, Chenel, Sandrine, all of them captivated by what Elenya was saying. And apparently very surprised.

Elenya went on, "They were part of my favorite stories while I was growing up. About the young woman who defied an entire planet and drew from nothing the records and the concepts that now shape our Assembly."

Anyon did not respond.

"Sean is an adept. You need to accept this. He has been given what may be a method to protect us, not just now but in the future. We need to pay attention and do what he says."

Sean resisted the urge to tell Elenya that she had sort of twisted the truth. The idea that had come to him wasn't so extensive, and wasn't about halting this particular attack, and wasn't . . . But he held his comments in check. Elenya was on a roll.

Anyon glanced once at Sean, but not long, as though he was too captured by this transformation in his daughter to give much weight to anything else. He asked, "What comes next?"

To her immense credit, Elenya replied, "That is for Sean to say."

Sean swallowed hard. What came next meant moving into the danger zone. "My brother needs to teach me how to hunt."

How do you do it?" Sean asked. "How do you release your-self?"

Dillon sat on the bed at the back of the clinic. He wrestled with the air before him, as he always did when he struggled to find the words. "I just . . . do it."

They could not bar the others from observing. But they could do their best to ignore their presence. Because they spoke English, Carver kept up a soft translation as Sean said, "Think back to the first hunt. Before it was natural. Take your time. No, don't look at the others. Forget them. It's just us now." Sean used the voice he applied when talking Dillon down from one of his schoolyard rages. Steady and calm. Giving him the space to focus. "Talk through it. I know it doesn't make sense. But we left logic behind a long time ago. Just relax and—"

"I sort of hunker down inside." Dillon stared at the blank white wall above Sean's head. Seeing only the event. "Deep down. Fit myself in a space that I make right there at the core."

"Where the power resides."

"Exactly there. I make a bubble like the one we've used to send thoughts, only tighter. And then I stick everything in there. Everything that's me." Dillon focused on his brother. "It's like I've already split from my body before I move."

"I understand," Sean said. And he did.

"Then I take a quick little right-hand turn. Just shift around. And step out. Like I step into a transit. Only I'm not using my feet because I don't have any." Dillon shrugged. "And I'm out."

Chenel said softly, "It took me months and months to learn what you just described."

But Sean didn't have months. He probably didn't have hours. He needed to do this now. He asked Elenya, "Will you anchor me?"

She was beyond solemn. "Will you take care? Will you come back to me?"

"Yes to both."

"Then of course I will."

He waited while she fashioned the invisible belt, then said to Carver, "You'll need to spot my brother, since that's been my job."

When Dillon translated for Carey, she asked, "Can I do that?"

"Later," Dillon replied, the affection crystal clear in that one word. "Soon. Right now you can time us."

"Okay," Sean said. "Let's go for it."

The first time was a lot scarier than Sean had expected. The moment of bodily separation felt too much like a small death. Sean's brain registered an animal panic, like he was underwater and only a second or so from drowning. But he formed the bubble and scrunched down, cramming all that he was inside, just like Dillon had described. Then he wrenched himself free.

As soon as he was out and hovering beside himself, the fear was gone. Like it had never existed. He had one brief instant to look down to where Elenya rested a hand upon his arm. Her affection radiated out and around them both, a unique form of shielding. Sean had never realized until this very moment that her love had a color all its own.

Then he turned to where Dillon hovered, waiting. Sean crossed the mental distance and connected with his brother. He had a fleeting sense of bonding with a fabric of emotion and genetic makeup that linked them in a unique fashion. Love and anger and frustration and all the impossible sentiments from growing through lives that were both individual and joined. Dillon must have felt the same, for he paused in the process of launching. He offered Sean a bodiless version of the warrior's grin. The schoolyard knight off to save the world. Sean was filled with the familiar surge of exasperation and pride and affection.

Then Dillon took aim. And they flew.

Walls meant nothing. Or space. Dillon aimed and they went. Sean's brother hunted like a bird of prey. Like he had been doing it all his life. Dillon swooped down the center of the station, a long, swift glide. As they moved, he turned them in a slow circle so their attention went out in every direction. Wherever he aimed, his attention was crystal, vivid, pinpoint. Dillon noted incoming and outgoing trains. Exits. Chambers. People. All of it in swift glimpses.

Gradually Sean overcame the newness and the sensory overload and focused with his brother. As soon as that happened, he sensed the wrongness. Whether it came through Dillon or he tasted it himself, Sean could not say. But it was definitely there. The lingering fragrance played over him like an acid mist. Fraying his shield in tiny gasps of wrongness.

They reached the far end of the station, and Dillon wheeled about, readying for the return. Instantly Sean saw the anchor's importance. The destination was unmistakable. Elenya's touch on his arm and her surrounding affection were beacons that guided him with a sureness so intense he was able to release his hold on Dillon and fly alone. Taking himself home.

He opened his eyes. Felt the gasping pleasure of breathing in and out. Reconnected with his body. Life coursing through him. Alive and there with the woman he was coming not just to care for but to *see*.

Elenya asked, "Are you all right?"

Sean took exquisite delight in sitting up, reaching out with his arms, and holding her. The moment was too intense to allow the smiles and gazes of others to intrude. He whispered, "I saw your love."

He felt her shift her face where his shoulder met his neck, and knew she was wiping away tears. Knew also it was not his return that frightened her so. But what this success meant. What was now going to happen.

Sean held her until she was ready to let him go. He made a process of settling her in close beside him, holding her hand, then asking, "How long were we gone?"

Carey replied, "Three minutes, sixteen seconds."

"Dillon, is it always that way, the scent?"

"Or taste, whatever. Yeah, that's how it seems."

"But they're not around now, right?"

"I'm pretty sure they haven't been back in a while."

"Me too." He turned to where Carver stood with Anyon and Tatyana. "Okay. This means the aliens have been here. Inside the station. Several times."

Anyon was clearly a man struggling with internal conflict. He wanted to doubt and dismiss, and at the same time he desperately wanted to raise the alarm. "You're certain?"

"Yes," Dillon said. "We are."

Sean only told the Watchers the absolute minimum. "You need to hold your hunts to the shortest possible time. I think this scent we've found is there because the aliens are making their own quick forays. They dart in, check things out, and leave before we detect them."

"And that's what you need to do," Dillon said. "Every time."

"Faster than us if you can," Sean said. "Just long enough to catch the scent and make sure they haven't come back. Then return."

Chenel looked at her partner. "Who is up?"

"You," Baran replied.

Dillon shifted off his bunk. As Chenel took his place, she said, "Describe to me what I'm seeking."

"Best not," Dillon replied.

"Go out there and see for yourself," Sean added. "Something this important, you need to decide without any prompts from me whether it's real."

Chenel moved slowly. Carefully. As though already practicing the caution of a tracker entering Indian country on a solitary foray.

Baran fashioned the invisible belt, then took station by her shoulder. One finger of one hand resting on Chenel's arm. "Ready."

Chenel shut her eyes. Sighed. And went still.

The entire room held its breath.

Ninety seconds and several eons passed. Then Chenel breathed again. Sat up. Looked at Carver. "Colonel, Counselor, Ambassador, I ask that you note the time."

Carver was the only one who moved. "Noted."

"Senior Watcher Chenel hereby gives official notice that the aliens have been here. We must assume they were scouting for an attack. I therefore urge you to raise the alarm."

51

Nothing happened for almost an hour. Carver explained, "There is resistance from some quarters, even with the Watcher's confirmation."

"Resistance," Dillon said. "Imagine that."

"They're asking a senior Watcher to come and confirm. Her name is Insgar."

Chenel, Baran, and Elenya all showed the same response to Carver's news. Shock and awe.

Dillon asked, "Who exactly is Insgar?"

"A legend," Elenya replied.

"The Watcher's Academy is named for her," Chenel said.

While they waited, they moved house. Sean didn't want to risk alerting the aliens. Two swift forays, one by Dillon and the other by Baran, confirmed there was no hint of alien presence beyond the station's confines. So they took over a café that occupied a small structure between the station and the thoroughfare. Sean's only glimpse of Cyrius was of a twilight snowfall. A few lights flickered through the wintry mist. A brief taste of alien air. And he was inside, the shutters drawn, the world outside lost once more. But Elenya saw his disappointment and moved in close long enough to whisper, "Soon."

Then they brought in the woman. She was the most ancient person Sean had ever met, a tiny stick of wrinkles and folds. The only things truly alive about Insgar were her gaze and her voice. She peered at them from a padded chair that moved without wheels, two attendants in tow. One wore a Guards' uniform, the other was dressed in white. Everyone treated her with great deference, including Ambassador Anyon. But she ignored them with the silent impatience of someone who had no time for inconsequentials.

The old woman waved her attendants away, took a slow breath, shut her eyes, and went still. The café was home now to several dozen people, most of whom probably had no business being there. But Sean's ability to command adults was as limited as ever. So he waited with the others, scarcely breathing.

Insgar opened her eyes, scanned the group, and asked in a voice made toneless by her years, "Where is the adept?"

Carver indicated Sean. "This one has shown the clearest evidence, Mistress. But there are indications that both twins move well beyond what we could class as normal abilities."

She waved them closer. Sean wondered whether they should bow or something, but decided simply to stand as erect as he could manage. Insgar inspected them with eyes that glittered fiercely. "Gifted and handsome both. Where is your home world?"

"Earth, Mistress," Sean replied. "An outpost planet."

She gave a fractional nod. "Which one of you first discovered the aliens?"

Ambassador Anyon demanded, "So you confirm their presence?"

She glanced at him, the swift look enough to silence him. Sean liked her all the more for that act. When Insgar turned back, Sean replied, "It was my brother. Dillon."

"Actually, it was both of us," Dillon countered. "Sean is the one with ideas."

"Not all of them," Sean replied. "Not that time."

She liked the exchange. How Sean could tell when there was no change to her expression, he had no idea. She spoke Serenese with a crisp cadence that belied her age. "Two adepts. Is it true what I hear, you can link your thoughts?"

"That move was definitely Sean's," Dillon replied.

Her eyes drifted over the silent throng, halting where Elenya stood next to Carey. "These are your mates?"

Sean hated how he was unable to stop his face from reddening. "We are trying to make it work."

Insgar lifted one hand and motioned. Elenya and Carey stepped forward. Sean noticed they were holding hands. The simple act warmed him immensely.

Insgar asked, "You can transit?"

"I can, Mistress," Elenya replied. "This one is from their home world."

She inspected them a moment longer. "You are up to the task of caring for adepts?"

Elenya translated for Carey, who nodded. Elenya looked at Sean and replied, "I will try, Mistress."

"You understand what I am saying, yes?"

For some reason, the question brought tears to Elenya's eyes. "I do, Mistress."

"Good. They need you both. More than any of these others will ever understand."

Elenya translated again, and Carey turned and looked at Dillon, her gaze molten.

Insgar nodded her approval. "You have a plan?"

"Sean does," Elenya replied. "He has been touched by the cloud of records."

Sean added, "Dillon was too."

Insgar said, "But you are the dominant one. The one who looks beyond the bend of time. Correct?"

Sean wanted to disagree, but Dillon said firmly, "Absolutely."

Insgar turned to the Ambassador. "I want you to listen carefully."

"Of course, Mistress. I am—"

"The adepts are correct. The aliens have changed tactics. They have made forays. Do as this one says. This world may yet survive." She did not wait for a response but instead turned back to Sean. "When this is over and we have won, you will come and visit me. We will have much to discuss."

52

Reluctantly Sean and Dillon accepted the presence of three more teams of Watchers. But only after authority for the newcomers was transferred to Chenel. The lady was one of them now and understood the need to maintain the lightning-fast forays. She monitored the newcomers until she was certain they both understood the gravity of her orders and obeyed. Sean did not speak with them at all. That first day, he stayed busy trying to teach Elenya how to hunt.

She was a remarkable student, though the process did not come natural, and Sean doubted she would ever find this a comfortable task. Elenya listened with her customary gravity, tried, and failed. Time after time they went through the motions, until they were both too exhausted to continue. She did not grow angry. Frustrated, yes. And her comments certainly took on a very crisp edge. But she swallowed her ire better than Sean ever could and kept at it.

The café now served as headquarters for Sean's team. He

and Elenya used what had previously been the café's office, where they dragged in a futon and laid it in a corner. Mobile residences were hooked up to serve as bunkrooms and showers and kitchen. Their café was now rimmed by more temporary structures that housed a growing number of people and equipment. Sean did his best to ignore them all. Having the job of teaching Elenya to fly without her body was an excellent way to stay focused.

That night he and Dillon shared a sleeping room, with the girls bunked next door. Before they cut off the light, Sean watched Dillon reach out and touch the wall separating him from Carey. As he did so, there was a soft knock from the other side.

Sean asked, "Have you tried the spook-speak with her?"

"All the time."

"And?"

"No contact with thoughts. But sometimes when she, you know . . ."

"Reaches out to you in love. I know."

"You too?"

"When we took off yesterday, I saw this light or something around Elenya."

"Carey calls it an aura."

"That's it." He smiled into the room's utter dark. Overhead the heating unit gave off a comforting hum. "I used that as my beacon coming back."

"Nothing better. Sorry, bro, but I'd much rather aim for Carey than you."

"Like I want to keep holding your hand one second longer."

Dillon rolled over. "Sean."

"Yo."

"You're planning something. Tell me I'm wrong."

Sean did not reply.

"You going to talk about it?"

"Elenya knows."

"Oh, is that so? And just exactly when were you going to share it with your wingman?"

"Wingman. I like that." And he did. A lot.

"And?"

"I needed to work out some things first. Like bringing Elenya on board. And making sure I could hunt."

"So you'll tell me tomorrow?"

"First thing."

"Good." A moment's silence, then, "And we're doing this together, right?"

Sean let his eyes drift shut. Satisfied and comforted both. "Wouldn't have it any other way."

***

Over breakfast the next morning, Sean explained what he had in mind. His brother was far easier to convince than Sean had dared hope. Carey was horrified, but Elenya's strong grip on her hand kept Carey silent.

Dillon only had one question. "It came to you like the hunt concept did with me?"

"Like it was a cloud of an idea, and I just walked through it," Sean confirmed.

"Then that's it," Dillon said.

Carey could not hold back any longer. "Are you serious?"

He gave a warrior's shrug, equal parts determination and grim humor. "If I had told you I was going to leave my body and go for a walkabout, what would you have said?"

"This is different!"

"Absolutely." Dillon was adamant. "This is one step further. And it's the right thing to do."

Elenya demanded, "You truly think this?"

"Totally." Dillon checked the wall readout. "We're up in five."

Elenya slipped into the place Dillon vacated. She pushed his breakfast tray to one side and reached for Sean's hand. "About the hunting exercise. Perhaps I should accept this is not for me and—"

"I had an idea last night. Something that might help." He explained what he had in mind.

Elenya gave him that look. The one where she opened her gaze and allowed him to see her hidden depths. "Whether or not it works, I like very much that you try to help me like this."

They stayed like that, holding hands across the table, until Dillon came for them. Sean felt Elenya's concern pass through her fingers and into his frame. He knew she was worried about what he intended to try later on, but there was nothing he could do about it. He wanted to tell her it was all going to work out. He wanted to say a thousand things. But this was no time for lies.

...

The café's main areas had been split into three sections. The largest was where they had breakfasted, what Chenel and Baran called the ready room. Beside that was the duty chamber. Up by the front door was a smaller room with two desks and a couple of chairs. Carver or Josef or Tirian manned that position and kept most of the others from setting foot inside. This became an increasingly difficult job with every passing hour, but not for Tirian. The former Examiner stopped traffic with his scowl.

Before he settled onto the duty room's couch, Sean shifted the curtains and looked out at the growing horde that surrounded them.

Dillon said, "I wonder how the Cyrian authorities are explaining this buildup."

Sean nodded to the snow-flecked glass. He thought his reflection looked scared. But there was nothing he could do about it, so he focused farther out, where the former park between the café and the main station was now jammed with equipment and mobile units and people.

Dillon went on, "Police carnival, maybe. Public display of angry egos. Has to be something."

Carver entered the room and asked simply, "Ready?"

"Absolutely." Dillon settled into the padded station and smiled at Carey. "Matter of fact, Sean is ready to take his own watch now. He's good to go."

Sean looked over. His and Dillon's pallets were separated by a low table holding a comm link and an alarm button, and the chairs for Carver and Carey and Elenya. He said, "I need to be sure we're in total sync for phase two."

Dillon offered a mimic of Carver's swift smile. "So why don't you take lead?"

"I like how things are."

Dillon snorted. "As if any of this was about what you *like*."

"Good point."

"So you take the hunt, I'll follow along." Dillon reached for Carey's hand, shared a look with his lady, then shut his eyes. "Carver?"

"Ready when you are."

Sean discovered a subtle pleasure in taking the lead position. He followed Dillon's pattern, though everything he did was somewhat clumsier. He tried to hold to his brother's speed and agility but knew he fumbled the job. Even so, Dillon stayed with him, searching where he missed, letting Sean grow comfortable with being the guy up front.

As soon as they returned and reported no change, Sean drew Elenya into the former office, settled her into position, and repeated his idea for how he might help her learn to hunt. He knew she didn't need to hear the instructions a second time. But he could also see that she liked him forming this verbal link.

Sean suspected she might be held back by the same terror he no longer felt. The panic attack that every new Watcher most likely faced could be the deciding factor of who actually graduated into their ranks. Sean imagined those who were least comfortable with their own world and physical life were also those who made it easiest through the fear barrier. Who let go and accepted the small death. Who could roam free. And hunt.

His idea was simple enough. Focus the energy at the core of his being and distill it through his feelings. Try his best to push aside all the nervous chatter, the pressure, the worries, the uncertainties, his own fears, everything but the chance to give this amazing woman what she deserved. All he had that was good and his to give. As she settled down and breathed and tried to still her fears, he fashioned his shield into a link and poured everything that might help create both calm and confidence . . .

And she was gone.

He could actually feel it happen. Like she had moved *beyond* him. That she was with him no longer.

And with a terrible start, he realized for the very first time what it would mean to lose her.

He knew there was no logic to this. But they had long since entered a realm where logic held no sway. Sean watched her lay there, silent and scarcely breathing, and suffered through a glimpse of the inevitable. That even if they succeeded in fashioning a life together, even if they lived all their days as one, someday she would depart. And she would not return.

Elenya sighed softly, opened her eyes, and asked, "Why are you crying?"

By the third day they had settled into a routine, and words like *cramped* and *boring* filtered back into their conversations. Elenya started making forays beyond the café perimeter. She visited with her father, mending fences, checking on the pulse of the mini-city growing up around them. Their little structure had become the center of a human whirlwind, even though most of the real tornado was off-world. The bureaucrats grew increasingly frustrated and resentful of being kept out of the loop. Which of course was ridiculous. Every Watcher reported in as soon as they returned. What the authorities meant was, they hated not being in control. And since Sean couldn't do anything about that, he wouldn't even talk to them. Even when Tatyana asked nicely. There was too much risk of giving in, and he couldn't afford that. None of them could. Everything depended on maintaining the status quo. And hoping they would hold on to the element of surprise.

Much as Sean chafed at their confinement, he couldn't

just leave. As Dillon put it, they were the ones who brought everybody to the dance. The station and its perimeter were now on a battle footing. There was no such thing as a day off. They were on full alert, even when sitting around watching the clock count down the Cyrian equivalent of seconds like a miser handing over gold.

But they could make temporary escapes.

That evening, Earth time, Dillon and Carey slipped away for a meal with her father. When they came back, Sean and Elenya followed suit. Elenya seemed thrilled with John's backyard grill, the roast chicken, the potatoes. It was amazing to watch her get excited over coleslaw. And raspberry iced tea — she actually moaned with pleasure over that one. It felt great to laugh, to share with John all that was happening, to feel a momentary freedom from the grim cadence of waiting.

The fourth day passed. And the fifth. On the sixth, the Cyrian leaders tried to insist on bringing Insgar back. The old woman was the last remaining Watcher who had survived an alien attack, and had been one of those responsible for tracking the aliens when they tried to spread via the transiters' occupied bodies to other worlds. She had led the Watcher's Academy for almost thirty years.

Insgar informed the Cyrian delegation they would ignore Sean's instructions at their peril, and sent them packing.

The sixth day gave way to the seventh, and the eighth. The disjointed meals with John and the few fleeting moments they could enjoy in the loft became a highlight of each passing day and kept the rising tension at bay, at least partly.

On the ninth day, everything changed.

54

A third couch had been brought into the duty room. Elenya was hunting with them now. Josef served as her anchor. She held back, staying firmly attached to Dillon's side. She did not venture out, nor did she ever express any real affection for the experience. She did it because she wanted to share in every aspect of Sean's world. And he loved her more for doing so.

Elenya's real duties lay elsewhere. With every passing day, her role as go-between became more vital. Carver related the arguments and the egos and the maneuverings. Josef then described observing Elenya handle the Cyrian leader's strident demands to be placed in charge. Both men smiled through their tales, taking evident pride in this woman coming into her own.

The one point over which the planet's rulers refused to budge was the station. Sean wanted it closed. The Cyrians would not even discuss it. Elenya's arguments got them nowhere, particularly because the Praetorian officers weren't certain it was a good idea. If the plan was indeed to pretend at normality, the station needed to look normal. Which required passengers and trains and business as usual. Elenya's urgent plea to create a fake power outage or rail problem fell on deaf ears. The bureaucrats spoke of public calm. The officers used terms like *collateral damage*. Sean tried hard not to loathe them all.

Sean had hardly seen Elenya the previous day, save for their hunting sessions and a hurried meal with John. All her remaining hours were spent on outside duty. Playing mediator. Keeping them isolated. Shielding them with the force of her will.

On the afternoon of day nine, she was so late getting back they almost left without her. When she finally appeared, Sean stifled Dillon's comment with a look that would have done Tatyana proud.

Elenya looked both drawn and angry, but all she said upon lying down was, "I'm ready."

They rose, linked, and passed through the station wall.

Sean froze eight inches inside the station. Less.

Under other circumstances, it probably would have been comic, how he managed to halt Dillon and Elenya by reaching out arms he didn't have and gripping them with hands that were back inside the former café. They both stopped, though, which was all that mattered.

Their entry point was the back of a kiosk that sold the veggie wraps, which had become their favorite Cyrian meal. They drifted behind and above the workers, watching the traveling hordes pass before their eyes.

A single instant was enough to be certain. Even so, Sean remained there a time. Scouring the distance, searching for the precise point of change. Once he identified it, he drew the others up and focused them on the location. Making sure they saw and understood.

The instant they returned, the very moment they opened their eyes and swung their feet to the floor, the entire world was filled with the tension they carried.

Carver demanded, "What is it?"

"Go get Chenel and Baran," Sean said. "Hurry."

When the Watchers arrived, Sean was seated on the same bunk as Dillon and Elenya, the three of them clustered together for strength and warmth, for they all felt chilled by the tense dread of having gotten it right. "Dillon, you tell them."

"You saw it first."

"You're better at all this. Go."

Dillon took a breath. "Take up position inside the kiosk. Don't move farther. Aim at the gate that is five degrees off directly overhead. There are three empty tracks. Right there inside the gate. That is your target."

Chenel asked, "What are we looking for?"

"You tell us," Sean replied.

"Go," Elenya said. "Hurry."

Chenel was back in three minutes flat. She rose, rubbed her face, then said, "I confirm their findings."

Carver protested, "They didn't say what they identified."

"They don't need to. Sound the alarm."

55

I t's like a jagged-edged hole into nowhere," Chenel said.

They gathered in the ready room because one of the other Watcher teams was out now. A team would be constantly observing from this point on, stationed by the kiosk that had become their blind. Sean sat with Elenya and Dillon and Carey, his back against the outer wall. Night had fallen and he could feel the cold through the window above his head. Blasts of wind drove tiny ice pellets against the glass. Sean decided he liked the season. Somehow it fit.

He let Chenel do the talking. She was one of them, but she was also a recognized senior Watcher. As far as all the authorities gathered in this room were concerned, Sean's own position remained in question. The leader of Cyrius was with them, along with a bevy of senior staffers, Ambassador Anyon, Tatyana, Carver, Josef, and a clutch of Praetorian officers. They shot Sean tight looks now and then. Taking his measure. Waiting for him to open his mouth. But Sean had no interest in becoming anyone's target. He sat and drifted. Whatever satisfaction he might have felt over getting it right was lost to the tension and the fatigue and the dread.

Chenel went on, "The first thing you notice is that the flavor of the station has shifted."

The Cyrian leader was an aristocratic woman with a grave bearing that matched the Ambassador's. "Define *flavor*."

"That is the accepted description for a Watcher," Carver said.

"There are records from the last several invasions," Tatyana added. "Ever since Watchers came into being. They all speak of a shift in the atmosphere, one they call *flavor*. Or *scent*."

The Cyrian leader accepted this with a terse nod and said to Chenel, "Continue."

"They have come and gone. I counted four recent forays."

"I saw six," Dillon said. "Each leaves a trail. Green. Like slime."

"I saw no colors," Chenel said.

"I did," Elenya replied.

"There will be time for comparisons later," Ambassador Anyon said, but without heat. "Go on."

Chenel motioned at Dillon with a jerk of her chin. "You tell."

"It looks like a flower that's opening. Green fire around the edges."

One of the Cyrian elders complained, "I have just walked through the station and noted nothing amiss."

"It's there," Chenel said.

"You don't need to see it," Dillon said. "That's why you have us. To see for you."

The Cyrians squinted angrily at Dillon. Dillon glanced at Sean and gave him another of those patented Carver-type smiles. Gone so fast it might not even have existed.

Dillon went on, "The flower or whatever you want to call it is an opening to the dark side."

Chenel said, "These new forays we detected were probably them checking up, making sure the station remains unprotected."

The Cyrian leader asked, "Is this standard practice prior to an invasion?"

"We have no idea." Tatyana had the decency to look at Sean as she spoke. "Never before have we known this level of advance notice."

All eyes tracked to Sean and stayed there. Finally Ambassador Anyon asked, "What do you suggest as our next step?"

Sean felt uncomfortable with the attention, but he knew what had to be said. "Ready the troops. Be sure to set up a secondary perimeter around the outside of the station, in case they break through."

The leader said, "Should we evacuate?"

Sean was about to urge them to do just that when a shriek arose from the duty room. The scream wrenched them all, a great cry of mortal distress. On and on it went, long enough for them to unfreeze and rush in and see the Watcher flail against the hold of her anchor.

Her limbs were not her own, that was how it seemed to Sean. Like she was a human form wrapped around something else. And that something was flooding into her, gripping every shred of her physical form with a convulsive force.

She flung her spotter across the room. The man weighed close to twice what she did, and he flew eighteen feet before crashing into the far corner. She did not rise from the bed. She catapulted to the side wall. And clung there. Snarling.

Sean looked into the face of death. The alien growled at him, taking in the scope of their planning and their intentions. And screamed again, this time in utter fury at the attack being exposed.

Tirian's blow was the first to slam into her. Then Josef, and Carver, and finally Dillon. Gripping the alien with invisible fists, squeezing out the alien life-form, and then striking the enemy with blasts of ice and fury.

Within the space of a dozen heartbeats, it was over. The woman fell to the floor. Inert.

Tirian leapt over the demolished comm link and touched her neck. "We have a pulse."

Carver fumbled through the wreckage, found the button, and slammed his fist onto the alarm.

56

All the station's doors were flung wide open. The alarm sounded throughout the vast building. The noise was deafening.

But no one inside the station knew what it meant.

The alarm had not sounded in over a generation. And never on Cyrius.

Most of the people simply froze where they were. And waited. Holding their ears. Trying to shout questions at whatever official was closest.

At Carver's directions, the generals and the Cyrian military formed wedges and powered through the doors.

Even with all their advance work, they were almost too late. The aliens were *fast*.

Sean and Dillon and Carey and Elenya entered behind the official formation, linked by clenched hands. They held to the outside wall and moved to a position that gave them a clear sight of the unfolding attack. Two minutes later, Chenel and Baran came racing up. Agape at the horror on display.

Sean thought it was like watching a high-speed virus invade a body. The aliens poured into the station through the portal that was now clearly visible. The aperture to another realm opened like a flower of death. The invading aliens spread with incredible swiftness, a greenish, translucent tide. They were not entirely visible. It was like viewing a confusing scene through heat waves. The aperture itself continued to expand, a fracture in the human realm.

The first Praetorian Guards who arrived froze in shock. It was easy to understand why. The aliens massed in a swirling mob that grew with exponential speed. Everything and everyone in their scope was consumed. The sight was both savage and gigantic. In the petrified space of a few seconds, there were so many aliens they formed a putrid cloud. The churning mass was lit from within by great roaring flashes, lightning bolts of furious pleasure.

Perhaps the one event that saved them, the first finger in the dike, was Tirian.

All the civilians screamed with one voice and rushed for the exits. Tirian's shield deflected one panic-stricken human after another. It was doubtful Tirian saw any of this. He moved with the single-minded purpose of a man who had finally, against all odds, been granted a chance for vengeance.

Against the surging human tide moved this lone individual, sucking up the fury and the fear, fashioning a huge ball of force that he flung into the alien mob.

Tirian might not have been the first to blast the aliens. But he was most certainly the first to take the battle to them. He raced forward, flinging one great bolt after another. His lone force was enough to slow the surging chaotic mass. At least, he did so for an instant.

Then the aliens counterattacked.

Streaks of green lightning blasted Tirian, over and over, halting him in his tracks. He fought back with single-minded fury. But the aliens gathered and formed an oval menace that swarmed over him. And ate away his shield.

Sean and his friends watched in horror as Tirian's shield melted under the onslaught. They saw Tirian react in shock as the first gap appeared in his shield, rimmed by the deadly green fire. A drop of electric acid oozed through the opening. Tirian screamed and jerked. But there was no escape. His shield was now his cage.

Then he gathered himself. Drawing in everything, all the force that was around him, a great heaving breath that even included the acid of death.

And he exploded. A blast of force so great it actually halted the aliens.

And galvanized the Praetorians into full assault mode.

57

The great bonging alarms now alternated with a recorded voice telling everyone to evacuate the station. Trains froze where they were, and all the doors flew open. Even so, some people still milled about in confused panic. After all, the Cyrians had known both peace and stability for decades. Only when they saw the alien swarm did they try to flee. But by then it was too late.

The swirling enemy overwhelmed the station's upper left quadrant, consuming all it came into contact with. The Praetorian Guard assaulted in a shock wave of fury. Carver led one contingent, Josef another. The Guards poured in now through numerous transit points. Instantly they were shouted into formation and sent on the attack.

The Guards fashioned a net of force that stretched over the entire alien mob, a wall between the humans and the enemy. The enemy attacked the net in a swirling mass of fury, like a poisonous stream seeking a conduit, an opening.

There was a subtle shift in the station's atmosphere, a grim hesitation in the onslaught of death and destruction. The Guards' barrier was being eaten away in a multitude of places. Each new hole was rimmed by the same green fire as the portal through which they continued to surge. Each grew into another flower of death. And through them flowed a new wave of attackers. Humans who were humans no more.

At their lead was a female in torn shreds of clothing, a slobbering beast that loped down the slanted wall on all fours. With each of her howls she released a gob of green fire, all of her projectiles aimed at the Guards. She duplicated as she ran, first two, then four, then an entire squad of howling mimics. Their fireballs struck the Guards' shields and clung and ate and burned and finally worked through. When they did, the Guards within had time for one terrorized scream of their own. Then they faced the same choice as Tirian. Many of those assaulted were too close to their fellow Guards to blast away. Those who did not went rigid, they howled, and they went on the attack.

Hordes of the tormented and their duplicates spilled out, leaping, flaming, racing. The noise rose and rose. The station was a battle zone now. And still the enemy's numbers grew.

But so did the Guards. They split and re-formed into tighter units, each squad small enough now to take personal responsibility for all the others in their group.

The battle flashed and flamed, while a new battalion formed by the far wall and began building a new power net, a barrier to hem in the swarming aliens and their replicates. The Guards flowed in through a dozen transit points now, hundreds of new troops arriving with each passing minute.

The fight was a close-run thing. When the turning came, Sean momentarily feared he was merely hoping for a shift. But within a few breaths he could see that the aliens were in retreat. Snarling, vicious, still inflicting casualties. But their surge had been stemmed. The battle was swaying now in favor of the human race.

Sean turned to the others. He saw that they knew, and they feared for him. He shouted it anyway. "It's time."

To their immense credit, they all nodded and transited with him.

The semi-wrecked duty room was cramped and uncomfortable with all the tension. Chenel and Baran had followed them back, and no one had the heart to tell them to leave. Sean saw the realization dawn on both their faces of what he was going to try. They made no attempt to disguise their horror. But at least they did not object.

Nor, astonishingly, did Elenya. She gripped his face with hands so tight she dug into the flesh of his neck and temples. But Sean did not mind. Nor did he mind the tears. Nor the fierceness of her voice, nor the fear in her words. "You will *come back to me*. Do you understand?"

"I do."

"You will *not* make me live alone." She shook his head, hard enough to hurt, and yet he felt nothing but comfort. "Tell me!"

"I love you, Elenya."

She kissed him, fierce as her grip. Then she released his

head and fashioned his invisible belt. She took hold of his arm, folding down over him. So close her tears fell on his hand. But she did not speak. She did not protest. Nor did she make a sound as she wept.

Sean looked over to where Dillon was stretched out on the opposite couch. "Ready?"

"For hours," he replied, reaching for Carey's hand.

Carey gripped him tightly. "Don't you need Carver?"

"Just hold my hand," Dillon told Carey. "Everything's good."

Chenel declared, "I must come."

Sean did not object. He did not point out that she actually didn't know for certain what he intended. Instead he merely asked, "Are you sure?"

She swallowed hard. "I am."

"You will serve as Dillon's wingman. You stay one fraction behind him. Linked to him like he is to me. Ready to make the move back. Drawing us with you."

She swallowed again. "Understood."

Sean turned back to his brother. "Dillon."

"Oh man, don't get all gushy on me, okay?"

"Thanks."

"You can thank me when this is over." Dillon shut his eyes. "I am three seconds from out of here."

Elenya released Sean long enough to fashion a second belt around Dillon. She gripped both one-handed and retook her fierce hold on Sean.

Sean asked, "Baran?"

"Chenel is belted."

Elenya kissed him again, tenderly this time. "Tell me what you are going to do."

"Make this happen. Come home. To you."

"I'm waiting here," Dillon said.

Sean shut his eyes. "Let's go."

59

The alien swarm had divided into eight different segments, with two Guards battalions fighting each. One group of troops maintained the shield barrier while the other attacked. The station was filled with great billowing surges of Praetorian force and green lightning blasts and the shrieks of the remaining possessed. But their numbers were lessening, and another four battalions cornered them and squeezed them and then destroyed the remaining aliens.

The station was holed in several places, great gaping fissures through which the snow fell and the flanking maneuvers could be seen. The sky was lit with battle and the air filled with the shrieks of the dying enemy.

Only one position remained unguarded. One place where the aliens could go. Back into the portal. Back where they had first swarmed through. And it was toward this point that Sean headed.

Sean would never have defined himself as brave. At that

moment, he was too scared to even spell *courage*. But he moved forward. Even when he could no longer remember why.

He had space for one coherent thought as he started forward, followed by Dillon and the Watcher.

Paradigm shift.

It was something from math class, his least favorite subject. The teacher had repeated those two words over and over. *Paradigm shift.* Moving outside the safety zone of logic and established rules. Ignoring the safe step-by-step procedure of whatever came next. Going off the rails. Changing the world in the process.

Sean hovered and searched for his target. Then Dillon shocked him into next week. His brother moved up and gripped Sean. Since Dillon had no arms, he used what was available—a warrior's fierce emotions. Loyalty and determination and aggressive, hardened pride. And love.

Then Dillon released him and shifted back.

And Sean was ready.

When viewed in this bodiless state, the mass of aliens looked entirely different. Which was why Sean was here. He had known this the instant the cloud spoke to him. That was how he recalled it. The impossible gift of communication from a timeless state, shifted into images he could fathom in the here and now.

The enemy's individual forms were much clearer now, like translucent jellyfish filled with venomous intent and the power to move at blinding speeds. The aliens were laced by violent shades of green and ochre, tight lines of force that shimmered and shifted with amazing swiftness. The alien portal was larger now, a great gaping hole laced in green fire, like it was intent upon eating its way into the core of the human world.

Then one of the battalion's nets dissolved, and the aliens spilled out, a heaving body of surging fury. Aimed straight for the portal. Fleeing. And the Guards let them go. Sean assumed the net's opening was intentional, to see if they would retreat. As soon as the Guards witnessed the blast of recoiling aliens, all the other nets revealed small holes on the side closest to the aliens' portal.

Sean drifted forward, a disembodied witness to the salvation of a planet. Intent not upon this battle or this world. But rather helping his civilization prepare for the next time.

His civilization.

The thought was enough to commit.

A lone alien swam past, much closer than the others. Flying so fast Sean almost missed his chance. Almost, but not quite.

He dove forward.

Into the alien.

The suspicions that had come with the cloud's images proved correct. The alien's shield did not halt him. Sean's bodiless state granted him the same ability to invade as the aliens.

Sean was overwhelmed by a myriad of impossible impressions. The energy he had witnessed coursing within the swarm was in fact their method of communication. And yet there was no leader. He knew this, just as he knew that the alien had sent out a panic alarm. Just as he knew the aliens had stopped their progress toward the portal. All of them. And turned toward him.

Sean saw the communication link did not begin with any of their number. Instead, it was emitted by the portal itself. A fierce awareness burned through now, hunting, hunting. Taking aim with a ferocity that left him utterly frozen. Incapable of thought, motion, response.

The electric communication between aliens burned away his host. The alien within which he had imbedded himself was gone. And still the lines coursed and lashed him, strong as razor whips. Tearing away his shield, his mind, his being.

He was lost.

Then the belt jerked him away.

As Sean was swept back, his vision cleared sufficiently to watch Dillon fashion a weapon of his own. He was glad for the chance to observe his brother come into his own. Dillon breached forty centuries of staid resistance to change and growth. He drew into himself all the lashing lines of communication and vengeance and force, turning them into one great, huge, massive . . .

Hammer.

Dillon turned their own force against them. He swung the great mallet of power and wrath in a huge arc, mowing through the aliens, stopping them in their tracks.

The last thing Sean saw was Josef and Carver leading a force of Guards, two flanking arms that rose up and surged forward, flaming the air with power of their own.

Then the darkness swept him up, and he was gone.

60

The face that greeted Sean when he opened his eyes was hardly the one he wanted. Sandrine bent over him, grave and professionally concerned. "Can you hear me?"

"Yes." His mouth tasted foul. "Water."

She fitted in a straw, let him drink, then held up her free hand and asked, "How many fingers do you see?"

"Oh, let the lad be. Move aside! You poke and prod me enough for ten patients!" The face that replaced Sandrine's was ancient and seamed and smiling. "Hello, lad. Remember me?"

The name swam up through the depths. "Insgar."

"Those dolts wanted to take you to the Praetorian Academy. Lock you away in some tower. Nothing to see but a continent of ruin and black rock. Idiots, the lot of them. I am two hundred and twenty-seven years old by Serenese reckoning. Do you know how I have survived this long?"

"Where is Elenya?"

"Eating a well-deserved meal. Pay attention. I survived, lad, by taking time for pleasure! And joy! Though both have been redefined by the limitations of age, I'll warrant you that. And the only way you can make room for either is by ignoring all the dolts out there and all their frantic little conversations that add up to absolutely nothing."

"How long . . ."

"Several days, thanks to the good doctor. Whom I have taken as my new personal physician. No doubt I'll run her off as soon as her government duty-time is done."

Sandrine said, "Never, Mistress."

"Humph. Give us a moment, would you please." When the door clicked shut behind the doctor, Insgar pushed a button on the side of Sean's bed, cranking him up to a seated position. She then touched a handle on her wheelless chair, lifting her up to where she sat at eye level. "How much do you remember?"

"Everything." Sean swallowed hard. "I remember it all."

"That's good, lad. Very good indeed. Because there's much you will be able to teach us once you're recovered. Vital information that we should have gone after long ago." She shook her head. "Still, the risk you took. Was this idea of yours truly gifted by the cloud?"

"Yes."

"I was envious of you when I heard, but only for an instant. All my life I've yearned for such a contact, since before I knew I could transit. But now, seeing what it cost you . . ." She shook her head again. "We will talk more in the coming days. But one thing I give you now. The reason I demanded you be brought here to rest. The one thing I can offer you in your hour of healing." Her voice was scarcely above a whisper yet carried the force of two long centuries. "An adept is not someone gifted with enormous abilities. Those dolts are a dime a dozen. We have a hundred worlds and more to draw from, you don't think we can find recruits with enormous abilities? Idiots, the lot of them. I should know. I ran the Watcher school for the first thirty years of its existence. Almost all of my students left as they arrived, content to carry out orders better than the next dolt. No. An adept is someone with the courage to see what needs doing, and then finding it within themselves to act."

For reasons Sean could not explain, the words caused the back of his eyes to burn fiercely. "I lost my courage."

"I know you did, lad. I know. Your valor has been eaten away, the audacity to act crushed, the daring to defy logic consumed, the flame of life almost extinguished." She touched her chair handle a second time, drawing closer still. "But all this will return, do you hear me? I know it for a fact because I have been where you are now. You will heal, and you will grow from your experience, and the next time such courage is required, you will be ready. Only take time for—"

Her words were cut short by the door slamming back. Elenya flew in, across the stone floor and into his arms. He held her and tried to reply to the woman at the same time, for Insgar remained where she was, smiling at them both.

The room had tall windows along both far walls, and the sunlight was gentled by the veil of white-blonde hair that spilled across his vision. Sean breathed in the warmth and the joy and the love, and tried to fight the rising wave of fatigue, for the moment was too precious to lose to slumber. But his body had a mind of its own. And he was soon swept away.

61

Insgar lived on Serena, her twin world. Many who retired from the service chose to dwell on the planet of their first transit. Sean doubted very much that he would ever select Cyrius as his home. Which was another thing the invasion had cost him, along with a decent night's sleep.

Sandrine gradually weaned him off the drugs that had kept him under for almost seven days. He didn't miss the grogginess. But his rest was now punctuated by nightmares of demons that chewed at his bodiless being and lashed him with green, electric fire. He spent his nights locked in battles he would never win, until he was drawn out by the chant of a woman who almost sang his name. *Sean.* He heard Elenya even when she was not around. And when she held him, she carried in her strength the drumbeat of life and the clashing cymbals of shared breaths, and above it all was the soaring joy of hearing her speak his name. *Sean.*

Insgar's home was a rambling country estate, all on one

floor, built in an open square with a vast courtyard at its center. Sandrine lived in a separate apartment in the back and was enormously happy with the arrangement. Insgar was a natural teacher and found in Sandrine a willing sponge. The doctor would have her choice of institutes for further study, if or when the time came.

The central courtyard held a formal garden, fountains, sculptures, and two small groves of blooming trees. Insgar spent many hours harassing the gardeners assigned to her flowerbeds. It was a happy home, filled with light and wind and space for reflection.

Dillon came every free day, often bringing Carey with him. He was preparing to enter the Academy, but for the moment he was spending time in the loft and visiting with their parents. Their parents showed mild curiosity over Sean's absence but accepted Dillon's excuse of a new temporary assignment. Sean tried to show interest in descriptions of their parents' new homes. But it all seemed to be filtered through the knowledge that he had moved on. He was setting up a life of his own now.

Carver visited as well, and Josef, and both men carried with them the quiet pressure of the unseen hordes who urgently awaited the chance to speak with Sean. But he never saw them alone, as Elenya remained determined to hold the world at bay until Sean was ready.

But his idyll could not last forever, much as he might like to pretend the choice was his. Insgar was bossy by nature and tolerated no argument once her mind was made up. Which was how Sean found himself facing the prospect of dining with Elenya's parents. He had already recognized that arguing with his host was a futile effort. So he agreed, but his sour countenance was enough to invoke her ire.

"You show that face to my guests, and I will make you sorry you still draw breath!" When angered, Insgar liked to raise her chair up high enough to glare down from imperial heights. "You think the aliens gave you a hard time? You wait, young sir! I will show you what real trouble feels like!"

"I said I'd do it."

"Aye, and I am ordering you to do so cheerfully! Now show me your smile of greeting. Phah. Elenya, talk sense to this dolt."

"Sean will do just fine by my parents."

"He'd better, or he'll find himself sleeping out in the fields! Listen to me, lad. The Ambassador and his wife are both powerful people. They will make you worthwhile allies."

"Or dangerous adversaries," Elenya said.

"That will not happen because I will not let it!"

"There is the small matter," Elenya reminded the old woman, "of my having run away from home."

"Ah, lass, I do like your spirit. You remind me of myself, back when I was still young enough to breathe fire. Now listen well, lad. What I am about to tell you will make all the difference in the world. When they arrive, you will greet them as a man in love. You will show them contentment and happiness. There is no wound, do you hear me, idiot? There is no lingering shadow. You will show them that all is well with you, because you and their beloved daughter are united against the world. And they will accept this because they must. No mention will be made of any past quarrel. If her mother brings it up, you will ignore the comment. You will show by example what the future holds. The four of you united. As a family. In peace."

"You sound like my father," Elenya said.

"Then he is a wise man indeed. Now go and fetch the tailor."

The two ladies fitted him out like he was a doll headed for a display cabinet. Sean protested once, or tried, but the two women joined together and smashed him down with such force even the tailor winced. After that Sean held to what dignity he had left, and submitted because he had no choice.

They dressed him in a civilian's counterpart to the dress uniform of a senior Assembly officer. The fabric was the most expensive available, similar to the grey sheath that Elenya wore. The color was one shade lighter than midnight blue, with darker seams running down both legs and forming his high collar and cuffs. But where an officer would use the attire as a backdrop for his or her medals, Sean's garments were completely unadorned. Even the buttons were hidden. It was a severe and elegant declaration of who he would someday become. Elenya said he was almost too handsome. Even Insgar declared herself moderately satisfied.

The dinner was served in the torch-lit central garden. Sean had no way of knowing for certain, but he suspected the bevy of servants was Insgar's strategy at work, reminding her guests that she was a woman of wealth and power she could flaunt. Which she did. The tablecloth was woven with jewels that caught the firelight, the service solid gold.

Sean had no idea what he was eating and had little appetite. But silence worked well enough for him. He responded when someone spoke to him directly, which Elenya's mother never did. The woman was elegant and severe and highly intelligent, a trained observer who radiated disapproval and yet who was caught off guard time and again. It was all Insgar's doing. The old woman punctuated every silence with a statement that rang with two hundred years of authority. How she was finally satisfied that she had identified a worthy successor. That thanks to Elenya's guiding hand, Sean would grow into the adept ready to lead them where they next needed to go. On and on the comments came, until even the mother's slow-burning ire was, if not extinguished, at least dampened.

When it was finally over and the guests departed, all Sean could think to say was, "Thank you."

Insgar lifted her chair up to where she could look down upon him. "You had best live up to my predictions, or I will redefine the word *misery*."

"I didn't ask—"

"Oh, hush with your nonsense. Why must the youth of every generation be forced to relearn the lesson of responsibility?"

Sean started to point out what he had already done in that regard, but Insgar lifted her chin a fraction, a gesture so like Elenya he had to smile.

When Insgar was certain she had stifled his response, she conceded, "You really are a handsome lad when you stop with your pouting and your nonsense."

"I don't pout."

Elenya moved closer and slipped her hand in his. "Sean, your pout could win prizes on several planets."

"There, you see? I knew she was the one for you." Insgar turned her chair about. "I suppose you two will be leaving me soon."

"I want to show Sean my twin world," Elenya said.

"There are several duties you both will need to perform first, mind."

Elenya squeezed his hand, stifling another futile protest. "Sean knows, Mistress."

"Well, come and visit with me when you're done gallivanting." Her voice remained firm even as she vanished into the shadows. "We have futures to plan. Two of them."

Sean's duties consumed a blur of days. First came Tirian's funeral, which Dillon and Josef and Carver had jointly insisted be postponed until Sean was able to attend. They buried the former Examiner with all honors in the field of lava bordering the Praetorian Academy. The cemetery was rimmed by the symbols of all the Assembly planets. The entire Academy and numerous other visitors filled the arena and the surrounding plain. Tirian's place was among those who had fallen in the Cyrian station, comrades in arms now. Sean sat upon the speaker's platform, chilled by a harsh winter wind. But for once he did not mind.

Then came the ceremony marking the reopening of the Cyrian train station. The planet's leaders insisted that Sean cut the ribbon, a ceremony that seemed as inane and useless on Cyrius as it did back home. Once that was over, Sean took a few days off at the loft, mostly because he wanted to reacquaint himself with his world. At least, he tried to convince himself of that. But especially in those hours spent with his parents, he felt increasingly that what he was actually doing was fashioning an internal farewell.

Then it was back to the Academy, this time for days and days of meetings and conferences and questionings. The one positive note to it all was the presence of Dillon and Carver. Their former instructor had accepted a senior role, at least for a time, so that he might help supervise Dillon's training and direction. They tried to talk about Sean's future direction as well, but he was not ready.

The hours were exhausting, made worse by the nightmares that followed every interview on what he discovered inside the alien's mind. Slightly better were the days given to teaching Watchers how to fashion duplicates of their own. When he could, Sean took to transiting back to the loft, where he and Elenya would have a quiet meal, sometimes with John, mostly alone. The professor missed his little girl, but he knew she was happy, even in the stark barrenness of Academy housing. Sean wanted to offer more, and tried to show the professor both warmth and gratitude. But the process of being squeezed dry by the senior Guards staff continued to open old wounds.

It was Elenya's patience that ran out first. She accused the officials of asking the same questions for the third and fourth time. And to both their surprise, their strongest ally in ending this process was Tatyana. The Counselor was being tapped to train as an Ambassador and considered herself in Sean and Dillon's debt. Sean didn't know how he felt about that, and Dillon's scorn was evident whenever they were alone.

The night before Dillon left for the Academy, they ate a

solitary meal on Insgar's patio. When they were finished, Dillon leaned back in his seat and asked, "You ever study the sky?"

"All the time."

"I don't recognize a single constellation. Hardly a surprise since we're on the other side of the galaxy." He gave that a beat, then asked, "You ever mind, you know, all the strangeness?"

"Not even a little." Sean slid back so he matched his brother's pose. Head on the rear of the seat, looking up at the gleaming river of light. And the three moons. One a whitish-grey sliver, one a ghostly pale touching the tree line, and one a ruddy golden globe directly overhead. "Not even at the worst moment."

"The aliens still invading your dreams?"

"Less than before. Elenya's helped. A lot."

"Sean . . ."

"Yeah?"

His brother was silent for quite a while. Sean didn't mind. When it came to something deep, Dillon always had trouble with his words. Sean listened to a night bird call, a melody of silver chimes. The sound heightened his sense of entering new realms. New adventures. He would heal, and he would go on. He was certain of that now.

Finally Dillon said, "We're going to stay pals, right? I mean, with all the changes . . ."

Sean straightened in his seat. When he was certain Dillon was not going to say anything more, he said, "Look at me, bro. Whatever happens. The bond stays the same."

"So . . . we're good."

"Totally. Permanently."

Dillon rose to his feet. Only then did Sean realize that was why he had come here. On his last night of freedom. "I guess I better go see Carey."

"Good luck tomorrow," Sean said.

Dillon flashed his grin. "What could they possibly do that's worse than what we've been through?"

Sean smiled back. After his brother departed, he leaned his head back on the seat and stayed there for hours. Watching the Serenese moons.

...

The day of his formal release, Sean wanted to return either to the loft or to Insgar's home. But Elenya was having none of it. "We have earned a break. Not just from work. From all we have ever known. I want us to discover my twin world together."

"You've already been there. Many times."

"As a child. And for brief visits with my family. But never far beyond where I first landed. Now I want to *claim* it."

"With me."

"Of course with you. Where are you going to call home, Sean? The professor's loft? Sneaking in and out of a world that rejects the Assembly's existence?"

"No. I'll go back, sure. Especially to see our folks. But that time is over."

"Then where? Cyrius?"

"Definitely not there. Not now, anyway. Maybe never."

She offered a smile that was far too beguiling for her age. "We could always ask my parents to take you in."

"Oh, right. Your mother would love that."

"My sisters think you are very handsome."

"I am not moving in with your dad. Ever."

"So this is a holiday with a purpose. I would love for you to consider Helene as a possible home."

All the messages included in those few words crowded in around him. He fashioned a single response, the only thing that made sense. "I'm ready."

KEEP READING FOR A SNEAK PEEK

of the next book in the
RECRUITS SERIES

Revell

a division of Baker Publishing Group
www.RevellBooks.com

I

The back roads of Virginia had always been Landon Evans's best friend.

In the months after his father died, Landon had started escaping the world by driving out here. It was incredible just how empty the Virginia countryside could be. Three hours to the east, the Washington sprawl spread like fungus. So many people, all of them enduring the terrible drive through terrible traffic, day in and day out, so they could sit at terrible jobs and pretend they were close to the nexus of power. And just beyond their reach was this.

Mailboxes saluted Landon as he passed farmhouses with acres of pasture, cows and horses and early summer crops. The world smelled sweet as the first dawn. Out here, Landon could pretend his mother wasn't hiding from life inside her prescription haze, that he wasn't suffocating in his community college classes, that he really could look forward to something better.

And finally, at long last, it did appear that he could. Look forward. Anticipate. Think of a future that was bigger than just getting by.

For one thing, his uncle, the senator, had offered him a gig as an intern. With pay, no less. Starting in eight days.

For another, he had been accepted at UVA. All his CC credits transferring. Scholarship. Not quite a full ride, but hey.

Which meant the money he was earning from this FedEx gig could go toward his share of an off-campus apartment. Because one thing was certain, he was *not* going to stay home and commute.

Landon had already given his notice to FedEx and was at three days and counting. Then he was moving into his uncle's garage apartment, spending a summer in Georgetown, working the Hill, learning what it meant to breathe the heady air of Congress in emergency summer session.

Right now he had two hours left in his eleven-hour shift. Landon had been at it since long before sunrise. Quick stops for breakfast at five thirty and lunch at eleven. His shoulders and neck and back were aching, but in a good way. He didn't even mind the grainy feel behind his eyeballs or the way the truck's cab was filled with the ripe smell of a long, hot day. Because he was saying good-bye. Not to the roads. He would always be coming back here. Hopefully someday to live. No, Landon Evans was saying farewell to somebody else's idea of a life.

Suddenly three people appeared out of nowhere, standing there beside the road, looking straight at him. Then a very weird-looking lady pointed something at his truck. Two seconds later, Landon's motor died.

···

Sean Kirrel suffered through the most boring class ever.

Current events and future trends. Each situation introduced by a list of wars and crises not even the planets involved still remembered. And taught by a professor named Kaviti. The name fit the guy perfectly. Kaviti was a pompous bore. He paced across the front of the class as he droned, "Recently in the news and on the minds of the Assembly is Cygneus Prime. Its history is marred by almost constant strife, which they claim is now behind them. The leader of the largest fief on Cygneus Prime at the onset of the Second Interplanetary War was Aldus, known to his loyal subjects as Aldus the Great and to his foes as The Butcher. Thirty-seven years ago, he defeated the last remaining opposition and established a governing council that rules the entire system, with one small exception known as the Outer Rim . . ."

Students at the Diplomatic Institute were called Attendants. Sean hated the word. It made him feel like a student in a school for glorified servants. Which, of course, was the intention. In truth, much of Sean's dissatisfaction had nothing to do with the school or his classes, and everything to do with Elenya. His soon-to-be-former girlfriend had been moving away from him for months. Sean felt increasingly helpless to do anything about it.

"The latest Cygnean conflict began as a dispute over the mineral-rich territories that form the entire planetary crust of the world known as Aldwyn . . ."

Professor Kaviti was one of the most highly decorated

members of the diplomatic corps. Not to mention a Justice in the Tribunal Courts and an alternate voting member of the Assembly Parliament. Sean figured the guy had bored his enemies to death, suffocated them with facts as dry as old bones. Sean endured two hours of this every day.

Kaviti liked to pick on Sean. Elenya insisted he was taking it all too personally. That was just the professor's way with all newcomers, she contended. But by this point in their relationship, Elenya had started treating all his concerns with an element of disdain. Regardless of what she thought, Sean knew the professor was taking aim. What was more, Kaviti was not alone. A segment of the faculty resented Sean's presence. He had been sent here after less than sixty days as an initiate. Most Attendants arrived with five to ten years of Assembly schooling under their belts. What was more, the institute had been *ordered* to take Sean. By a planetary Ambassador and the founder of the Watcher school, no less. The fact that he and Dillon had saved an entire world from alien invasion only heightened this group's desire to find fault. There was no question in Sean's mind. Kaviti intended to down-check him and kick him out.

Kaviti's drone swam into the background as Sean picked at the open wound in his heart. He replayed the arguments that had laced his last three meetings with Elenya. She had a beautiful woman's ability to show outrage when she did not get her way and the intelligence to win every fight. She was gone now, off on some research assignment she would not discuss. Elenya had also told Sean not to come visit, which had pleased Elenya's mother to no end. The last time Sean had stopped by their home, the lady had actually smiled as she bade him farewell.

Sean was so lost in the misery of love gone bad, he almost missed the Messenger's alert.

The first *bong* resonated through the classroom like a musical punch. After the second and third, Dillon popped into view. It was almost comic, since Sean was pretty certain Dillon had no right to use the Messenger's official alert. His twin brother was a cadet at the Academy, the military arm of the Human Assembly. The twins shared a contempt for the Messenger Corps and the kinds of transiters who settled for that life. The Messenger's know-nothing existence was too close to the bureaucratic lifestyle that had framed their parents' world.

But Sean did not grin at his brother for two reasons. First, he would have gone into serious debt for any reason to leave this class behind.

The second was Dillon's expression. As grim as his uniform. Dillon threw the teacher a parade-ground salute. "Apologies for the interruption, Ambassador. But Attendant Kirrel has been summoned."

"Summoned?" Another thing about Kaviti was his ability to dismiss with a sniff. It was claimed that, years after graduating, classmates of the Diplomatic school still greeted one another with an elongated snort. "By whom?"

"That is none of your concern, Ambassador. Sean?"

"See here! Just one minute, cadet!"

But no scrawny arm-waving was going to stop Sean's escape. He was midway up the aisle and asking, "Where to?"

"Treehouse. Go."

"Already there," Sean replied. And he was. Bang and gone.

Dillon arrived an instant later. The air was compressed by his tension.

Sean demanded, "What's the matter?"

"Landon Evans, remember him?"

"Sure. Carey's cousin."

"He's been kidnapped." Dillon pointed at Sean's closet. "Change into civvies. Jacket and tie. Hurry."

Thomas Locke is a pseudonym for Davis Bunn, an award-winning novelist with worldwide sales of seven million copies in twenty languages. Davis divides his time between Oxford and Florida and holds a lifelong passion for speculative stories. He is the author of *Emissary* and *Merchant of Alyss* in the Legends of the Realm series, as well as *Trial Run* and *Flash Point* in the Fault Lines series. Learn more at www.tlocke.com.